15468

MW00876486

DATA
RUNNER

The Data Runner series is dedicated to my family,
without whom it would not be.
This book is for my father, who always believed.

Diversion Books
A Division of Diversion Publishing Corp.
443 Park Avenue South, Suite 1004
New York, NY 10016
www.DiversionBooks.com

Copyright © 2013 by Sam A. Patel
All rights reserved, including the right to reproduce this book or
portions thereof in any form whatsoever.

For more information, email info@diversionbooks.com.

First Diversion Books edition May 2013
eBook ISBN: 978-1-626810-60-0
Print ISBN: 978-1-62681-084-6

DATΛ RUNNER

SAM A. PATEL

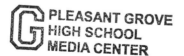

PLEASANT GROVE
HIGH SCHOOL
MEDIA CENTER

DIVERSIONBOOKS

Strength is the outcome of need; security sets a premium on feebleness.

—H.G. Wells

It's hard to imagine that a little rubber stopper can almost break your nose, but that's exactly what happens to me when the rooftop door flies open so hard it bounces off the stop and back into my face. This sends me tumbling straight into two empty garbage cans like they're the last two pins in a spare. Garbage cans. Who the hell keeps garbage cans on a rooftop?

I groan.

Okay, so maybe there is no good way to come crashing through a door when Blackburn's goons are on your tail, but there are plenty of bad ways to do it and this is definitely one of them.

I jump back to my feet and wedge the door shut behind me.

I hurry around the roof looking for an out, dripping sweat in the cool night air. That's when I see them perched above me on the adjacent rooftop. Three Complex soldiers wearing full capsule body armor, laser goggles glowing red like the lit-up retinas of a pack of nocturnal creatures. Each of them holds a sundrop gun—you can tell by the accordion tubing that wraps around to the packs on their backs—but that works to my advantage because we're back in the Free City now and they can't fire those here. That's why they just stay there tracking me. It's all they can do. They sure as hell can't make that jump with all the gear they're carrying and there's no other way down here.

I skid to a halt at the edge of the roof.

I know what you're thinking. *Didn't you tell Red Tail that the key to a gap jump is to keep going?*

I did, and when it comes to gap jumps that's true most of the time, but there are times when you have to stop and weigh what's in front of you against your skillset, and this is one of those times. Standing on the brink of the building looking over the edge to the adjacent rooftop, it isn't the horizontal distance that bothers me. That's only ten feet, and I can clear that easy. What bothers me is the drop, which I'm figuring to be about twenty-five feet.

Twenty-five feet.

Have you ever cleared a twenty-five-foot drop?

Maybe you have, but that was probably into water, right? Off a diving board, or perhaps you took the plunge off a short cliff into a lagoon. Something along those lines? If that's the case then the worst thing that happened was a little bit of slap rash where your body hit the surface. Yeah, I know that feeling. That whip-like sting, like your entire body has just been snapped with a giant rubber band, and when you finally climb out a few minutes later all you can see are patches of tender skin all over your body. That's a sting to be sure, but let me assure you, it's nothing compared to what I'm facing.

I turn around. The soldiers with red eyes watch me from above like the alien gods of some ancient mythology.

I hear a crash from the floor below, which can only be the big steel chair I knocked over just minutes before on my way to the roof. They must have picked it up and thrown it into the door I jammed with a broomstick. I knew it would only buy me a minute or two, but in a clutch situation like this, even a minute can make all the difference in the world.

Their footfall races up the stairs to the rooftop door behind me.

There is no going back. Right here, right now, for all the chips on the table, I am all-in. I guess this is what they call painting yourself into a corner. The only difference is, my corner just happens to be on top of a twenty-five-story building with the next rooftop ten feet over and twenty-five feet down. And just in case you're wondering...yes, I am wearing my body armor... but body armor won't do squat for my ankles if I don't stick the landing just right. If I end up with a twist or a sprain, I will be done. And then there's the matter of the cortex chip in my arm.

Even if I do stick the landing, I have to be sure to protect the inside of my forearm when I roll out of it, because if that chip should happen to burst…

Full Tilt.

Game Over.

No Replay.

The footfall reaches the other side of the door. The wedge won't last long. Even now as they throw their shoulders into it I can see it begin to slip.

I take two steps back.

The men behind me aren't Complex soldiers like the ones above. These guys are internal security. They wear suits over light body armor and carry weapons that can be fired within city limits. Glock 21s, if I am not mistaken, and they are already drawn. That means they are shooting .45 caliber bullets. I can still feel the time I had Dexter fire a 9mm round into my body armor from ten feet out just to make sure I could take it. I took it all right, even if it did nearly fracture my rib. But a .45? I have no desire at all to find out what that feels like. That's just too big a caliber for a 17-year-old body to handle. Seventeen. That's something I still have to remind myself of from time to time—that no matter how gifted I may be intellectually, I still have the physical body of a 17 year old.

The wedge slips another two inches.

I hear the grumbling curses of Blackburn's goons as they squeeze their hands through the opening. If ever there was a moment for a leap of courage, this is it. I am ready. I have to be.

I take two steps back. Three. Four. And run.

The door flies open behind me. The clamor of their voices immediately turns to full-on words like *there he is*, *there's the Carrion*, *don't let him get away* as they raise their guns to my back. But I am already in motion. Committed, as the tread of my boot grips the edge of the building. I leap.

A shot is fired.

The bullet whizzes past me as I soar, suspended in thin air like I'm hanging by a thread hooked to the crescent moon, until the Earth takes over and I drop.

Feet running across air.

Arms swimming against wind.

I sail clear into the night.

And as the crushing blow of an impending landing that could go either way quickly approaches, I can think of one thing only—

That gravity, just like the blackjack table that started this all, is also a zero-sum game.

THERE ARE NO LIMITS, ONLY PLATEAUS

1.

It's something I have done countless times before, but for some reason when I press my thumb to the biometric pad on this particular morning, it gets me thinking. The high-resolution scan converts the ridges and valleys of my thumbprint into a data matrix. This data matrix is then buffered into a volatile memory chip so that the internal processor can measure it against the two thumbprint matrices already stored in the EEPROM. Obviously, the comparison with Martin Baxter's will fail. But when the comparison with Jack Nill's authenticates...

BEEP!

The system trips the tumblers, and I open the basement door to a whiff of burnt silicon from overclocked processors. Grab both railings with gloved hands. Lift my legs and slide down the steep stairs into my father's workshop. "I'm off, Martin."

Yeah, I call my father Martin. That started when I was 14, and he and I got into a huge argument one day about the Queen's Pawn Game. I kept trying to illustrate to him why the Indian defenses offered much more immediate counter-play for black than d5, but he just kept insisting that d5 was the best response to a d4 opening—the same old, boring counter-opening that he felt was still the best overall and second to none in versatility. Anyway, I made some point, I don't even remember what now, after which I blurted his name emphatically at the end of a sentence. Something like "I bet you didn't consider that...did you, *Martin?*" I don't know why, but it stuck. Now I call him Martin all the time.

You may be wondering why, if my father is Martin Baxter, then my name is Jack Nill. That's easy. The name comes from my mother, Genie Nill, the only thing of hers besides my olive skin, dark hair, and hazel eyes that she left me with when she disappeared. I wasn't even 4 years old at the time, so what memories I have of her are vague. Random images. A porch swing. Sitting on her lap. A beautiful woman with a carefree smile hovering over me as the sky moved behind her. Things like that, nothing more. If you want to know the reason why she left, then you'll have to get in a very short line that begins and ends with me. And if you do get in line behind me, I wouldn't advise you to hold your breath.

"Martin?" I repeat.

"Did you see this?" he asks, referring to the news stream on one of his transparent screens.

I read the scroll over the active video. *"More allegations arise in the Blackburn scandal. Brand new evidence suggests that Blackburn, Ltd.—primary defense contractor and standing army for the North American Alliance—has been conducting backroom deals with Caliphate Global, the corporate arm of the Islamic empire.* What else is new?"

"Not that one." Martin turns his attention to the trans screen, throws that stream aside and brings up a local feed from the Free City News Stream. "This one," he says, pointing to a dolled up newswoman reporting live from the riverbank. Behind her is a long strip of yellow tape, and behind that, a bloodstained sheet covering a corpse. "They found another data runner with his arm cut off."

You know that moment when someone breathes a sigh of relief? Well, this is the exact opposite. Because unlike the Blackburn scandal, which—let's be honest—has nothing to do with me today, this news affects me directly. Dexter is already running the sneakernet, and it looks like Pace is about to get into it as well. "Is it the same as before?" I ask.

It isn't unusual for data runners to turn up like that. All those random bodies that are always washing up missing an arm—you always know they were killed for whatever it was they were transporting at the time. Running data isn't just a dangerous game in a dirty world, it is quite possibly the most dangerous game—and you accept that risk when you get into it—but this is different.

"Same kind of cut, same kind of weapon," says Martin. "Apparently, there's some nut running around the Free City hacking off people's arms with a samurai sword."

"*Katana*," I correct, "and it's not just random people he's after…" Obviously, there is only one reason why an interceptor would cut off the arm of a data runner… "he's going after their cargos. He must be searching for a particular load that he just hasn't found yet."

"Do you have any idea what he's looking for?"

"How would I know?"

"Your friends on the sneakernet." Martin pushes back and turns in his chair. Underneath his lampshade of shoulder-length curls and the thin rectangular glasses he's worn for years, he's actually a good-looking guy. The chic geek who simply got old. "They must have some idea what this rogue interceptor is after."

I shake my head no. "But I guarantee you he's not a rogue. Interceptors are just like data runners, they always work for somebody."

"Somebody like the Hermes Agency?"

The Hermes Agency is a pretty decent outfit when it comes to information couriers. Obviously they're not Arcadian Transports. No other outfit even compares with Arcadian Transports. But if you're a potential client or a potential data runner, you could do a lot worse than Hermes. That's the agency Dex runs for. It's also the agency that has tried on several occasions to recruit me, most recently after our big parkour exhibition in the Free City. Martin knows I'm not crazy enough to run the sneakernet, but he also knows I've been getting offers from them, which is why he mentions it. "Somebody just like them," I reply.

All of a sudden Martin gets that look. You know the one. It's the same look most people of his generation get any time they take a drive down memory lane. "Running data," he says. "It's still such a foreign concept to me."

Here we go. Martin's childhood. Growing up in the halcyon years of net neutrality when everything was secure, and you could actually send information over open channels without having to worry about it getting stolen. Hell, in those days you could actually send correspondence through the post without having to worry about it getting scanned for content. But that was then, and *then* is a world away from now.

Don't get me wrong, it's not that I don't appreciate Martin's point of view, I just don't see it the same way he does. Maybe it's just one of those generational things. Martin grew up with the old Internet, so he still remembers what it was like when virtual space was public domain. He actually remembers net neutrality. But for me the aggregate internet—or *aggrenet*—is all I've ever known, so net neutrality is just another idea in history. For me, it kind of makes sense that virtual space would have ownership rights same as everything else in the world, and that a single megacorporation like Grumwell would own it all. I mean, *somebody* has to be the largest GDP in the world. Better them than Caliphate Global, right? But try telling that to Martin and you'll get an earful about Keynesian economics and the anti-democratization of the free market. I still don't fully understand it. How could I? How could anyone? It's all so vast.

"Well, look at this way," I say. "Maybe the sneakernet was an unintended consequence of the aggregate Internet, but so was the undernet…"

The undernet. Because the more they locked the aggrenet down, the more people like us found a way to tunnel beneath it.

"…and so was Morlock."

Morlock. The group of hackers who run the undernet.

Martin smiles. "Still haven't gotten the tap from Moreau yet?"

Moreau. The one who runs Morlock.

"How did you get yours?" I ask.

Martin shrugs, which isn't something he does often. "One day I ported into the undernet and there it was."

"There what was?"

"The tag. There's no official invitation or induction or anything like that. One day you're an isolated hacker/phreak working on your own, the next you discover that your work has been tagged as Morlock." Martin snaps his fingers. "Just like that, you're part of the collective."

"Tagged by Moreau himself?"

Martin shrugs again. Twice in one morning, that had to be a record. "Every Morlock operates as an independent cell, so there's no way of knowing why some are selected and some aren't. I'm not sure there's any rhyme or reason to it."

"I'm sure Moreau has his reasons."

"You'd have to ask him that."

"Oh, I will. When I find him, that's going to be the first thing I ask him."

I remember the security panel upstairs. The nice thing about talking to Martin is that he isn't big on segues. You can just jump from one topic to another. "The biometric security system upstairs…you know how in the movies they're always cutting off someone's thumb to get past it? Well, couldn't you just pull one of the stored thumbprint matrices from the EEPROM and ghost it into the buffer to trick the authenticator?"

Martin answers without even giving it a moment's thought. "Those EEPROMs all use a modified Floating Gate MOSFET for their storage mechanism. It works like a built-in failsafe. Any attempt to pull the data matrix directly from the EEPROM will trigger a hot-carrier injection into the gate dielectric and wipe it out completely. Besides, any security panel worth its salt is going to put at least two inches of reinforced steel between the front-side scanner and the logic board. You wouldn't even be able to access it without some heavy-duty cutting tools."

"What's a MOSFET?" I ask.

"Metal–oxide–semiconductor field-effect transistor."

Okay, that's a few steps above my knowledge base. If integrated circuits are like Legos then I can use them to build anything to spec and, to a lesser extent, to create things on my own. But Martin isn't limited by what comes in the box; he can mix his own polymer and pour his own custom-designed Legos. His building blocks are the molecules and compounds that make up my building blocks, which allows him to build on a whole other level than me. Where I see a single EEPROM, Martin sees the transistors and semiconductors holding that integrated circuit together.

"I hate to say it," says Martin, "but cutting off a thumb is still probably your best way in."

Hacking off arms. Cutting off thumbs. It was a very strange morning in Martin's basement. Normally our day doesn't start with so much dismemberment.

Martin rolls across the basement to a worktable covered in felt and turns on the card shooter. After a brief mechanical whir, the machine spits out six hands in a perfect parabola followed by a seventh with the bottom card down. I know at once what this means. Blackjack at the syndicate gaming parlor. "I thought you were banned from that game?" I ask.

"The pit boss owes me a favor. He convinced Vlad to let me in for one more game."

"Why would he do that?"

"They made an event out of it. They've bumped it up to a thirteen-deck shoe, so people are going to show up just to watch the game. A lot of whales."

Whales. Suckers with fat wallets. "What are the stakes?"

"It's a zero-sum game. Fifty grand, heads-up."

"Fifty grand? Where did you get fifty grand?"

"On margin."

Of course. If we had fifty grand to start with, Martin wouldn't need to play. He was playing to win that fifty grand, which meant he had to borrow the buy-in to win the pot. If you think that sounds crazy, it's only because you're not Martin Baxter. His system reduces the gambling coefficient down to nearly zero. In that sense, Martin Baxter doesn't gamble—he works the numbers and trusts the math. For him, blackjack is like a cash machine.

"See that?" Martin glances at me as he wins five out of six hands against the card shooter. "They haven't invented a shoe yet that can beat me."

That much is true. That's the thing about people like Martin—even when they're unemployed they're never really out of work. How could they be? Minds like his are far too active to ever go limp; they're always cooking up something, and they always find a way to get by. That's one thing Martin always says and I believe: when you're smart, you can always think your way out of a jam. And it isn't just true of mental smarts either. It applies to physical smarts as well. You know, muscle memory.

"PK training in the Free City today," I remind him as I turn and hoist myself up the stairs.

"Okay," he says. "Stop, drop and roll!"

Stop, drop and roll. It takes me a second to figure out why that sounds so familiar. Until I realize…"that's what you're supposed to do if you're ever on fire. But I guess the principle applies to PK as well."

"Bowling too, I would imagine."

"Sure, why not. Why waste a perfectly good mnemonic?"

"Why, indeed."

"Good counting," I say as I reach the door at the top of the steps.

"Good jumping," he replies behind me.

We don't say *luck*. Martin and I are both dedicated to math, logic, and the laws of the universe. Neither one of us believes in luck.

●　　●　　●

Pace waits for me at the end of my driveway with two bladders full of water slung over his shoulders. Today is his turn. He and I are both members of the TerraAqua water collective, Chimpo and Dexter aren't, so we take turns bringing extra water for them. Although that's probably going to change very soon. In the last two billing cycles, Pace's family has been past due on their fees, and with the overdue deadline coming up fast, I know their days are numbered.

We tap fists. Pace is shorter and leaner than me and wears a constant quarter-inch buzz cut. Constant. Seriously, he must buzz his head twice a week to keep that length because I have never once seen it grow out of that quarter-inch setting. As for the barely visible stubble on his chin, I suspect it's all his Filipino genes will allow.

"Have you heard the news?" he asks.

"I just saw it on the Free City newsfeed."

"Newsfeed? What are you talking about?"

"They just found another runner with his arm cut off?"

"They did?" Pace jerks back with surprise. Clearly this is the first he's hearing of it.

"Why, what were you talking about?"

The distraught look on Pace's face says it even before the words. "Hermes offered me the job."

"Congratulations," I say.

Pace gets oddly defensive. "I don't have a choice," he says. "I'm not stupid. If it was just the TerraAqua fees, we could find some other way to get by. But now we're behind on everything. I don't really want to, but what choice do I have?"

"It's okay Pace." I understand why he's freaking out, but he needs to get over it if he's going to survive out there. "Maybe they'll even let you run with Dex. Then at least the two of you can watch each other's backs."

"Yeah," he says, instantly relieved. "Yeah, that would be good."

Worry is not the right description for the look on Pace's face but neither is fear. Something in between maybe. "Come on, Dragon. You'll be fine." I slap him on the back and recite the parkour club's motto. "There are no limits, only plateaus."

Dex's words, not mine.

2.

Dexter Drake is the black kid in the white hoodie who plants his hand on the railing and kicks his feet high into the air, so high that all I see are his sneakers sailing across the clear blue sky as I hurdle over and push off the same. I'm half a foot behind him. I'm always half a foot behind Dexter. That's a fact permanently cemented into our heights. He's an inch over six feet tall, I'm five inches under—half a foot between us. Fifty yards back, Pace and Chimpo bring up the rear.

Just ahead, a woman in designer clothes carries two big Fifth Avenue shopping bags in each hand as she chats away to the person inside her comm shades. Blind. Even though she can navigate her surroundings through the transparent image inside her lenses, she is completely oblivious to the world around her.

Dexter points her out and gives me the motion to scissor around. This is one of the things he loves most, what he calls popping a bubble. Getting in so close that you shatter the illusion of their tiny little world. I'm sure most people would regard this as a bunch of kids making trouble, but what we do is neither rowdy nor unruly, it's just the Dragons' way of announcing that we too exist. We are here, and we deserve a bit of your attention, even if we do have to startle it out of you.

Dex and I pick up speed and run straight for her. I mean straight for her. And soon she's gaping at us and screaming something that must be shrill and unsettling to the person on the other end of her call who can't see us approaching beyond the borders of their screen. Three steps away.

"Oh my God!" she screams, drops her bags, and covers her face with her hands.

Dexter leaps off the ground and pushes to the left. I leap

and push to the right. And with a wisp of air that makes a strand of her hair dance, we sail around her in a way that touches no part of her but the electrons of her aura.

"Top of the morning to you, ma'am," Dex says with a tip of his cap.

"Have a nice day," I say, coming around the other side.

The woman is still shrieking through her fingers when we land and keep going.

Pace and Chimpo will not attempt this. In fact, after seeing us do it, they'll go out of their way to give her an extra-wide berth. Pace may have the skills to execute such a stunt but he lacks the personality to get away with it. And Chimpo? That one still makes me laugh. Chimpo once attempted this on a very large suit who must have been a wrestler before he put on the tie, because in one fell swoop the guy dropped his briefcase, caught Chimpo in midair, and let out a giant guffaw as he lifted poor Chimpo over his head and body-slammed him into the gutter. Needless to say, Chimpo won't try that again.

Dexter heads for the subway station two blocks from the Free City magnet academy, the same one that used to be my stop less than a year ago. That gives me pause. I know it shouldn't, but I can't help it. Following on Dex's heels, I have to wonder what my life would be like right now if Martin hadn't lost his job.

If things had gone according to plan, I would have graduated the magnet academy one year early with one full year of university credits already under my belt. That would sound impressive to most people, but that's because most people get to accomplish things against a normal benchmark. I have Martin Baxter as mine. Martin who got his PhD at 20, authored his first major paper at 22, and formulated his proof for the nonlinear transgression of imaginary variables by the time he was 26. That's my benchmark. Even still, entering the New England Institute of Technology—Martin's old alma mater—one year early with another year of credits would have been a very respectable accomplishment. But then one day without so much as a warning, Delphi Advanced Microdesigns, the tiny outfit that Martin had co-founded, was swallowed whole by Grumwell. Grumwell, the one corporation that Martin always said he would *never* work for. And just like that my whole life changed. One day I'm setting up a physics lab in the best secondary school in the Free City, the next I'm the new kid walking through the blighted halls of Brentwood High.

Dexter and I stop at the subway kiosk and wait for Pace and Chimpo to catch up. They've all done the track jump before. I'm the only one who hasn't. You might even say that this is like my initiation, though none of us think of it in those terms. The Brentwood Dragons parkour club isn't just a bunch of kids playing jungle gym. It's an entire philosophy of movement. A system for navigating the world. For us it's a way of life, and we are dedicated to it.

As a rule, the Brentwood Dragons only ever take part in exhibitions of parkour, never competitions. There are PK competitions out there, but that isn't what we're about. As a team, the Brentwood Dragons hold true to the core principles of parkour, which are as ancient as any martial art. We're like the Buddhist monks who believe that every movement is the thing that speaks for itself. The essence of parkour is a spiritual journey of self-discovery—to find one's balance with nature, to find one's balance within oneself. We're not like the new breed of traceurs who are only in it for the money. What they fail to realize is how that mindset destroys the essence of parkour. That's not us. We don't train in secrecy. We don't hoard our techniques into secret playbooks to use against our fellow traceurs. We share all. For us, it isn't about who gets there first and how fast, it's about being the best you can be. It isn't about beating someone else's score, just getting there the best way you can. That is what we believe. That's real parkour.

I catch sight of myself in the front window of the corner café where I used to get my blueberry muffins. This might be the same subway stop, and I might be the same person, but the reflection in the window looks nothing like it did back then. Back then I dressed like a preppy even when I wasn't wearing the magnet academy uniform. Since then, the dress slacks have become chinos, and the Oxfords have been replaced by cross-trainers. I still wear collared shirts, only now they're untucked and made of flannel. My hair is still a mess, probably even more so now that there is more of it. I never did care for brushes, combs even less. I suppose that's one of those things a mother would have gotten on me about, if she'd bothered to stick around.

"You ready?" Dex asks.

I turn away from my reflection. "As ready as I'll ever be."

Dexter grins and slaps me on the back.

It's hard to imagine sometimes, but if you look hard enough, you can always find the silver lining in every darkened cloud. For me that silver lining is Dexter Drake.

The first time I ever saw Dexter was on the run. Three guys from school had chased me down the abandoned part of Main Street and into an alley where I managed to trip over my own feet and fall into a pile of boxes before they even touched me. I used to do that quite a bit—trip over my own feet. After knocking me around a bit, they finished up by taking my Urban Dweller backpack—the City Sport model in bright orange canvas with black suede trim that comes equipped with watertight utility compartments and a removable hydration vessel. I didn't want to lose it, but I wasn't about to take a beating over it. Keep in mind that this was before I grew six inches in a year, so there wasn't much I could do about it yet, just lay on the ground and wait for them to finish robbing me.

Suddenly as if from nowhere, literally nowhere, this six-foot-something kid comes crashing down like a superhero in the middle of the alley. The very first thing I noticed about him was the downward furrow in his brow, which formed a sharp V with the wide arch of his nose. It gave him an expression that was altogether menacing. And he snarled.

"Give the kid back his bag."

The three guys all took a step back before they remembered there were three of them.

"Get lost, Drake. This is none of your business."

"I'm making it my business."

"Come on, let's get him."

And the next thing I knew, it was three on one.

Watching Dexter fight was like standing before a giant

waterfall. There was something fluid in the way he moved, even amidst this violent rush of fury that could chop off your head if you got too close. He could not be contained. With every shove, every kick, every twist, and every flip, he let loose a full blast of gravity and water that came crashing down upon them until they ran off.

Dexter tossed me my bag. Then he did something I never would have expected. He ran to the wall…and kept going. Ran two steps up the wall and grabbed the old fire escape. Hoisted himself up and continued climbing. All the way up, using ledges as steps when he had to. The next thing I knew, he had scaled the building and was disappearing over the ledge onto the roof. I kept my eyes trained. Somehow I knew he wasn't done yet, and I was right. A moment later Dexter leapt off the rooftop and sailed clear across the gap five stories over my head and onto the opposing rooftop. I just stood there amazed by what I had just witnessed, on the ground and above.

Dexter and I were destined to become best friends. Not because there is such a thing as destiny, but because the outcome was inevitable. I knew that if I was going to survive in Brentwood, I was going to have to learn one of two things: how to fight or how to run. I guess that's what they mean by having a fight-or-flight response. The trick, regardless of which you choose, is to make the choice and stick to it. Like Martin always says, proficiency is the key to success. So the very next day I checked the bulletin board at school and was faced with two options. The first was the Brentwood High mixed martial arts team, which practiced a combination of Krav Maga and Keysi Fighting Method. I took one look at that and knew that was just asking for trouble. The second option was the Brentwood High parkour club, officially known as *Brentwood Dragons PK*. I knew that was more my speed; now I just had to become proficient at it.

That was how I became a *traceur*, which means "tracer" in French, the word used to describe people who practice parkour. And that was how Dexter and I crossed paths once again. But even if I had gone the other way, chosen fight instead of flight, it wouldn't have mattered. You see, Dexter was the captain of both teams. That's what I mean about inevitable outcomes. Fight or flight, our friendship would have happened.

Three turnstiles stand between us and the platform stairs. With Pace on my left and Chimpo on my right, the three of us Kong vault over them in unison. You know that move where you dive headfirst to plant your hands on either side of the gantry, swing your legs up and over the turnstile, push off and land on the other side? That's a Kong vault.

Dexter takes another way down altogether. It's a twelve-foot drop from the upper deck to the subway platform. Dexter vaults over the railing—reverses—and grabs the floor of the upper deck on his way down. It's a tough grab that requires an incredible grip, but he hangs on like it's child's play as his legs swing wildly to shake off the excess momentum. Now lowered by his height and the full length of his arms, his feet are just a short drop to the platform. He releases and lands. That particular combination is a simple vault–180°–lache, otherwise known as a Turn Down.

The local train has just gone through and cleared the platform of passengers. The next train coming up the tunnel is an express that will not be stopping at this station. It will just shoot through and continue on its way.

The train bears down. Pace and Chimpo are already bouncing on their toes. Dexter is next to me. The four of us will do it together but in the end it's my leap to make. I'm the reason we're here.

Dex puts up a fist. I bump it.

He turns to me with a look of courage. Not for him but for me. He's doing this for me. He must see the nervousness on my face because he grips my shoulder and gives it a squeeze. Even through two layers of clothing I can feel the hard calluses on his hands. Calluses from jumping. Calluses from fighting. His courage surges into me and fills me with a sudden rush of bravado.

"Remember, Jack," he says in a voice so deep it flows like cough syrup. "There are no limits, only plateaus."

3.

Pace and Chimpo go first. Run to the edge of the platform and leap off. Fly over the tracks and land their toes on the concrete ledge on the other side. Grab onto the molding that separates the upper mosaic from the dirty white tiles below. Hang on.

This one is called a *precision jump* because it requires leaping off one object and landing on a precise spot on another. This precision jump in particular is not nearly as difficult as it might seem. The molding has a deep lip for a solid grab, and the ledge is large enough to land half your foot on it if you know how. Dexter knows how. He turns 270 degrees in the air and lands with the outside half of his foot along the ledge, grabs the molding with three fingers and turns into the wall to plant his other foot and hand.

The headlamp of the train lights up the mouth of the tunnel.

I run.

A slant of light comes racing across the tiles as the train comes screaming into the station. I plant my foot on the edge of the platform and hear Dex's reassuring voice.

There are no limits, only plateaus.

I leap off the platform. All I see is a blinding spot of white as the train comes at me in slow motion, and through the large front windows, the conductor's eyes go wide. I pass the crest. Now it's not the train but the wall that comes rushing toward me. This is when I realize I've put way too much into the launch. No matter how well I land, it won't be enough to keep me from...

SLAM!

Straight into the tiles. It flattens my nose, but I manage to hang on. Hug the wall.

Behind us, the train roars past with a billow of debris and

the loud mechanical clank of carriage wheels hitting track joints. I can feel the train at my back, only inches away, its seams and rivets tugging at my shirt as it races by. Even after the final car goes by, and I turn to see the back end of the train disappear down the tunnel, the adrenaline is still pumping through my body.

Pace and Chimpo have already released and are running up the tracks into the tunnel. Dexter hangs on a bit longer before he releases and lands perfectly on a single tie.

"You did it, Jack," he calls up.

"Yeah," I reply, still unable to make my hands let go of the wall.

Dexter sees this and realizes I might need a minute to gather myself, so he hops onto the concrete blocks and takes off after the others. But just before he enters the tunnel, Dexter jumps straight up into the air—pirouettes 180 degrees—lands in step and continues his forward progress walking backwards. "I've got a load to run. They're heading over to the wall at Riverfront Park. You remember the way, right?"

I doubt if he can see my nod, but I do. There isn't a single inch of Free City subway tunnels we haven't trekked. I know them all like the back of my hand. We all do. But Dex can see that I'm a little shaken up, so he double checks to be sure. "Yeah, I'm right behind them," I say.

At this, Dexter spins around and disappears into the tunnel.

Finally I release off the wall and spin 180 degrees to land. But unlike Dexter, my feet don't land on a crosstie; they land in the grimy flood channel between the rails. My head is so buzzed that the ground doesn't even feel real. My heart is still racing. I take a moment to shake out my hands and feet. It helps. Then I start up the tracks after the others.

Because I'm in the flood channel I can't see over the edge of the platform, which is why he seems to come out of nowhere— the well-built blonde kid in his late teens or early twenties, dressed all in black, who jumps off the platform and lands on the tracks between me and the tunnel.

I halt. The first thing I notice is the way he lands. Flat on his feet, letting the impact bend his knees instead of the other way around. I know at once he's not a traceur. If he intends to chase me then he doesn't stand a chance. He's bigger than me—that's a fact—but the fact that he's bigger than me doesn't mean anything at this point. I'm too light on my toes. I'll be up the stairs and over the gantry before he's even pulled himself back onto the platform…if that's what this is.

He doesn't move.

Now I wonder. *Who is this guy, and why is he standing in my way?*

From the platform above, I hear a scrape of hard-soled shoes approach, until the white-haired man in the dark trench coat and matching hat towers over me. I'm sure I haven't seen him before. I would know it if I had. For a moment I just stand there looking between him and the blonde kid, cautious enough to be on my guard but not enough to bolt.

The man speaks. "Would you care to come up or shall I come down?"

This I can do. In one continuous motion I hop onto the track rail and one-hand myself onto the platform. Shaking the grime off my hands, I watch the blonde kid do the same. That's when I reconsider. I guess the way he moves isn't so clumsy, it just seems that way to me.

"That's Bigsby," says the man. "Don't mind him."

I don't mind him. In my head I've already navigated two lanes out—one to the upper deck and the other into the tunnel. Just in case.

"My name is Cyril." He reaches into his pocket for a sterling silver business card holder and ejects one. It rolls out crisp. He hands it to me.

The card is a beautifully textured ivory. There isn't much by way of information, just a few lines embossed in gold and a topaz-blue 3D barcode hologram in the lower right corner.

ARCADIAN TRANSPORTS
when security is the only option
Cyril Murphy, Agent

Arcadian Transports. I could hardly believe it. And not just because they're the best firm out there; these guys had proven themselves nearly impossible to find. You can't even reach them. They have no known office, no address. They don't even have a telephone number. All they have is one very simple portal on the aggrenet. That's their only means of contact, and it's entirely one way. If you need their services, you send them a message detailing the job. If they're interested, they call you back. That's all. A bunch of hackers once tried to track them down by backtracing their portal but only ended up getting pinballed off all the proxies until they landed at a live show in some strip club in Little Ukraine.

I could just hear Dexter laughing in my head. *A bunch of hackers?*

Alright, it wasn't a bunch of hackers, it was me. I did it. Dex asked me to do it, and that was where we ended up before I broke off the backtrace. Ever since I've known him, running for Arcadian Transports has been Dex's dream job. The trouble was the way it works; you don't seek out Arcadian to become one of their runners. They have to come to you.

"I don't have to ask if you're familiar with our firm," says Cyril.

I'm not sure if this is a statement or a question. "I know who you are," I reply.

"Very good. You know who we are, and you know what we do, so let's get down to brass tacks. I've been following you very closely, Jack. Your times at the Open last month were quite impressive; your lanes through the course very clever."

Cyril was talking about the Free City Open PK Exhibition that we participated in a month earlier. "If you're going by those numbers then Dexter Drake is the person you're looking for. His skillset far exceeds mine."

Cyril kind of smirks. At least I think that's what it is. "I think you know that's not true. Trust me, we know all about Dexter Drake. He may have a few more moves than you on the run, but you're just the kind of person we're looking for. You're smart. Quick on your feet. Highly intelligent. Very capable. We could use someone like you on the sneakernet. Consider this an offer,

Jack. I want you to come run for us."

I'm bothered by the way they so easily dismiss Dexter. If they've been following my traces then they know I've gotten pretty good at it, maybe even real good, but not as good as Dexter. Plus he has the fighting skills to boot. Or maybe that's just the thing they don't want. If your only training is in flight, then fight is never an option. So maybe Dexter's ability to choose is actually working against him. Regardless, there is a much bigger issue here than that. Tracing the sneakernet? That is a very steep curve of calculated risk.

"Don't answer yet," says Cyril. "Go home and think about it. Remember, a year or two of this could pay your way through school. You were supposed to be enrolled at the New England Institute of Technology by now, weren't you?"

I nod. Silver lining aside, it still burns that I'm not.

"You still could."

The words are like honey to my ears. How could I not be tempted by such an offer? "How would I get in touch with you?" I ask.

"The card's tagged. Scan it and I'll find you."

"Scan it where?"

"Anywhere," he replies. "It's a trigger code. The scanner will report back an error on the local system, but the code will pipe out to the aggrenet and do what it's been designed to do."

I look down at the shiny hologram in wonder. Writing a trigger code is easy. Writing a trigger code that is completely undetectable, that's the hard part. That's top-level national security type stuff. "How do you slip the data stream past the packet-switching monitors?" I ask.

This time I see it more clearly. Cyril actually smirks. "Smart kid," he says.

Cyril turns and heads toward the stairs. Bigsby takes a moment to fix on me with his cold, slate blue eyes. I don't know what it is, but there's something about him I just don't like.

"Nice talking to you," I say as he turns to follow.

This seems to amuse Cyril. "He doesn't say much, but Bigsby is one hell of a runner."

Right, I think. *I'll be the judge of that.*

I return to the card. *Arcadian Transports*. The name alone reminds me of all the time and effort I spent trying to track these guys down for Dexter. All to no avail. Now it's all right here in the palm of my hand.

"Why so hard to locate?" I ask.

Cyril answers over his shoulder. "They can't compromise what they can't find, Jack."

4.

Later that night, legs shredded and arms dangling like rubber, I make my way home from the bus station after a long day of training. Tonight, I'm not thinking about that. I have other things to think about. I know that running the sneakernet is crazy, but I can't stop thinking about what Cyril said about making enough money to pay for school. The worst part about having to leave the magnet academy was that I lost access to all the proprietary grants and scholarships that would have paid my way through college. Without those awards, the best schools weren't even on the table anymore. My plan was to work three or four years after graduation to save up for it. But if I go with Cyril's offer, I could earn the same amount in one or two. But—is it worth two years of risk to save two years of my life? To be honest, I'm not really sure. But I would be running. Running, even if it's running from danger, has to beat sitting on my ass for ten hours a day variable-checking the sloppy code of mediocre programmers. Just the thought of it makes me cringe. If ever there was a digital-age analogue to Bartleby the scrivener, that has to be it.

The stop sign at the end of the block glows octagonal red as a pair of headlights approaches from behind. Ordinarily, a slow approach at this time of night would have me bouncing on my toes, but this one comes with a familiar squeal that I know all too well. I let the beat-up pickup truck pull up alongside me.

"Hello, Jack," smiles the old teacher through his Santa Claus beard. It's Mr. Chupick, my faculty advisor.

"Hey, Mr. Chupick."

"Can I give you a ride?"

"If it isn't out of your way."

Mr. Chupick shoots his thumb at the giant water tank

mounted to the flatbed that still has some slosh to it. "Hop in," he says, "I'm just running the rest of the water around town."

Mr. Chupick lives on a small farm on the outskirts of town. He grows some produce and maintains some livestock, but mostly he draws water from his well and supplies it to those around town who can't afford the hookup to TerraAqua. If he sounds like a nice man, that's because he is, but make no mistake. Beneath his pleasant exterior he is also a tough man, and he can do almost anything. Whenever Mrs. Bach's car wouldn't start, he was always the one who got it going. When three pallets of sheetrock donated to the elementary school were left collecting dust because there was no money to hire a contractor to do the job, it was Mr. Chupick who went in on the weekends to put it up. That is something that has always impressed me about him, how good he is with his hands. I'm good with my hands when it comes to electronics—wires, transistors, antennas, that sort of thing. Mr. Chupick is good with his hands when it comes to the stuff that really matters, the stuff that people can't live without. I know about things that can change the world; the stuff he knows could rebuild it from scratch.

I get in and yank the door closed behind me. "So where's the water going tonight?"

"The food trucks. They could use a topping off."

I suppose it's irony that Mr. Chupick says this just as we pass three boarded-up storefronts that all used to be restaurants.

Like many towns across North America, Brentwood was once a decent suburb that tried to become an affluent suburb by selling its energy rights. And just like many other towns across North America, things went very bad very quickly. In Brentwood, it wasn't mercury in the dirt or dioxin in the air, it was a major hydrofracking mishap that caused a slurry of chemicals and natural gas to poison the town's water supply. Just like that. One day you had the cleanest spring water coming out of your tap, the next you could set a match to it and light the stream on fire. No joke, people could actually set their taps on fire. After that, many of the former residents left town, mostly because they could afford to leave. They took their settlement checks and moved into gated communities further upstate, and Brentwood became just another halfway suburb for people whose former residences were out in the squatter settlements. People who previously could only ever dream of living in a suburb like Brentwood. But now that the local water was toxic, who else could ever hope to live there?

"There's something I've always wondered about," I ask Mr. Chupick, "how come your well wasn't ruined in the disaster?"

"A lot of people wonder about that. The spill happened above the water table. It affected the reservoir and all the surface water, but mine is a deeper well that taps into an isolated pool of groundwater."

"So how much water do you have down there?"

"That's the sixty-four thousand dollar question. The Blackburn Corps of Engineers came into Brentwood and did a complete topographical survey a few months ago. That would tell me the answer, but I can't get them to release the results. If I could see those surveys, I would know exactly how much there is."

"Why won't they show them to you?"

"Because even though they're contracted by the North American Alliance, they're still a private company. There used to be this thing called *freedom of information*, but that went out with the bathwater once the corporations took over."

"So how come you never joined the water collective?"

"Oh, they've tried. Ever since the disaster, the water collective has been after me to join. Sure, I could let TerraAqua take over the management of my water rights. They would come onto my property, cement up my well, drive a pump into the ground and turn it into a relay in their water system. In return, I would receive a monthly revenue from the collective. But who would that benefit? Right now, I draw the water myself and distribute it as I see fit. I don't need TerraAqua to manage that." Mr. Chupick steers the truck onto my street.

"Is that why you didn't leave like everyone else?"

"I didn't leave because this town is my home. After Mrs. Chupick passed away, I couldn't see moving anywhere else.

It may not be much, but all of my memories are in that little farmhouse." We pull up to my house. "If you want to have a real sense of community, you have to marry a town like you marry a person. It's for better or worse. Brentwood may have a sickness right now, but I vowed to stay in sickness and in health. Understand?"

"I do." The Free City had a lot of things going for it, but a sense of community was never one of them. Even at the academy, being a year younger than all my classmates made it tough to have any real friends. Moving out to Brentwood was the first time in my life I had either, so I do understand where Mr. Chupick is coming from.

"Besides," he says as he lifts the shifter into park, "where would I go?"

Where indeed. I thank him for the ride and throw the door closed behind me.

•   •   •

I hear Martin mumbling something in the living room. He does this sometimes when he's trying to figure something out. Whatever it is, he can tell me about it in the morning. I grab the rotted banister and start upstairs but then stop for a moment to listen to some of Martin's mumbling. I can't make out the words but they sound unusually spastic.

What is it that has him so frazzled?

It's only two steps to the landing but it hurts every inch of my body. Toes, knees, the balls of my feet, they're all sore. I drag myself around the stairs and into the living room where Martin is pacing back and forth in a stylishly loose-fitting black suit with polished black shoes. His white shirt is unbuttoned at the neck. His unlinked cuffs dangle haphazardly from his jacket sleeves, and his hair is tied back cleanly. If James Bond were a nerd, he'd be Martin Baxter.

"Bollinger Bands," he keeps saying. "Bollinger Bands."

I have no idea what that means.

"It's just Bollinger Bands applied to a card distribution."

"How was the game?" I ask.

"You expect abnormalities in the data set, of course. You expect those abnormalities, but over time those abnormalities should be normalized by the moving average. The standard deviations do allow for a margin of error." He places his fingers on his lips and purses them. "I did everything right," he says.

"Martin?" But he isn't listening.

"I did everything right. I kept the count. I calculated everything, *everything* on the fly. I kept a forty-card moving average and bound it high and low with one standard deviation. That tells you your entry and exit points, right?"

"If you say so." I barely grasp what he's saying.

"I tracked it all. I knew exactly which way the table was trending. When it was trending up, I pressed up accordingly. When it started going the other way, I pressed back down. I split my tens exactly when I was supposed to, doubled when the numbers said to double, stayed when they said not to. Hit. Stick. Double. Split. I did everything right. Even on the insurance, which is normally a sucker bet, I knew precisely when the numbers favored hedging. I did everything right." Martin turns to look at me. "I did everything right. The numbers were not wrong." Now I can see the fear in his eyes. My stomach drops as Martin lifts his glasses off the bridge of his nose and pinches his sinuses. "Fifty thousand."

"You owe the entire stake to the syndicate?"

"It was a zero-sum game," says Martin. "All or nothing."

He doesn't need to say it. We both know what that means. This is exactly how the syndicate operates. First they get their hooks into you, then they own you. In general, you don't ever want to owe the syndicate any amount of money, but I've seen people get in deeper over far less. Chimpo's uncle once took a galvanized pipe to the kneecap over just a few grand, but that was only because Chimpo's uncle had nothing else to offer, so when he couldn't pay, they put him on disability and collected that. But not Martin. Martin is far too valuable for that. He's someone they can exploit. Currency transfers, money laundering, wire fraud—all the things that would land Martin in prison if he got caught. "How long do we have?" I ask.

"I can make payments for thirty days. After that, I'll have to make other arrangements."

Other arrangements. That's always how they get you.

"My back is to the wall now, isn't it?" Martin mumbles. "There's no other choice now, is there?"

Martin looks to me as if for confirmation.

"No, there isn't," I say. But that's only because I fully expect him to say that he's going to have to take the offer from Grumwell. I mean, that would be the reasonable assumption, wouldn't it?

"We're going to have to run."

Run? "Run where?"

"Into the squatter settlements. It's the one place the syndicate won't come after us."

My jaw hangs open. Was he kidding? "It's the one place the syndicate won't come after us because even they won't mess with the settlement cartels."

"Don't worry, we'll be fine."

I immediately think of Dexter, who had to move into the squatter settlements when he was 5 after his family lost everything they had in the big asset crunch. The Drakes didn't have any choice at the time. We do.

"No. No way. We're not moving again." It's not a response but an assertion. "This is our home, Martin. We're not leaving it. What about the offer from Grumwell?"

I can see Martin grind his teeth. "That's not an option. There is no way I would ever work for Grumwell!"

Even in a storm of fifty-foot waves, or in our case one giant fifty-thousand foot wave, Martin clings to his ideals like a life preserver. Ever since the takeover of Martin's old company, Grumwell has had a standing offer for Martin loaded with benefits, perks, and a substantial signing bonus. I know this because they never let a month go by without reminding him of it. They want him, and they are willing to pay anything to get him.

"Do you have any idea what they did to me?" he says.

"I know, Martin. They stole your company away from you."

"No, Jack. If only it were that simple. Companies get swallowed all the time. That's business. Grumwell didn't just take Delphi away from me, they blackballed me among my own peers. Do you think it's just *bad luck* that no other firm will touch me?"

I know it isn't because Martin and I don't believe in luck.

"Grumwell made it known that any other firm who hired me would suffer the same fate as Delphi."

"Why would they do that?"

"Because that's the way Miles Tolan operates. When he wants something bad enough, he doesn't just take it by force. He orchestrates it so that the thing he wants comes to him. He removes all other options until Grumwell is the only one remaining, then he sits back and waits for his prize to come to him." Martin drives his index finger into his head like he's tapping at his brain. "This is what they want, Jack! This is what they're after! But I will never let Miles Tolan have it. You have to take a stand for something in this world, and this is mine. I believe that knowledge is the shared intellectual property of all who seek it—not something to be owned by the few, or controlled by the one. My intellectual property is my own, for me to share with whomever I choose. It is not for sale to anyone. Especially not Miles Tolan."

Now I'm the one who's grinding my teeth. "That's great, Martin. That's just wonderful. Every time you take a stand, I'm the one who ends up paying for it. I worked my ass off at the magnet academy so that I would be a shoe-in for every award. Then everything fell apart and you brought us out here. But did you hear me complain about it even once? No, I didn't. I just accepted the fact that I would have to work a few years and save up the money to pay for it myself. And that's fine, Martin. I'm willing to do that. But I am not willing to do this. I'm not leaving again." If Martin has any kind of rebuttal, I don't give him the chance to make it. I'm already marching out the room.

"Thirty days, Jack." He calls after me. "I can cover us for thirty days."

"A lot can happen in thirty days," I reply.

Upstairs, I slam my bedroom door shut. I didn't tell Martin

about Arcadian because I know he'll never let me do it. However, that's not really his call anymore, is it? If Martin can make rash decisions that affect our future then surely I can do the same. Martin made his decision, now it's time for me to make mine. Martin may be all out of options, but I'm not. I can do it. I can run us out of this mess.

I dig my thin screen out of my backpack and drop it onto the desk. Place it in hologram mode and call Dex. "Hey, Jack," he answers. "What's going on?"

I don't say anything, and he sees it almost immediately.

"What's wrong?"

"Dex, I need you to tell me everything I need to know about running the sneakernet."

Dexter stares at me with surprise. "Hermes?"

I shake my head and hold up the card for him to see. "Arcadian."

Dexter's surprise turns to disbelief. "How the hell…"

"They tapped me in the tunnel this afternoon. And then just now I found out about this thing between Martin at the syndicate … I have no choice, Dex. I'm going for it."

Dexter sighs. I know he's not jealous of me, but I also know what it's like to watch someone else get the thing you want more than anything, even if that someone is your best friend. Dexter always thought he'd be the one running for Arcadian one day. We all thought that.

"Are you absolutely sure you want to do this?" he asks.

"Yes."

"I mean it, Jack. Tracing the sneakernet is nothing to play at. It's all or nothing. You either get into it with everything you've got, or you don't get into it at all. That goes double for Arcadian. All of their transports are high value."

I look down at the card. *When security is the only option.* Then back to Dex. "I know that," I say. "I know that, and I'm in."

WHEN SECURITY IS THE ONLY OPTION

5.

The beige sedan is so nondescript that I don't even notice it until it pulls up alongside me. Bigsby is behind the wheel. I guess it's implied that he's there to pick me up. The front door is locked. I release the handle and wait for him to unlock it, but he flicks his thumb at the back seat instead. I get in.

The beginning of the ride is strained. Bigsby doesn't respond to the simplest of platitudes. Whether it's by orders or by choice, his lips are sealed. Even when I ask him about the work. "So how long have you been running for Arcadian?"

No answer.

"You don't have to go into details, I just want to know what to expect."

Hands two and ten on the wheel, eyes on the road.

"Come on, Bigs. Don't be like that. We're on the same team here."

Bigs eyes me in the rearview mirror, his way of saying he doesn't like that one bit. That's when I let it go. I don't know what his problem is, but it's of no concern to me. We ride in silence for a few minutes until Bigsby turns on the Free City news stream. More discussion about the Blackburn scandal. More about the company's finances. More about how broke they really are. And much more speculation about how badly this whole thing could compromise the security of the Alliance.

Blah, blah, blah.

The thing is, even if Blackburn has done business with the Caliphate, just what does the Alliance Senate think they're going to do? Blackburn, Ltd. isn't just the biggest standing army in the world, it's *our* standing army. Blackburn *is* the Complex. Sure, there are other defense contractors out there, but none that could even come close to handling the full military needs of the North American Alliance. If Blackburn really is *too big to fail*, as they used to say back in the Old-50, then those other companies are all *too small to succeed*. So my guess is, after all is said and done, and the people responsible are given their slaps on the wrist, Blackburn won't be going anywhere.

But still they continue belaboring the discussion. Like any debate, it goes on and on and nothing is said that hasn't been said a thousand times before, so I pull out my thin screen and enjoy the ride into the Free City of Tri-Insula, or what used to be the old City of New York. That's when it hits me, right as my thin screen flashes alive, whoever came up with that trigger code for Cyril's business card had to be Morlock. I mean, to pipe across the aggrenet completely undetected like that, it had to be piping through the Morlock layer.

That's right, the Morlock layer, otherwise known as the undernet.

That invisible layer of packet switching that lies beneath the aggrenet, the one most people have never heard of, and the few who have simply dismiss as urban legend, it's real. It is very, *very* real. Martin is Morlock, officially. And though I'm technically still waiting for my work to be tagged, I consider myself Morlock as well. I can't tell you how many of us there are. That's kind of the point. We all use the same handle; not just for anonymity, it hides our numbers as well. For all anyone knows, there could be five or five thousand of us behind that tag. Only one person knows for sure—the only Morlock with a unique identifier is the leader, Moreau. But if you think that tracking a single individual would be much easier than tracking an entire collective, you're wrong. If you know where and how to look, you can always find traces of Morlock, but over the years Moreau has proven to be completely untraceable. Believe me, I've tried. I've scoured the furthest regions of the undernet looking for him, only to come up empty every time. To say that Moreau is very good at covering his tracks is an understatement. Lots of people are very good at covering their tracks. I'm very good at covering my tracks. But there are those people in the world—you know the kind—who are so good at avoiding detection that they never leave tracks in the first place. Moreau is one of those people.

Nevertheless, finding him has become a personal mission. I can't even say why, really; I just want to be the one who does. It's not *him* I'm after per se, it's the challenge of finding him. And on that subject, I do have a theory. The way I figure it, his base of operations has to be somewhere out in the squatter settlements. That makes the most sense. With so many people creating so much transmission in such close proximity, you can't pinpoint anything in all that noise. Not unless you were to sneakernet in and do it in person. But that would open up a whole other can of worms. Like any refugee camp, shantytown, or favela, the squatter settlements has its own laws, its own system of justice, and its own set of rules. The first rule being—if you're not from the settlements then you are an outsider, and they hate outsiders.

We take the bridge into the Free City.

Now my nerves take over. Scanning the card was the easy part, but the closer we get to those massive buildings whose secrets I will shortly be tasked with carrying, the more it becomes real. As we pass over the river, I try to take my mind off it by staring out the window, but all I see is the famous Grumwell building towering more than a kilometer into the sky. The largest building in the world, it is a monolith of black marble and mirrored glass that gleams in the sun like a modern-day Great Pyramid. But what else would you expect from the biggest corporation in the world? So enormous is the Grumwell building that looking at it from the moving car seems to make the entire world go by in slow motion.

But that slowness ends the moment we take the off-ramp. Bigsby tosses me around the back of the car as we make our way through the Free City traffic until he takes a sudden turn into an underground garage. That makes me wonder; why would a firm who goes to such great lengths to remain hidden just give up their location like that? I mean, I have no intention of revealing their location, but you'd think they would have taken some precaution. Put a blindfold on me at the very least.

But everything makes more sense when Bigsby delivers me

to the eighteenth floor suite that is little more than a gutted space. Scattered all around the room are silver cases lined with foam cutouts. Each shape corresponds to some piece of gear that has already been set up in the room. In the middle of the room sits a medical chair under a blast of sterile lights. Next to that is a rack of surgical equipment. But the most interesting thing of all is the link. These guys aren't porting into the aggrenet through the building's infrastructure; they have their own rifle antenna pointed out the window.

The first person I see is the big bald guy who looks like a prison thug working the hardware. He has tattoos all up his neck and even on his scalp, but the tattoo I notice most is on his enormous forearm. That one depicts a large eagle with a snake dangling from its beak.

I don't even see Cyril approach from the side. "It's good to have you on board, Jack."

"Thanks."

He checks his watch. "We've got a lot to get through today, so what do you say we—"

"—get down to brass tacks?" I offer.

Cyril smirks in that nearly imperceptible way of his. "Smart kid."

6.

The bald guy's name is Snake, which I soon learn refers not to the slithering reptile but to a type of eagle that feeds on it. The *Snake Eagle*, as it is known, is exactly what is tattooed on his arm. Snake was once the best runner Arcadian had, until his age finally caught up with him and he developed chronic tendonitis in his knees. Now he's their head technician. Apparently it helps for new runners to be ushered in by someone who's actually been in their shoes. I can see why. Snake isn't what you would call personable, in fact he's not very friendly at all—surly if anything—but he is not unsympathetic. As hard as I try not to let my nervousness show, Snake can smell it all over me. He doesn't say anything at first, not until Cyril steps aside for a moment to make sure all the paperwork is in order. Then he leans in close.

"You're a little scared," he says.

I nod.

"You should be."

I—what? If this is supposed to be a pep talk then his technique could use some work.

"Fear is a survival instinct. Maybe the best survival instinct we have. You will need it out there." We lock eyes. Snake's are dark and narrow, but I can see at once he's trying to help. "I've seen over a hundred Aves come and go. Take my word for it, it's always the cocky ones who are the first to get clipped. A little bit of fear is a good thing. Fear will make you hypervigilant, and hypervigilance will keep you alive. Just don't let it take you over. Remember, a paralyzed runner is a dead runner."

Cyril returns holding a titanium box with a laser-etched serial number. A hiss of escaping air fills the room as he opens it and shows me the injection cartridge inside. He holds it closer for me to examine. Inside the cartridge is a small translucent blob with hanging tentacles suspended in a clear aqueous solution. It is about the size of a dime and looks exactly like a jellyfish.

"This is the bioidentical cortex chip that will be implanted subcutaneously on the inside of your forearm. It is a proprietary biocircuit developed in our labs specifically for this purpose, and it is unlike any other in the world." Cyril picks up a UV light and runs it over the box, making the chip inside glow an iridescent purple as it reveals the vast network of micro-optical fibers running through it. "Right now it's inert, but once it enters your body, it will hardwire itself into your neural axons to form a synaptic link with your central nervous system."

Snake snaps on a pair of latex gloves and takes the chip from Cyril. He places it in the injector gun.

"You are the power source, Jack. The chip draws it power electrochemically from your body. That means there are certain precautions that you will now have to take. We'll go over those in a minute."

Snake aggressively rubs an alcohol swab over the meaty part of my forearm.

"I won't lie to you, Jack…" The hairs on my forearm stand straight up as the cold steel tip of the implant gun touches my skin. "This is going to hurt."

Before I even register Cyril's warning, Snake braces my arm and fires the gun.

"Ow!"

Imagine the biggest wasp you've ever seen. Now imagine five of them. Five stingers digging into you all at once, all on the same square inch of flesh. Like five serrated claws clamping down on a single patch of skin. The bite is so great it makes my arm twitch, which only makes the pain worse. This lasts for what feels like minutes but is probably no longer than ten seconds. It lasts until I can feel the lump. Just under my skin at first, but soon it sinks deeper. I feel what can only be the cortex chip's tentacles piercing through the tendons beneath as the wasp stingers sink deeper into my arm.

Until I feel the jolt—like an electric shock running down the entire length of my arm. Then my arm is on fire. Burning deep inside my skin like every pore has been filled with piping hot acid that is now dissolving its way through my flesh.

I lurch ten inches out of the chair, but Snake shoves me back down and holds me there.

"Something's wrong!" I scream.

"No, that's normal," says Snake. "Nerve pain is the worst kind there is."

It feels like my arm is blistering red bubbles of oozing flesh from my wrist to my elbow. Only it isn't. The only physical mark on my arm is the small red ring at the injection site. The rest is all nerves.

"You just have to wait it out."

I close my eyes and focus. Deal with it as best I can. It takes a mountain of effort just to endure it—more that I have to spare—but just as I reach my breaking point, it begins to dissipate. Slowly at first, then all at once, it goes as quickly as it came. I check my arm. Other than the injection mark, there's no real damage, even if it does feel like it's just been dipped into a 12-molar bath of hydrochloric acid.

"There now, that wasn't too bad, was it?" says Cyril.

Snake flashes me a private look as he releases my arm. *Right, like he would know.*

Cyril continues. "Every other firm out there is still implanting its runners with decades-old silicon chips. That's why so many of them get dismembered. It's simply easier to grab the entire limb and dig the chip out later." Cyril runs the UV light over my arm until it finds the glowing purple spot just beneath the skin. Considering how deep the pain was, I'm surprised how close to the surface it is. Snake circles it with a surgical marker. "This chip is now part of your biology. Hacking off your arm will do no good. That will only destroy both chip and cargo."

For the first time I feel a sense of relief. "At least I don't have to worry about waking up in a ditch minus an arm."

But Snake shakes his head. "That just means they'll have to drag you back to the lab and strap you to a table to get at it."

Wonderful. That's just great. Leave it to these guys to make getting my arm cut off the better of two options.

"Now, there are three things you have to know," begins Cyril. "First, you must protect the circuit from a targeted impact. It can take a minor bruising, but if the blow is concentrated enough to burst the chip while you're loaded up, the release of live data cells into your bloodstream will be toxic."

Toxic! Was he kidding? "If the chip is part of my biology then how can it be toxic?"

"It's like your appendix," says Cyril. "That's part of your biology too, but if it bursts open it'll poison you from the inside. Don't worry—the chip is resilient. You can see we injected it through a pinhole. In most cases you won't even have to worry about it, but it is something you need to be aware of.

"Second, you must keep your body's core temperature between 95 and 101 degrees Fahrenheit. Outside of this range, you risk permanent damage to the chip and/or complete loss of cargo. Avoid heatstroke. Avoid hypothermia. Drink lots of water when you're hot and bundle up when you're cold.

"Third and most important, since it's the one you can't avoid. This cortex chip draws its energy directly from your body. As of now, it will draw a very small and constant amount to remain active, but your body will adjust to that in no time. The energy required to maintain cargo, however, will be much larger. It will impact your metabolism. The bigger or more complex the cargo, the more energy it will take to maintain, which means your hypoglycemic curve will be very steep. What that means is, you will have to keep your blood sugar up. Right now you can probably go a day without eating before you start to feel faint. When you're carrying cargo, that window will shrink to about four hours if you're lucky, even less if you're under strenuous pursuit. Once you start to feel faint, you'll have twenty minutes to get some fuel into your system before you pass out. Thirty minutes tops."

That doesn't sound good at all. "What happens then?" I ask.

"What happens if you pass out in the middle of a run? Oh, I don't think you want to find out, Jack."

Cyril's remark is followed by an ominous pause during

which I definitely wonder what I have gotten myself into. I wait for Cyril to continue, but he has nothing more to add. It is Snake who finally breaks the silence.

"It's time for you to get branded," he says and swings another machine over my arm.

I inch back in the chair. "What is that?"

"It's just a plain old laser-guided tattoo iron," he says as he slaps it into place. He seems surprised that I even have to ask. "Standard equipment found in any tattoo parlor around the world."

Tattoo? Okay. I'm not bothered by the idea of getting one; it's just one more thing I wasn't expecting.

"From here on out, you will not be just another runner," says Cyril. "This the moment when you become one of our Aves. Runners are a dime a dozen. Our Aves have been handpicked for the job. That is why Arcadian Transports is the best at what we do, Jack. You can take pride in that. You are about to become part of an elite group of data runners."

Snake hands me a thin screen loaded with an index of birds. "No one beyond this room is to know your name," he says, "not even other Aves. It's a security issue. From this point forward you will be known only by your tag, which is why you should pick something that represents you." He takes a moment to eye me up. "You're in good shape, but you're very lean, so don't go with a massive bird. In fact, you don't look like the kind of person who would attack trouble head-on, so I would stay away from the birds of prey altogether. Think about your traits. Every human characteristic can be found in the avian world, so find the bird that best represents your strengths. This is the tag that will define you as a runner. Don't just pick it at random, let it be an extension of who you are."

It seems pretty clear to me why he chose the Snake Eagle. It takes a certain kind of understated bravado to be able to swoop in undetected and pluck a snake off the ground—the perfect mix of stealth and strength. I can see that in him. Unfortunately, that doesn't help me any as I scroll through the taxonomy. I haven't got the slightest clue what bird best represents me. But then I remember something I once saw about crows. Crows are incredible problem solvers, capable not only of using tools but of fashioning those tools from scratch. The amount of wit and reasoning skill this requires apparently makes them one of the most intelligent creatures on the planet. So there's that. But then I start thinking about ravens, which may not be as intelligent as crows but have other traits that I admire. Like their vocal ability to imitate certain sounds. That's a form of ghosting, right? Which is very similar to what I do whenever I ghost the aggrenet. Ravens also have a much longer lifespan: something like thirty years to a crow's eight. So there's that as well.

Crow or raven. Raven or crow.

I wonder. "Is there a cross between a raven and a crow?"

Snake takes the thin screen back in a way that tells me he knows exactly what I'm looking for. Working with new Aves like this, he probably has every species of bird memorized.

"*Corvus corone*," he says. "Literally *raven crow*." He goes through the index until he finds exactly what he's looking for and shows it to me. "Commonly known as the Carrion Crow."

The Carrion Crow.

I'm not even done considering it when Snake renders an image into the tattoo iron and adjusts it over my arm. "Wait, I'm not sure that's the one I want."

"Yes you are. If that's what your gut is telling you, don't second-guess it."

Snake opens a lacquer box, revealing a series of ink jars inside. He pulls out the large one of black and holds it up for me to see. The color inside is thick and rich and leaves curtains on the glass as he turns it in his hand. "This is irradiated scorpion ink. It will help block your chip's signal from being tracked."

Okay, the irradiated part I get. I assume it's similar to what they use in hospitals, and equally safe. What piques my curiosity is the other part. "What do you mean *scorpion* ink?" I ask, thinking it has something to do with their venom.

"The pigment that is used to make these inks comes from the pulverized exoskeletons of scorpions."

Snake fills one vial with black and another with a very dark purple that looks almost metallic. He attaches both vials to the tattoo iron and starts the machine. The laser guides the needle array over my forearm. On any other day this might actually sting, but today it's just a prickle compared to what I have already endured. In the meantime, Cyril presents me with a large aluminum case. He opens it. Inside is a full set of upper torso body armor, gunmetal gray with gold trim, so new it still has the plastic film on it. Cyril peels it off and removes the armor from the case.

"Titanium meta-aramid ultramesh," he says with a rap of his knuckles. "The best you can get. It's a bit heavier than a strict titanium microweave, but you get that back tenfold in tensile strength."

I'm not worried about the quality of the armor. What concerns me is why he's giving it to me in the first place. Everything has happened so fast that I can hardly wrap my head around it, but this pushes everything else to the side. This is different. Seeing the body armor brings it close to the chest. Maybe a little too close to the chest.

Cyril seems to know exactly what I'm thinking as he returns the gear to the case. "I won't lie to you," he says. "Arcadian cargos are always high value, and we've had some unexpected challenges as of late. It's getting pretty rough out there. Hopefully, you'll never need it, but you won't be doing yourself any harm by wearing it. Just think of it as a safety net."

"Has anyone ever been shot?" I ask.

It's a simple question, but it seems like Cyril has to consider how to answer it. "They've been shot *at*," he replies. Then he taps the case. "The body armor works."

The tattoo iron zips to a halt as the carriage returns to the base. I have to wait for Snake to finish blotting the blood and ink off my arm before I can see it, but when I do, I am amazed by the result.

The image is of a Carrion Crow in flight. Drawn in black with just enough purple mixed in to give the plumage an iridescent sheen. Wings spread. Feathers splayed at the tips almost as if it's swooping. Beak slightly open, ready to caw. But the most captivating thing of all is the eye, the one visible eye that looks outward. Not at me but at the outside observer looking back at my arm. It stalks. Like the eyes in those paintings that appear to follow you wherever you go, the eye of the bird on my arm draws you in. Mesmerizes.

The eye does have a functional purpose too. It happens to be exactly where the chip is. "What do you think?" Snake asks.

"It's perfect."

"It gets better," he says, picking up the UV light. "Scorpions produce a fluorescent compound called *beta-Carboline* in their cuticles, which intensifies with each molting until the hardening of their final exoskeletons."

Snake shines the UV light across my arm, and I am immediately awestruck by how the dark bird lights up. It glows indigo like some sort of mythical creature. All except for the vigilant eye that shines pale purple from the chip beneath.

"The Carrion," says Cyril. "From here on out, that will be your tag."

It isn't until Snake removes the UV light and the bird on my arm stops glowing that I recover my senses. "Okay, so what now?"

"Now you wait." Cyril opens another package to show me one more item nested in foam. This one needs no explanation. It's a standard Superconducting Quantum Interference Device, or SQUID, interface. The same kind doctors use to communicate with surgically implanted components like pacemakers. "I assume you know how to use this."

"There's not much to know," I reply. It's totally noninvasive. All you have to do is stick the sensor over the implant. The link will form magnetically through the skin. Truth be told, I don't even need it because Martin and I already have every interface known to man down in his workshop. But ours are piecemeal, and those SQUIDs are expensive, and this one is brand new and surgical grade, so I'm not about to turn it down.

"When the chip in your arm vibrates, use the interface to link it to your thin screen. That will give you the pickup location. Go there. They'll load you up and give you the destination.

Deliver the cargo. Once delivery is made, the job is done. We're going to keep you local for a while, so your runs will always be point to point within the Free City. Payment gets wired into your account upon completion of each job. It's that simple. If all goes well, you won't see us again for a while."

"What if I need to get in touch with you?"

"Just like the business card, run your chip over any scanner ported into the aggrenet. The scanner will return a local error, but there's a trigger code in there that will get back to us."

"Then what?"

"Then we'll find you."

7.

"This is the stupidest thing I've ever heard in my entire life," says Dexter without a hint of exaggeration.

To be fair, it is the stupidest thing I've ever suggested in my entire life. "But you did bring it?" I ask anyway.

"It's in my bag," he says. "But let me just say again for the record how completely moronic this is."

The old public library is a three-story building that's been boarded over. This particular section of Main Street got hit pretty hard by the downturn, so the library is just one in a string of abandoned buildings that's been fenced off at street level. The only way in is from the top.

Three buildings over, Dex and I use the fire escape to get to the rooftop of the old gym. I guess it's kind of ironic. Back when the town had money, people would use machines with hologram projectors to simulate climbing up a wall when all they had to do was go outside and do it for real. Although looking at it now, I guess it could only be people like us who see the forest through the trees. All those open-faced buildings. All those heaps of rubble and half-crumbled walls. All those towers of vacant Blackburn Corps of Engineers scaffolding that are just enough to make it seem like a reconstruction effort is underway when really there is none. All those exposed pipes and jittery old fire escapes. All the steel cables running down empty elevator shafts. It all makes the perfect training ground for the Brentwood Dragons. That's what makes us different. While everyone else compares Brentwood to its former glory, we embrace it for what it is now. We see the beautiful playground beyond the blight. Because for us, there are no obstacles that are not challenges. Obstacles are like plateaus, and there are plenty of plateaus, but those plateaus are never limits. There are no limits.

From the rooftop of the old gym, Dexter and I gap jump the buildings to get to the old library.

All week long I've been tracing in dressy clothes with my body armor underneath to get used to both of them. I figure if I'm going to make it on the sneakernet then I'm going to have to blend in, and there is no way I'm going to do that in the Free City looking like a kid from Brentwood. The shoes were harder, but Dexter helped me find a pair of black lace-up boots that are both stylish and functional, protective but light. The new clothes I got used to quickly, since that was how I used to dress anyway. The armor is a different story. It's a big change, that's for sure. Particularly when rolling out of a landing. I've grown accustom to feeling the ground across my back as my frame absorbs the energy. But now I have this shell between me and the ground that doesn't absorb but transfers the energy, so each time I come out of the roll there is all this extra momentum popping me off the ground like a spring. Which isn't necessarily a bad thing. I might even use it to my advantage once I get used to it.

Dexter and I make our way down the stairwell to the third floor. The entire floor is empty. All that remains are the concrete pillars and load-bearing walls holding up the ceiling. Everything else is gone. Even the pipes in the walls have been gutted.

"Are you sure about this?" he asks.

"Cyril said that other runners have been shot at."

"Shot *at* doesn't mean *shot*," says Dex.

"Yes, but getting shot at means that sooner or later one of those bullets is going to hit the target. Think of this as a dry run."

"Dry run in stupidity."

"It's a controlled experiment."

Dex shakes his head. "This is so stupid, Jack."

"No, it's not. I have no idea what it feels like. The first time is going to be a shock no matter what, and I don't want that to happen out in the field. By doing it like this, I'll at least know what to expect. It's building the muscle memory, that's all. I'm just desensitizing my body to it."

"Are you even listening to yourself? You're talking about

PLEASANT GROVE HIGH SCHOOL MEDIA CENTER

desensitizing your body to a bullet, Jack. A bullet."

"Not the bullet itself, Dex, but the impact." Actually, now that I do listen to myself, the whole thing does start to sound a little crazy. But then aren't half the things we do crazy? "It's not like the bullet will pass through the armor."

"How can you be sure?"

"Because this gear is certified to stop a 9mm slug at point-blank range."

"Says who?"

"I read the instructions."

"Oh, that's different," mocks Dexter. "If that's what the instructions say then this isn't stupid at all."

"Give me a few feet just to be on the safe side."

"I don't think there is a safe side here, but I'll give you five."

Dexter opens his bag and removes an old pillowcase rolled into a tight bundle. He puts it on the ground and carefully unrolls it to reveal his uncle's gun. I just stare at it. All my life, this is the closest I've ever been to one.

"What kind is it?" I ask.

"It's a Beretta. I don't know the model."

"But you're sure it's a 9mm?"

"If it isn't then we've been using the wrong bullets all these years."

Because of the new gun-control laws, it is impossible to get a carrying license for modern weapons. However, because of the way the laws were written, any handgun manufactured prior to the formation of the North American Alliance is automatically grandfathered in. That's why the market for "loophole guns" is so big. The carrying permits for those are as easy to get as a driver's license. That's what makes them so valuable. The newer the loophole gun, the more valuable it is.

"I wouldn't do this for anyone," says Dexter. The way he handles the gun, working the slide and hammer with confidence, you can tell he's an expert. There's a certain authority in the way he holds it, even in the way he always points it at the ground. He knows exactly what it is, what it's capable of, and how to use it. You can tell he respects it as much as he commands it. "No one else but you. You know I hate guns."

"I know."

Out in the squatter settlements, guns are a fact of life. Not only did Dexter have to learn how to use one at a very early age, he had to be ready to use it. Not because he was a thug, but just so he could protect his mother when his father and uncle weren't around. The things that can happen to a woman left alone in the settlements are unspeakable. Unspeakable. For that reason alone, Dexter didn't have the luxury of being her child. He had to be another man in the house.

In a way, I think that's why he and I get along so well. Our backgrounds couldn't be more different, but the one thing we do have in common is our independence. He and I both had to learn early on how to take care of ourselves. Another thing we have in common is our ambition. When the Drakes finally made it out, it wasn't just the settlements Dexter left behind, it was everything that went along with it, including all those facts of life he once had to live by. Like guns.

Dexter points the gun away and inserts the empty magazine, pulls back on the slide until it locks open, inserts one bullet directly into the chamber, and eases the slide forward. "Last chance to come to your senses," he says.

There really isn't a soft spot to catch my fall, but that doesn't matter anyway. According to the instructions, I should let the bullet throw me off my feet and land on my torso. The way it's been designed, the ultramesh is supposed to disperse the energy of the bullet throughout the armor. The harder I hit the ground, the more energy is dispersed throughout the gear. Basically, the way the instructions read, if I do have to take a bullet, I should go with its trajectory and let the body armor do its job. To that end, I rock backwards onto my heels.

"Do it."

With his finger well off the trigger, Dexter palms his grip-hand and raises the gun to my chest. Even in his oversized hands it looks large. This is when I begin to wonder if I really am crazy.

I flinch as Dexter pulls the trigger, but nothing happens. He tries again. Still nothing. Dexter thumbs the safety and points the gun to the side. Pulls back the slide about halfway and releases it. Returns it to my chest. Flips the safety off.

"What hap—"

The blinding flash strikes my chest so hard it throws me off my feet with a thunderous bang that I don't even hear until I am already sailing backward through the air. Much further than I ever would have imagined. I land hard on my back. The next thing I see is through tears. Dexter hovering over me.

"Jack! Jack! Don't move. Are you okay?"

"Peachy," I gasp.

What does it feel like to get shot? Lying flat on my back, it feels like a 7-foot muscle man has just wielded a 10-pound sledgehammer over his head and brought it straight down onto my chest. Even though I've done exactly what I was supposed to do, I can feel the impact of the slug like a dent in my endoskeleton.

Dexter hovering over me, "Jack, say something."

"You were right, Dex. This was a stupid idea."

But I have to get up. Out in the field I won't have the luxury of catching my breath. I roll to my side and push myself back onto my feet—barely. Between me wobbling back and forth and the room rocking side to side, I'm amazed I can even remain upright, but I do. My entire body is sore, even my legs, and my chest feels like it has just been punched in, and there is one rib in particular that feels cracked.

I remove my sweater. Underneath it all, I am amazed at how small the bullet looks compared to how it feels. It's just this tiny little thing caught in the mesh. Dexter rifles through his bag and comes out with a pair of pliers. He grabs the slug and twists it out of the mesh, leaving behind a tiny dent in the weave. I hold out my hand and Dexter drops it into my palm. Such a tiny little thing.

"What was my down time?" I ask when I finally catch my breath.

"I don't know. Less than a minute."

"That's from the shock." I unbuckle the armor and reach inside to my rib. The bruise is so big that my fingertips run into it by accident.

"Are you alright?"

"Yeah," I wince. "Yeah, I am. I think next time I should be able to roll out of it."

Dexter's expression is something between shock and amazement.

"You've never been shot at while carrying a load?" I ask.

Dexter shrugs. "My loads aren't high value. I don't get paid as much, but I don't get shot at either. Anyway, I'm more concerned about that guy with the samurai sword who's running around the sneakernet cutting off people's arms."

"*Katana*," I correct. Just as I regain my balance I feel a tingle in my arm. I'm not even sure what it is at first. Until I suddenly realize, the chip inside has started to vibrate.

8.

I'm not sure what to expect when I show up at the address given
to me by my cortex chip, but the one thing I don't expect is that
it will be such a dump. It isn't even a high-rise, just a crummy
12-floor walkup that smells old.

The suite is one large room in which people sit at long
tables sectioned into workstations. There is nothing dividing
one workstation from the next, so everyone can see and hear
everyone else. The only private office is located in the back
corner. Figuring that's where I'm supposed to go, I start down
the narrow aisle between the last row of workstations and the
wall, but before I get there a hand reaches out and pulls me to
the floor. Normally it wouldn't have, but my legs are still weak
from the bullet. Not to mention the bruise on my chest the size
of a softball.

I try to get up but a second hand grips my shoulder and
shoves me back down.

I glance up. Sitting above me are two guys in white shirts
who look identical except for their chins and ties. One makes a
shushing motion with his fingers. "Arcadian?" he asks.

"Yes," I answer, wondering if any of this is normal.

"Good," says the other. "We've been expecting you."

He motions for me to stay down as he does something at his
desk that I can't see. A moment later he lowers his hand to pass
me a SQUID sensor, and I wonder again if any of this is normal.
I pull up my sleeve, exhale hot breath onto the contact and stick
it over the crow's eye. For some reason, this is when it hits me
that I am actually doing this. I am a data runner.

The data stream enters my chip in magnetic pulses that feel
like the ball end of a sewing pin tapping Morse code into my

arm. It has no discernable mass of course, but it's almost as if I can feel its weight loading into me. This goes on for about thirty seconds while the two guys above me act as if I'm not even there. Then comes a two second pause followed by a quick series of five rapid pulses, then nothing at all as the light on the sensor goes out. The same guy who handed it to me reaches down with a scrap of paper. Scribbled on it is an address. I try to take it but the guy won't let go. I try again but his fingers hold tight. I guess I'm supposed to memorize it. I do, then fold the SQUID into the paper and let him retract both.

The other one warns me to stay down. "I'll tell you when it's clear."

I take a moment to admire the bird on my forearm before pulling down my sleeve. It really is a beautiful image. I have to be sure to give Snake my compliments when I see him again, if I ever see him again.

"There is a brown envelope taped under the desk," he says. "Grab it."

I see it immediately, a small padded envelope. I peel it off. The rip of tape is louder than either man is comfortable with; both look around the room nervously.

"What am I carrying?" I ask.

Now they eye each other. "We were told there would be no questions," says the man with the address.

"That we could rely on it," says the other. "We were told there would be discretion."

"Alright," I say. "So what do I do with the envelope?"

"That's your red herring."

Red herring? I wonder.

"It's your ticket out of here," says the other. "Security will stop you on the way out. They will search you. When they find that envelope on you, they will take it. You should make a fuss over it, but let them have it. Then deliver the real package."

I slide my backpack off my shoulder and stuff the envelope inside. "Anything else?"

Neither guy answers. Neither guy says anything until, all of a sudden, "Go now!"

I crouch-walk along the wall to the beginning of the row before popping back to full height. If anyone else notices me, they pretend not to. I nearly turn around and look back at the two guys but manage to check myself. I'm pretty sure that's the last thing they would want. Moving toward the door, I keep looking for the security they mentioned, but I don't see it anywhere. For a moment I think I might avoid it altogether, until I exit the suite and find him waiting for me outside. Not *that* big, as security guys go. He'd probably be about Dexter's size if not for all the artificial growth hormones.

"Stop right there!" He rips the backpack off my shoulder and pulls it open with far more zeal than necessary. I've hidden the envelope in the hydration compartment to make it look like I'm trying to sneak it through, but it doesn't take him long to find it. He removes the envelope and drops the bag.

Seriously, would it have been that difficult for him to just hand it back to me?

He turns the padded envelope over in his hands. "This is a secure work environment. All shipments in and out are processed through Consolidated."

Consolidated, or what used to be the Postal Service. Nothing is secure in their hands. They're a huge part of the reason we have a sneakernet to begin with. Trust me, it isn't the Consolidated salary that's put so many postal carriers in luxury vehicles and vacation properties.

"Look, I've got a job to do," I say and make an attempt for the envelope.

"All shipments are processed through Consolidated," he repeats. "Your services are not required here!"

He whips it away and widens his eyes like we're about to have a problem. We aren't about to have a problem. I think I've played the part convincingly enough. I throw up my hands. "Okay, fine. But if you don't want me showing up then you should tell your people not to call. I don't have time for this crap." As soon as I say it I realize I might have pushed it too far. The last thing I want is for him to start grilling me about which employee handed me the envelope. "Whatever, man. I've got another job downtown."

I move to pass. He stops me. I step back and stare at him. Neither of us blink. I should be plotting my lane past him, but somehow I know it's not the right move. He has the envelope. I have no reason to run. Running now would only arouse suspicion. So I don't. Finally he lets me go. I move past him and down the stairwell.

Behind me, I hear him take the envelope back into the suite. This is of no concern to me. I make my way out the building and head for the nearest subway station. I have real cargo to deliver.

9.

According to the monitor, the next train is only three minutes away. I check my watch and lean over the platform to scan the tunnel. There is a very sharp bend coming into the station so I won't see the train's headlamp until the last second. I look around.

Standing there with my backpack over my shoulder, I look like any other upscale student on his way to a Free City charter school. And now that I've introduced a dollop of hair gel into my mane, I blend into the Free City crowd even more than I did when I was an actual member of it. It throws me at first. Every time I catch sight of myself in a reflective surface it's like I'm looking at a much more stylized version of myself. Dare I say, a cooler me? It reminds me at once of all those rich kids who would return to school each fall glistening with Mediterranean tans, sporting styles so new they haven't even made the fashion magazines yet.

Passing a few girls on the platform, I catch a few looks that might even convince me I am one of them, if not for that damn itch on my arm. Well, not an itch exactly—just an acute awareness of the chip in my flesh loaded with data. I try not to favor my arm in any way, try to remain calm, nonchalant, but it's hard. It's hard because I know it's there, and now I have this uncontrollable urge to clutch it. I know it's all in my head, that the data itself is just a bunch of zeros and ones that has no tangible feeling whatsoever, but in my mind it's like I can feel its pulse in that spot on my forearm. It's like that phantom limb thing, only in reverse.

A glint of light appears on the tunnel wall.

By now I have strolled to the end of the platform so I can see everything at a glance. I look around as casually as I can.

Mostly it's men and women in business suits with a handful of students mixed in.

I check my watch. Observe my surroundings. Wait.

The splash of light on the tunnel wall grows stronger by the second until the train finally comes barreling into the station.

The doors open to let passengers off, and I find myself scanning them as well, wondering if this is what Snake meant when he told me to be hypervigilant. I hope it is because at that moment I'm not sure what else I can do. I step aboard the train. There are plenty of seats but I figure it's probably better to stay on my feet. The doors chime and close behind me. The train lurches forward. I grab a strap and hang on. Because I was standing at the end of the platform, I am now riding in the last car of the train. I figure this is smart because the end cars usually have the fewest riders. Fewer people means fewer people to keep my eye on.

The train picks up speed. And soon the fast dolly of the empty platform through the window of the subway car abruptly wipes to darkness, leaving only my reflection in the interior glass.

A girl my age wearing comm shades stares despondently into her music.

A girl in a black hoodie sits with her arms folded and her head down.

Two men in business suits chat.

A cute redhead wearing a crested blazer over a tartan skirt operates her thin screen. She's the one I linger on. Her legs have minor scrapes here and there that are probably from field hockey or some other extracurricular sport. I can't make out which school her crest belongs to, but it is definitely one of the Free City charter schools.

A few others.

This is how it is for the next few minutes, me minding all of them as they mind themselves, frozen in their daily commutes. I begin to wonder if maybe I'm taking the whole thing a bit too seriously. I take a breath and let my shoulders relax. Body armor. Hypervigilance. It's all well and good but I'm on a moving train now. What could possibly happen?

As if on cue, the sliding door to the forward car gets thrown open so hard it actually rebounds closed and has to be opened again.

The Japanese man who enters has a large curl of hair not unlike a surfing wave covering the top-right quadrant of his face. He is slender and wears a very expensive suit under an equally fine overcoat. Behind him enters a big round blob of a man who only takes shape after he squeezes through the door. This one has a shaved head and thin goatee and wears an electric-blue tracksuit with white stripes running down the arms and legs. I see the trouble in his eyes the moment he enters.

Neither one looks at me. For a moment it seems as if they will pass right by me. Maybe they have business with someone else on the train, the two guys in suits perhaps, or maybe they just want to be at the back of the train. Who knows, who cares? Just so long as it doesn't involve me. But that all goes out the window the moment the big one turns to face me, effectively trapping me in the tiny nook between the seat and the door. The suited one grips my wrist with surprising strength for a man his size and forces two layers of sleeve up my arm. Smiles.

"Well, well, well, Gendo. *Miru* what we have here."

The guy obviously speaks English, but for some reason he addresses me in Japanese. "*Ave-u desu ka?*"

He's just playing with me. It might have worked too, if I hadn't studied a year of Japanese back at the magnet academy. I nod. *Am I an Ave?* Yes, I'm an Ave. He's already seen the tag. There's no point denying it now. "*So*," I answer

"*So ka?*" he sings. "*Nihongo o hanashimasu ka?*"

To the question '*you speak Japanese?*' I responded in the affirmative. "*Chyoto*," I add. *A little.*

"*Subarashii!*" he says in a way that can only be sarcastic. "That is wonderful. You Aves are getting smarter with every new flock."

I am in trouble. There is no question about it. I am in deep, *deep* trouble. I can't even scan the train for options because the big one is blocking my view.

"That is Gendo," he says, referring to the mountain standing before me, "and you may call me Mr. Ito."

"I'm not carrying anything," I blurt. The moment the words leave my mouth I realize how desperate it sounds.

"No?" Mr. Ito shakes his head mockingly like an adult toying with a child. "Okay, then. I guess Ito and Gendo leave you alone."

Everyone else has either exited the car or is standing by the far doors waiting to get off at the next station. They don't know what's going down, and they don't want to know. They just want to be off the train. I just want to be off the train.

Mr. Ito throws open his coat.

"Oh, no!"

"Oh, yes!"

Strapped to the inside of his coat is a katana.

Mr. Ito twirls it around the back of his hand and raises it to his downturned eyes. Slowly he pulls the steel from its sheath. Meticulously. Keeping a perfect line as he stares me down over the edge of the blade.

"What the hell is that for?" I press my back to the door, as if I don't already know.

Mr. Ito smiles. It is a gangster's smile, offered strictly for his own amusement. "This," he catches my reflection in the blade, "this is not for making ice cream." He pauses for drama like a bad actor. "Not *I* scream," he finishes, "this is for making *you* scream."

My mind starts racing. Best-case scenario—I come out of this a cripple.

Gendo grabs hold of my arm and pulls me off my feet. The next thing I know, I am on the floor of the train turning my body into his hold. The more he twists, the more I turn. I have to. It's the only way to keep him from breaking my arm. But even getting my arm broken would be preferable to what Mr. Ito has in store for me, as Gendo extends it for him. Mr. Ito rotates the blade in his hand.

"Wait, that won't work!" I yell over the screech of the train. "Cutting off my arm will only destroy the cargo. You won't get anything."

The lights flicker.

"*Get?*" Mr. Ito laughs. "Who says we want to get anything?"

I have no idea what that means. I can't even imagine it. My mind draws a complete blank. My heart thumps a mile a minute as Mr. Ito raises his sword.

Then comes a girl's voice. "Excuse me."

Gendo and Ito both turn, but from the floor of the train I can't see past them.

"Do you have the time?" she asks.

Her voice is timid, almost childlike.

"Time?" growls Mr. Ito. "This is the time for you to go away, little girl, before I cut you."

Mr. Ito turns his attention away from her and back to my arm as he lifts the blade high over his head. *This is it*, I think in a full-fledged panic. *What a disaster. I'm going to get clipped on my very first run.* Mr. Ito's eyes go wide as his hands tighten around the grip. He clenches his teeth. The sword is ready to drop at any second. He tightens his hands even more, until they are too tight. Almost shaking. Shaking. And soon spittle flies out of his mouth. That's when I know something is happening. Even Gendo wonders what is going on as he turns to see what Mr. Ito is doing.

Then I hear the buzz, barely discernible over the noise of the train, but there nonetheless.

Mr. Ito collapses onto his side with the sword still in his hands, revealing the girl in the black hoodie standing behind him with a Taser. She pulls off her hood. For the first time I get a good look at her. She's not as young as she sounded. My age, maybe a year older. Her hair is jet black and curls just under her chin, and her skin is pale; a combination that makes her sky-blue eyes shine that much brighter.

Gendo yanks my arm to throw me into her, but I manage to slip free and clear his grip just in time to avoid the transfer shock when she hits him with the Taser in her hand, plus a second one she produces from her pocket.

"Get to the back door!" she screams, sounding nothing like she did before.

Gendo is still on his feet, shaking but able to move. The girl clearly knows this is the best she's going to get as I reach the back door. She releases the voltage. Gendo has to grab the nearest pole to remain upright, but he does. Running in my direction, the girl in the black hoodie sweeps a shoulder bag off the floor that I don't even notice until it's in her hands. Gendo stumbles behind her like a drunken sumo wrestler, but as the train slows into the next station he is able to find his balance.

"Pull the emergency release!" she yells.

She is talking about the lever to release the rear door, which she's now running full speed toward. I grab the lever and pull it just as she leaps into the air. Grabs the poles on either side of the door and uses both her legs to kick it. The door flies off its frame and topples over. She climbs over it and maneuvers out the back of the train. I follow. Gendo staggers toward us. The girl grabs my elbow and pulls me to the edge. I look over. The train might be slowing but the tracks beneath us are still going by rather quickly.

"There's no easy way to do this," she says. "Just jump."

She's right. There's no easy way to leap off a moving object. But we do. And this is where my training kicks in.

The whole point of training is to teach your body what to do. That way, if you're ever in a pinch and your brain has other things to worry about, your body can take care of itself. That's why they call it *muscle memory*. Just like your brain, your body always remembers.

Which is why, the moment we're in the air and without even thinking about it, I'm already doing a 180 and adjusting my body to roll out on the landing.

It's a move I've done countless times before, but it feels like the very first time. My body armor keeps the ties from bruising up my torso, but that doesn't stop my arms and legs from taking a beating as I tumble behind the train and come to rest on my side with my legs bent across the rail.

There's no time to dally. I pop back onto my feet. The first thing I see is Gendo, who has lifted the detached door over his head and now throws it at me. I step back even though it'll miss me by several feet. Twenty feet up the track the train stops. Now

Mr. Ito is back on his feet and coming up behind Gendo.

A hand grabs my shoulder and pulls me so hard I nearly stumble.

"Come on," she says.

I know exactly where we are. Up ahead is an access point to one of the abandoned MTA tunnels that was once part of the old City of New York subway system. I start to point it out but she is already veering in that direction.

Whoever she is, she knows these tunnels as well as I do.

10.

We slow from a jog to a brisk walk.

"What the hell is the matter with you!" she chides. "Are you crazy getting on a train carrying cargo? And on the last car no less. Talk about boxing yourself in. Where did you think you would go?"

"I—" I try to answer, but right at that moment a pit opens up in my stomach, and the tunnel around me begins to spin. Hot. Faint. I've never felt like this before. The onset is so sudden it causes me to keel over. I feel like I'm about to drop to the ground. The girl appears unsurprised by this. In fact, she's already on top of it. From her bag she removes a large energy bar, catches the corner of the wrapper in her teeth and tears it open, folds back the foil, and practically shoves it into my face. I grab it. Take a huge bite. Chew. Swallow. She tears open another for herself as I gobble up the remains of the first.

"Well?"

"I…didn't."

"Birdbrain."

"Wait a second, who are you?"

"You mean besides the person who just saved your ass?" She steps under a tunnel light, leans over, and raises the leg of her cargo pants. Tattooed on her calf is a regal looking bird about to perch on a stump. Hers is colored all in brown except for the scarlet tailfeathers stretching down toward her ankle, but it has that same watchful eye.

"I'm Red Tail," she says.

"Red Tail…" I hadn't thought about what I might say if I ever met another Ave. The way Cyril made it sound, it wasn't likely to ever happen. "What is that, a hawk?"

Great, I think. *Wonderful.* Here's someone who can possibly answer any question I might have about running for Arcadian, and I ask her about her bird.

"Yes, it's a hawk."

A very long and awkward moment passes between us as she just stands there looking at me like I've forgotten something.

"Well?"

"Well, what?"

"Haven't you ever played this game before? I showed you mine now you show me yours."

Oh, my tag. I raise my sleeve to show it to her. Clearly she is impressed.

"Nice work," she comments.

"Thanks."

"That was meant for Snake."

"Oh." There is a noise in the tunnel behind us. Something like a wooden stick hitting a metal pipe. "Are they following us?"

"Not likely," she says. "Ito doesn't like getting his suits dirty, and Gendo is just dead weight in the tunnels. But we should keep moving."

Red Tail and I continue down the tunnel. For a moment I consider inquiring about her real name but decide against it. That's something Cyril was adamant about. Besides, if she told me hers then I would have to tell her mine, right? Quid pro quo, just like the tags.

"Who were those guys?" I ask.

"Data disruptors."

"Why would they cut off my arm like that? Don't they know it'll destroy the data?"

"They're counting on it."

"Huh?"

"There's something you need to understand about this business. Sometimes destroying your rival's data can be just as valuable as stealing it. There are two kinds of interceptors you will run into in the field—retrievers and disruptors. Retrievers are the easier of the two to elude because their primary objective is to recover your cargo intact. That means they can't do anything to you that might damage what's in your wing."

"My wing?"

"The arm that carries the data. That's your wing. Disruptors are different. Their mission is to terminate the transport at all cost, usually by destroying your cargo en route. Disruptors have no interest in recovering your cargo. Their primary objective is to stop you from making delivery. Ito and Gendo are independent contractors. Until recently, we never had to worry about them because they were mostly contracted by midlevel companies who farmed that stuff out, and we're mostly chased by megacorporations who do all that stuff in-house. Shanghai International, Caliphate Global, Grumwell—they all have massive internal security divisions to handle these things. Not to mention Blackburn, whose entire concern is paramilitary security. Believe me, they're the last one you want on your tail."

"Okay, so if Arcadian runners never had to worry about Ito and Gendo before, what changed?"

"They got hired by a mega."

"Wait, you just said—"

"I know what I said," Red Tail interjects. "The rumor is, somebody stole something so big it could potentially bring down an entire megacorporation all by itself."

"I thought the megas were too big to fail."

"Too big to fail is never so big it can't be destroyed. Apparently, whatever this thing is, it's so damning that the people looking for it can't even trust their own internal security. That's why they hired disruptors. They don't even want it back. They just want it gone."

"So why did they come after me?" I recall the crappy little office where I made my pickup. "I don't know what I'm carrying, but I'm pretty sure it's not that."

"Because whoever stole the information loaded it into a data runner and put it on the sneakernet to keep it secure. Now there's a blind relay going on. Nobody knows where or when, but each day the cargo is passed from one data runner to the next. They're not running the cargo for delivery, they're just running it to keep it in motion. Ito and Gendo must be completely out of leads, because now they're clipping every runner they come across. Hacking and stacking arms until they find it. That's why they came after you."

"Is it possible the load is being moved by an Arcadian runner?"

She shrugs. "Anything's possible."

Red Tail stops for a moment and produces her thin screen from her bag. The translucent glow lights up her face like a ghost as her fingers navigate the device, and I know at once that hers is no ordinary thin screen. Trains and stations all have open signal relays to the surface, but the tunnels themselves don't, particularly the old abandoned ones. The only way to get a signal this far off the rails is by tapping into the nearest service relay. Which means that, just like mine, her thin screen has been flashed to port into the undernet. And that can only mean one thing.

"You're Morlock," I say.

She confirms with a quick nod. "So is Snake. Most of us are. I think it's one of the things Cyril looks for." It's only as an afterthought that she asks about me.

I nod. "Kind of."

"Kind of?"

"Not officially, but I've been operating as Morlock for years so it's really just a technicality. For some reason Moreau refuses to reach out to me. I don't know why, but when I find him that's the first thing I'm going to ask."

"When you find him?" she asks with incredulity. "Don't tell me you're tracking Moreau?"

"He's my white whale."

Red Tail stares at me through the glow of her thin screen.

"That's from *Moby Dick*," I add.

"Yes, I know the white whale is from *Moby Dick*, birdbrain. I just don't know what to make of it. Ahab lost his leg to the whale. What's your reason? And don't say it's because he hasn't invited you into the club yet. That's stupid."

Now I'm left without a response. It may be stupid, but it's the only reason I have.

For the second time in fifty feet Red Tail stops and looks around.

"What is it?"

She shakes her head. "Have you noticed that we haven't seen a single rat since we've been down here?"

"Oh, there's a reason for that," I tell her. It never would have occurred to me that the thing she found odd was the lack of rodents. I was so used to it by now that I would have been surprised if we had seen one. I open my backpack and remove a homemade device that is basically just a small project box with an on/off toggle, three stub antennas, and a red LED indicator that is currently on. I hand it to her. The way she turns it over in her hand, examining it closely and with genuine curiosity, that's when I know for sure she's a techie. "It emits a signal that drives away all rodents within five meters."

Red Tail turns the box to examine a second switch on the side. That one is inset and locked to prevent it from being flipped accidentally. "What does this do?" she asks.

That was Dexter's idea. I still had no idea what the application would be; I just built it because I wanted to see if it would work. Unfortunately, we never got around to finding out because neither one of us wanted to be the person standing there with the device in his hands when the switch got flipped. "I haven't tested it yet," I say, "but it inverts the signal."

Red Tail considers this as she hands it back. "Interesting."

We continue down the tunnel for a while and veer left at the split. That's when I realize we're heading in the exact direction I need to go in order to make my delivery. Red Tail knows exactly where I'm supposed to be, and she's taking me there.

"What were you doing on the train?" I ask.

"Liddy sent me. She couldn't let you step into the grinder on your first run. She told Cyril that it was way too soon to put you on a decoy run. Nobody gets red-herringed their first time out. But Cyril disagreed. In case you haven't noticed, he's a real sink-or-swim kind of guy. You should be flattered. You didn't hear this from me, but Cyril has real high hopes for you. I think this was his way of throwing you against the wall to see if you'd stick. That's why—"

"Wait, wait. Hold on." She's going a mile a minute and I

have no idea who or what she's talking about. "Who's Liddy, and what's a decoy run?"

"Boy, you really are a newb. Alright. Don't worry about Liddy. As she always says, her job keeps her in the blinds."

"Who is she?"

"She's the Birdwatcher. You won't know it, but she'll always have eyes on you. As for the decoy run, sometimes when a cargo is especially valuable, they'll hire two Aves to make the run. One carries the real cargo; the other carries the decoy. The second is called the *red herring* because it diverts attention away from the real transport. In this case, that's you. You're the decoy, my fine feathered friend."

"No, that can't be right. They gave me an envelope to get me out of there. That was the red herring. Why would they have done that if—"

But the more I talk, the more obvious it is. I've been duped. A brown envelope? Just who was that supposed to fool? I mean besides me. It's like a game of chess. The brown envelope was a gambit. They knew security wouldn't buy it, and that was their plan all along. They wanted security to finger me as the runner because really I'm not. My whole cargo, this whole run was one big brown envelope. I am the red herring.

"You see?" she asks.

"I see."

"Decoy runs are particularly rough because they're designed to draw the fire. They always meet resistance. The only runner who's ever gotten through one without incident is Snake."

"How'd he do that?"

But Red Tail only shakes her head. "He calls it the Lemmon–Curtis Bluff. If you want to know any more than that you'll have to ask him yourself. Anyway, the Birdwatcher knew you would need some help so she sent me to shadow you."

"But you were already on the train."

Again she shakes her head. "Gendo and Ito were tracking you from the top of the stairs where you couldn't see them. They came down and jumped on at the last second. I was on the other side of the pillar less than five feet away from you. I stepped onto the train two seconds after you did."

"I didn't see you."

"That's because your eyes were on the redhead, who by the way had *NOT ME* written all over that pretty little face. Her body language was all wrong. That's lesson number one, birdbrain. Keep your blood in your head."

"Stop calling me birdbrain."

Red Tail laughs. "Come on, you have to expect a little hazing."

Red Tail turns her attention back to her thin screen, and we walk in silence for a few minutes, giving me a chance to take in everything she's just told me. But soon her expression changes, seemingly from some disturbing piece of information she's just received.

"What is it?" I ask.

"Look, you've come into this at a very awkward time. This is going to sound paranoid, but it's the best piece of advice I can give you right now. Trust no one. Do you hear me? *No one.*"

"Wouldn't *no one* include you?"

"That's your choice. If you don't trust me, it's on you. And if you do trust me then you can trust Snake as well, because he's the only one I trust right now. Him and Liddy, but like I said, she's always in the blinds."

"What's this about?"

"It's better that you don't know. I'm only giving you a heads up so you don't get blindsided when you least expect it. What I'm saying is, expect it. Even from someone inside Arcadian."

Everything has happened so fast that it's only now, as I replay it in my head, that I finally realize I'd be lying on a train in a pool of my own blood right now if it weren't for her. Even if I survived it, my arm would be long gone. So I guess at the very least I owe her an arm's length of trust. Besides, if she had meant me any harm, all she had to do was sit back and let it happen. So when Red Tail tells me not to trust anyone else at Arcadian, there is no reason I shouldn't trust her about that.

"I have a load to pick up," she blurts suddenly. "You can find your way to the drop-off point from here."

"But if I'm just the decoy runner then do I even have to

make the delivery?"

"Always. Most of the time you won't even know when you're a decoy runner, but even if you do, you always have to make the delivery. That's the job. Remember, people hire us when security is the only option. We can't mess around with that. Even when you're the red herring, you have to keep going until the cargo is secure."

Before she goes, Red Tail gives my arm a squeeze. Not just my arm but my wing. "Don't worry, Carrion. You'll do fine. Your powers of observation are good, they just need to be retrained. Just remember, the people to watch out for are the ones who don't want to be seen. Learn to filter everything else out until all that remains is the thing hiding in plain sight." She starts back the other way. "And stay off the trains! You'll live longer."

"Wait," I call after her. "What if I need to get in touch with you?"

She thinks about it for maybe half a second before she begins spitting numbers at me. "5 2 6 5 6 4…"

"Whoa, hold on a second." I can memorize twenty digits without even batting an eye, but I have to know in advance that that's what I'm supposed to be doing.

"…2 0 5 4 6 1…"

"There's no way I'm going to remember all that."

"…6 9 6 c." She smiles. That much I see even in the faint light of the tunnel. That and the blue of her eyes. "You must be something special, Carrion. I don't give out my digits to just anyone."

The *c* at the end gives it away. "What is that, hexadecimal?"

She makes a tiny gun with her hand and fires it with a click of her tongue. That is exactly what it is. "Just code *Red Tail* in base 16. Upload it into your cortex chip and scan it into the aggrenet. The Birdwatcher will find me, and I'll find you."

RUN LIKE HELL

11.

These disruptors aren't afraid to get their suits dirty. They're on my tail the entire run. Then I feel it for the very first time, about ten yards behind me in the main tunnel.

Pop. *FLASH.* BOOM.

The whiz of a bullet through the tunnel.

And by the way, having a gun fired at you inside a tunnel is nothing like having one fired at you up on the surface. The echo alone makes it different—a dislocated sound that toys with your senses and plays with your mind. Suddenly it isn't just the space that feels tighter. Everything feels tight. Everything is cramped. Everything carries a different weight down here. Even the twisting trail of wind zipping behind the bullet with my name on it, even *that* adheres to a different law of physics down here. The only thing I can do now is run. Leave it behind. Run faster. Run until the dim light of the tunnel can no longer illuminate the distance between us. The only thing I can do now is run like hell, and that is exactly what I do.

By now it's easy to see what Red Tail meant about disruptors and retrievers. Data retrievers can't fire their guns blindly into a dark tunnel. Most of the time they can't fire their guns at all. With them it's like a game of tag; they actually have to lay their hands on me. But these guys trying to stop delivery on my load from Wexler Pharmaceuticals, they have no interest in recovering the cargo stored in my wing, they just want to shoot it down. And even though I'm just the data runner who's not supposed to know what he's carrying in his wing, I know why.

I was told a lot of thing about running the sneakernet, given a lot of tips. But the one thing I figured out on my own is how invaluable it is for my trade to follow the news closely, particularly the business news. I know that these interceptors have to be from Applied Microgenetics. Two days ago the *Journal* reported that Wexler Pharmaceuticals was within hours of filing a long-awaited patent application for a brand new type of molecular gene therapy that could be worth billions right out of the gate. This was a very big deal in the biotechnology world. Apparently, for the past ten years, Wexler had been in direct competition with Applied Microgenetics to see who would bring their molecule to market first; and whoever did would essentially wipe out the other guy.

That's how I know, even without seeing the load, exactly what Wexler Pharmaceuticals has tasked me with when they load me up and give me the address for the Free City branch of the patent office. This is the final lap in a very long race—ten years long to be exact—and I am the one they are trusting with the baton. It's a pretty big run for someone who has been on the job less than a month. Probably the biggest I've been given so far. But I can handle it.

Whatever reticence I had on my first couple of runs is gone. Now I don't think twice about switching over to an active track and running straight for the headlamp of an oncoming train. The interceptors from Applied Microgenetics dig their heels into the dirt and slide to a halt. They have no idea what I'm doing. And because they have no idea what I'm doing, they have no idea what to do themselves. With a train coming straight at me, there is no way out of this passage. No way out...but over. But surely I'm not about to leap over an entire train, am I? Not quite.

As the train bears down I wall-run up the side of the tunnel until my toes find footing. It's just a tiny little nub, but that's all I need to push off. I use everything I have to pop vault up to the overhead beams and hang on for dear life as the train roars past beneath me. And just as my pursuers dive for cover, I drop onto it and sail past. At moments like these, the tunnel wind in my hair feels good. Like victory. I don't even care that the air down here smells like urine and is so thick with grime that I can taste its gritty chalkiness in my mouth. I don't care because I've earned my wings. As a bird, I can fly.

It's all about adaptation. Adaptation is the key to success when you're running data. And in that sense, it's like I've been training for it all along. Parkour is all about adaptation. Adapting to one's environment. Only the unskilled barbarian hulks his way through life's barricades and leaves a wake of disaster in his trail. The traceur doesn't do this. The traceur doesn't knock an obstacle out of the way unless it's absolutely necessary. He meanders his way past it. Over. Under. Through. Around. He gets past not by moving the obstacle but by moving himself. That is parkour, and working this job I use every technique I know just to get it done.

People on the platform look at me like I'm crazy when I throw down my backpack and slide off the top of the train before it even stops, catch the ground with both hands, and roll out. My body armor rocks across the tiles and springs me back up. I pick up my bag and keep moving. I'm downtown now, and the patent office is just—

Interceptor. Somewhere. I can't see him, but I can sense him. I look.

One by one the crowd around me disappears as I filter it all out. Just like Red Tail advised, I disregard everyone who does not register as a threat until all I see is the sneakernet. Just like the undernet is a network hidden beneath the aggregate Internet, the sneakernet is a world hidden in plain sight among the commuters and trains. But people act differently on the sneakernet, and that's what you learn to spot.

The guy with the newspaper. You know why? I can smell it on him. But it's more than that. I think he wants me to smell it on him. I mean, come on, sitting out in the open like that with his comm shades on, it's almost like he's trying to be obvious about it. Until I realize, that's exactly what he's doing. He wants me to spot him.

There are two sets of stairs leading to the upper deck. The guy with the newspaper is covering the left side. There doesn't appear to be anyone covering the right, which is how I know they're there, lying in wait. It's a bottleneck. The guy with the newspaper thinks I'll see him and go for the other stairs, whereupon the others will come out of nowhere and have me trapped. So which way do I go? Easy. I don't go for either stairs. Rather, I head for the guy with the newspaper. Why? Because I've already spotted him, and I know his position, and I can see his hands, and it's exactly what he won't expect.

"Hey, disruptor!" I yell and run straight at him until he has no choice but to stand and drop his paper. But it's too late for him to do anything else. I leap through the air with a flying kick that knocks him off his feet, step off the tile and vault over the railing to the stairs behind him. From the corner of my eye I see three more disruptors come racing down the opposite stairwell. But before they hit the bottom, I'm already at the top.

The turnstiles are backed up with people trying to get out. I head for the gate. Leap. Kick the release button with my toe and fly straight into the wrought iron gate that swings open with my momentum and lets me out. One more set of stairs and I emerge from the underground.

To a clear blue sky and the bright of day.

And just across the street, the building housing the Free City branch of the patent office.

● ● ●

Dexter meets me outside afterwards. It's not even noon and we've completed one run apiece. I look around. "Where's Pace?"

Dex doesn't even have to say it. I can tell by the look on his face.

"Still?"

"I don't think he's cut out for it," he says.

"It hasn't been that long. Give him time."

"Time has nothing to do with it. This is a sink-or-swim profession. Look at you. They threw you straight into the deep end, and you stayed afloat."

"I had help from Red Tail."

"Are you saying I haven't been helping Pace?"

"No, of course not."

"Because I've helped him out as much as I can. But I

can't keep holding his hand. I do have my own loads to carry, you know."

"I know."

"I dropped two loads a week to run with him, but I can't afford to do that anymore. If Pace can't do it on his own, he's going to have to find another gig."

"Yeah, I hear you." That's when I see Pace coming up the street, jittery as hell and sweating bullets like he's having a nervous breakdown, looking in every direction at once but nowhere in particular. It reminds me of Snake's warning about not letting the hypervigilance take you over because that is exactly what's happened. Pace has let the fear take control. "Pace!"

He jumps like a frightened cat as he jerks his attention in our direction. *This is bad*, I think. Dex and I are barely ten feet away, and he didn't even see us. He's looking everywhere but not processing any of it, and he's not seeing what's right in front of his face.

"Hey guys. Hey, Jack. Hey, Dex." Pace spins around like he's checking the environment. Like he's actually trying to take in every single variable at a downtown Free City intersection at the busiest time of day. "Hey, Jack," he repeats, not even realizing it.

I grab an energy bar from my bag and offer it to Pace even though I don't think he's in any condition to eat. Dex declines as well. I keep forgetting that they're using regular old silicon chips with a built-in power source. Theirs don't use metabolic energy like the cortex chip from Arcadian. Oh well, more for me. I tear it open and wolf it down, even though the three of us have met for lunch. There's always room for more.

A bit of construction noise from somewhere down the street causes Pace to grab his arm. Dex looks at him confused. "You're loaded up right now?"

Pace frantically scans the buildings around us like he's looking for snipers. "I couldn't make the drop."

"I left you five blocks from the drop-off point," says Dexter. "What happened?"

"They were waiting for me," he says. "They were waiting for me on the platform so I ran back into the tunnel."

Dex doesn't say it but he's obviously peeved.

"It was two against one," says Pace. "What was I supposed to do?"

Improvise, I think. *Adapt.*

"So you're overdue," says Dex. "Again."

"I thought you could come back with me and help me suss it out," says Pace. "Just this once."

"Can't do it this time," says Dex. "If I'm even one minute late for my pickup this afternoon, they'll abort the entire run. I can't afford to lose that paycheck."

"Sure, sure," says Pace. "I understand."

There's no question about it, Pace is a mess. I can't let him go back to the sneakernet in this condition. He is after all a Dragon. And if nothing else, Dragons always look out for one another. "Don't worry, Pace. I've got your back."

"Yeah?"

I nod.

"You sure?" Dex asks.

"Yeah, I got it." We pound fists. "By the way…" I pull out my thin screen to check the balance in my account after the Wexler delivery. I've been running like hell for nearly a month. Twenty-seven days to be exact, to the detriment of everything else. Even PK club. For the past twenty-seven days, running data has been my only form of parkour. But in some strange way, the past twenty-seven days have shown me more than I ever thought I was capable of. Because for twenty-seven days, I have done the best parkour of my life. The best part though, twenty-seven days of running has not been without its rewards. I am just one run away from the magic number. Martin's note. "You feel like taking a little trip tonight?"

Dex knows exactly what I mean. "The syndicate?" he asks.

I nod.

Dexter offers a congratulatory bow. "Well done."

"Pick me up after dinner."

"Not a problem."

With Pace's load overdue and afternoon pickups waiting for me and Dex, lunch is off. We part, Dex going off in one direction, Pace and I going in the other.

●   ●   ●

Pace begins to hyperventilate when the interceptors come at us from both sides of the tunnel. "Breathe," I tell him. "Just breathe."

"They—re—goi—ng—to—ge—t—us—"

"No they're not. Give me your sweatshirt."

"Hu—huh?"

"Just do it."

Pace gives me his sweatshirt, and I hand him my sweater. He's a full size smaller than me so neither one fits right, but it's enough to get the job done. Behind us, one interceptor approaches. In front of us, another awaits.

Pace begins to calm down. "They're going to shoot us."

"No, they're not. They're retrievers, not disruptors. Their mission is to recover your load. But they're not going to do that either. You hear me?" Pace seems to zone out. "Pace!" He finds his way back. "Listen to me. We're going to run straight at him and scissor around. Just like popping a bubble. Wall run around him and keep going."

"What if he gets me?"

"He won't. He can only go one way, and he'll come after me." I indicate Pace's sweatshirt, which I am now wearing. "You just get around him and keep going. Do not stop. Do not turn around. Don't even look back."

"What about you?"

"I'll be fine. You just keep going. Okay?" The answer doesn't come as quick as I would like. "Okay?"

"Yeah," he says. "Yeah. Thanks, Jack. I really owe you one."

But I wave it off. "Dragons don't keep tallies. You just keep going. Keep running until you make the delivery."

I put out a fist. Pace pounds it. We go. Straight for the interceptor. Pace running at my heel, until we break. The interceptor stretches out his arms to grab both of us, but as we split apart he has to choose, and he chooses me. Pace takes two steps up the tunnel wall and skirts past him as I get thrown against the other side. My only concern now is that Pace will stop, but he doesn't. He keeps going.

The other interceptor catches up to us. He turns on a torch to give us light. One is bald, the other is getting there. Both look like ex-athletes. Meaty, but nowhere close to lean. The balding one with the torch pulls out a large bone saw from a holster clipped to his belt.

"You're making a mistake," I say. "You've got the wrong runner."

"Yeah, we're always making that mistake," they laugh. "We always got the wrong runner."

The bald one throws up my sleeve and suddenly freezes. Both of them freeze, especially the guy with the bone saw, who shines his torch closer to my arm. Now they look at each other. "This guy is Arcadian."

Bald guy keeps me secure but loosens his grip as the other one scratches his head with the butt of his bone saw. "I think we got the wrong runner."

Suddenly the bald guy flares his nostrils and shoves me into the wall. The sad part is, I'm not even carrying my own load. I'm getting all this over an empty briefcase. "Where's your friend?" he barks.

"Friend, what friend?"

"Don't play dumb," he says. "The other runner. Where's the other runner?"

"How should I know? I just ran into him a few minutes ago." It's true, every so often you do come across other runners down here, but when that happens you usually just nod and go your own way. There's no way of knowing who you can trust down here, so most runners just ignore each other whenever they pass in the tunnels. "We were just running in the same direction is all."

They eye each other. You'd think they'd recognize Pace's sweatshirt from when they chased him earlier, but I don't think these guys are all that bright.

"So what do we do?" he asks.

"Should we take his arm anyway?"

"That's pointless," I interject.

"Shut up!"

"I'm telling you, it wouldn't serve any purpose."

"Shut up! You just shut up!" He scratches his head with the bone saw. "He's right, though. They got those fancy chips that can't be removed."

"So what do we do?"

"There's nothing to do."

He puts away the bone saw. The other lets me go. I figured as much. As far as I can tell, Ito and Gendo are the only ones hacking off arms indiscriminately. Like I told Martin before—retrievers are like data runners, they always work for somebody. No contract, no money. No money, no point.

"Hey, you know where that other guy was headed?" he asks.

I shake my head. "Just that way," I say and point up the tunnel.

Knowing Pace's speed, he is easily at the next station by now. There is no way these guys are going to catch him. We part with a mutual grumble. The data interceptors go their way, I go mine.

12.

The plan is for Dexter to wait outside in his uncle's junkyard Buick while I run inside to fix Martin's account with the syndicate.

"Does Martin know you're here?" Dexter asks.

"No. He doesn't even know I've been running data for the past month."

"How could he not know?"

"He's been preoccupied."

Martin and I haven't really spoken since that night. I mean, we've spoken the way we normally speak, but neither one of us has brought up the elephant in the room. I suppose Martin just figures I'll have to come around when our thirty days is up, and I know I won't have to. But that conversation is coming. Martin had to take a trip for a few days—something about meeting with some investors, I'm not quite sure about the details—but he said we'll talk when he gets back tomorrow. Yes, we'll talk, and then I'll hand him his note with the syndicate. And when he asks how, I'll show him the tattoo. He might not be too happy about it, but what can he say? Anyway, this isn't just about Martin's note. If I keep running, I can save up enough to pay for school. I've always had the brains to get into NEIT, now I have a way to pay for it too.

"Keep the engine running," I say.

"Why?" he asks.

"In case it goes sideways."

Dex agrees. "Say Jack, I got a special run tomorrow."

"Special how?"

"It's a parity run, and they're offering triple pay for it."

"Parity run. Don't tell me you're going to use Pace."

"No way. You know he can't handle that."

Running data isn't always a one-to-one ratio of cargo to runner. Sometimes you work in teams. There is of course the decoy run, where one runner carries the real cargo and the other carries a dummy load. I learned about that one firsthand. The redundancy run consists of two or three runners carrying the exact same cargo. That one is less secure because there is two or three times the chance of your cargo being intercepted on the sneakernet, but you also have two or three times the chance of making delivery. Clients use that model when the importance of making delivery far outweighs the risk of being intercepted. The parity run, on the other hand, takes the opposite approach. In a parity run, you have two runners carrying half a load each, or three runners carrying two-thirds of a load each with full mirroring so that any two put together delivers the full cargo. Clients use that model when protecting against interception is far more important than making the actual delivery, since the retrievers have to snag not one but two runners to steal the cargo.

"It's a new client," says Dex.

New client. High-value cargo. Parity run. That's a lot of variables to have going for a single run. Maybe too many. I know Dex, he wouldn't ask unless the hairs on his neck were standing straight up. "So maybe I watch your back on this one."

"You know, I think that might be a good idea." He turns his attention to the building in front of us. "How're we going to stay in touch when you're inside?"

The gambling parlor jams all signals from the outside to prevent cheating. For Dex and I to stay in contact, I'd have to sneak inside, find the signal-jamming apparatus, open a port without raising any alarms, sneak back out. Then pipe into the syndicate mainframe using that port, write a quick code to mask our transmissions by piggybacking them onto the existing wireless traffic, and finally, sync our thin screens to in-ear devices since comm shades are out of the question.

Or, we could just go lo-tech.

"Oh, that is sweet," says Dexter when I hand him the old walkie-talkie held together with electrical tape.

"They're staticky as hell but they should get the job done."

Dex hits his push-to-talk button and nearly jumps at the giant burst of noise that comes through my monitor.

"It's probably best to maintain radio silence unless absolutely necessary."

"I hear that."

"You good to go?" I ask.

"Eyes wide, ears back."

"There shouldn't be any problems. I'm just being extra cautious."

"Don't worry, a Dragon's got your back. Just do what you came to do and get out. You should be fine."

Dex is right. But even still, *should* is the operative word.

● ● ●

The gaming parlor is managed by a slobbering, sleazy, sweaty lump of flesh named Vlad.

"You come to pay me Baxter's debt?"

I nod. The note is already on his desk. I hand him five $10,000 currency cards, all bank-issued with the seals still intact.

"Cash?" he says with surprise.

"You do accept cash?"

Now a smile creeps onto his face. Until that very second, I don't think he actually believed I was there to pay him his money. "Do I accept cash," he mutters with amusement.

I watch him break the seal on each card and run it through the reader on his desk. Each time he does, the full value of the card flashes momentarily on his screen and then abruptly drains to zero as the funds are deposited into the syndicate's accounts, until all that is left is plastic.

"Are we good?" I ask.

"We good," he says and hands me the note.

I rip it in half twice and stuff it into my backpack.

"Tell me, how a kid like you pay off such a big note?"

"I run numbers."

Vlad laughs like I have just said something funny even

though I haven't. I guess he just assumes it's a joke. At least it puts him in a better mood. Before I go he comps me a $10 chip.

"Here," he says, "have a play on the house. See if your luck is any better than Baxter's."

I take the chip and try doing that thing where I walk it down my knuckles, but all I end up doing is dropping it on the floor, where it lands on its side and rolls away from me. Then as I try to grab it, I kick it even further with my toe. Finally I chase it down and retrieve it, looking far less cool than I would have if I'd just pocketed the stupid thing.

Vlad slaps his leg like he's watching a Looney Tunes cartoon. I hold up the chip. "Thanks."

I can still hear him laughing behind me as I leave his office.

The gaming floor at that hour is still relatively quiet. There is a jam-packed hustle and bustle of high-stakes players that the syndicate parlor is known for, but that won't start for hours. Right now it's mostly scattered people playing low-limit games. The only game of real interest belongs to the suited gentleman playing heads-up poker against a house player.

It isn't long before I pass by the roulette table and decide to throw the comp chip down on black while the ball is still in orbit. Then I wait, not for an integer but for a color, as the ball does its obligatory bounce around the spinning wheel and lands on zero. Green zero. Neither red nor black, odd nor even, high nor low, it is one of two slots on the wheel that belongs to the house. Figures.

I'm just about to head for the door when something interesting happens over at the poker table. The man in the suit pushes all-in ahead of the flop. The house player calls. At a glance it looks to be about twenty grand or so. They show their cards. Suit's got pocket Aces, while the house player turns over a 7♣ and 2♥. I can't even believe what I'm seeing. Seven–Two unsuited? Statistically, that is the worst hand you can start with in Texas hold'em. There's no straight draw. No flush draw. Even a pair of sevens is likely to get beat. There are few rules in card games that are sacrosanct. In blackjack, you always split your aces and double down on an eleven. Always. In poker, you never bet a Seven–Two unsuited on a pre-flop raise. Never.

But surprising as this is, it's nothing compared to the next three cards dealt up on the table. 7♦ 7♠ 2♠. The house player flops a full house that blows away the Suit's Aces. There's only two cards that can help the suited gentleman now. The dealer reveals the turn. A♠. Yep, that's one of them. Aces full of Sevens beats Seven full of Twos. It's not quite over. The house player does have one out left. One slim, highly unlikely out. The dealer taps the table, burns the top card, turns over the river. 7♥. Four Sevens to make four of a kind. Suit loses it all to the house player. What are the odds?

Actually, what *are* the odds? I can't tell you the exact percentages, but I know they're not good. Probably the same as landing a little white roulette ball in the zero. It happens. It just happened to me, and I'm sure it was just chance, but then I didn't have twenty grand riding on that spin. If I did, would that little white ball have found the house slot by more than just chance?

I wonder, because after the man in the suit wanders away with his tail between his legs, and the dealer gathers the house's chips and closes the table, it is not the dealer but the house player who takes up the deck of cards used in the game. That's strange. I may not be an expert on the inner workings of gaming parlors, but I do know that house players are supposed to be treated like any other player. In no instance does a house player ever walk off with the cards when the game is done. That's beyond strange; it's downright suspicious.

I should just walk away. Go back out to where Dex is waiting and be done with it. But something in my gut won't let it go. I follow him across the floor and up the steps. I trail a short distance behind him as he punches a code into a restricted entry. His fingers move quickly, but not quick enough to elude my eyes. 2–2–6–3–2.

I check to make sure no one is around and pull out the walkie-talkie.

"Dex," I whisper.

Even with the volume turned all the way down the static that comes through the monitor is so loud I have to cover it with my hand.

"Go for Dex…over."

"Something's going on here. Go around back and wait for my signal…over."

"Did you get the note?...over."

"Affirmative…over."

"Then what do you care what's going on in there? Get your ass out and let's blow this joint…over."

"In a minute. Go around back and watch for my signal over."

"Signal! Who are you, Batman? What signal?...over."

I haven't thought that far ahead. "You'll know it when you see it…over."

"Roger tha….over and out."

2–2–6–3–2. A green light grants me access. This puts me in a dimly lit hallway with a bunch of back rooms where who knows what goes on. Thinking about it now, there's a back door in Vlad's office that can only lead into this hall. At present, all the doors are shut except for the one at the end. I get there just in time to see the house player remove a set of contact lenses. He moves out of view. I skirt to the other side of the opening and see him disappear into the bathroom. A moment later I hear the sound of running water.

I enter.

Inside, I find an antique desk littered with the appurtenances of casino games. Single decks of cards. Two heavy wooden card shoes. A box of dice. Three roulette balls sitting idle in an ashtray. The only thing out of place is the contact lenses. I lift one to my eye and peer through it like a spyglass. There doesn't appear to be anything corrective about it. It's just a transparent lens, or so it appears, until I happen to pass it over the deck of cards. At that moment, a heads-up display of fifty-two playing cards splashes across the lens.

"What the—"

I turn the top card over, which matches the first one in the string. Then I quickly rifle through the rest of the deck, watching every card go by as expected. That was how the house employee did it. With these lenses and that deck, he knew exactly what was coming.

But that wouldn't matter in a game of blackjack. The dealer has to hit according to the rules, not by choice, so seeing the next card wouldn't benefit him in any way. I turn the lens to the blackjack shoe, but all I see is the back of the next card. It doesn't matter. Even if the cards aren't transparent, I know it has to be fixed in some other way. I take a moment to examine it. On the outside it's indiscernible from every other blackjack shoe on the gaming floor.

I slide out the next card. 6♥. Then a few more. 8♦ 7♣ 6♠ 9♦ 9♣ 6♣.

That's weird. Seven cards in a row without a single high or a low. I go to draw another card and happen to catch the edge. Not much, just enough to slide it back a few millimeters, but that's enough to reveal the tiered edges of two other cards hiding beneath the top card. I know at once what I'm looking at as I reset the top card. Then, just like a pro, slice it back and draw the card directly beneath it. The mechanism is so smooth you can't even see it happen, but it does. 2♥. I do it again knowing they'll all be low. 3♦ 4♠ 2♣ 5♥. Then I draw from the slot beneath that one, knowing before the first card is even turned over that they will all be a Ten or an Ace. Sure enough. 10♦ K♣ Q♥ A♠ J♦ 10♦ A♥.

This is the reason Martin lost. He wasn't beaten by thirteen decks; he was taken by a rigged shoe.

I rifle through my bag and find my LED torch just as the water in the bathroom cuts out. The only window in the room faces out the rear of the building, which is where Dex should already be waiting. I press it to the glass and flash three times. Dex and I haven't agreed upon an actual signal, or what it would mean, but I figure he would know enough to be ready for me. I slip out of the room just in time to avoid the house player coming out of the bathroom.

But now I have a different problem: the sound of voices coming down the hall in the direction from whence I came. I can't go back that way. Not to worry, there is an emergency exit at the end of the hall. I hurry to it and throw my hip into the release bar, only to slam the entire side of my body into a door that does not budge. I push it again. Same result. I survey the door looking for a catch or a pin or a release—something, anything—but find nothing.

Not good. I pull out the walkie-talkie. "Dex," I whisper. "Dex, I'm in trouble here."

A blast of static sounds like it contains a voice but it's so faint I can't make it out.

"Dex, the door won't open!"

The voices turn the corner and become three shadowy figures. The round one in the middle can only be Vlad. There's no point hiding it now. I turn the knob all the way to the right and call for Dex again, but this time the static contains nothing.

"Dex cannot hear you," says Vlad as he steps close enough for his silhouette to take on color. In his oversized hand he holds a mechanical jammer, the kind that also works on radio signals.

I try the door again. Again. Again and again.

"That won't open. These doors have all been locked by remote security. Why you come back here?"

Okay think, I tell myself. If I can't get out of it, I may as well get some answers. "You cheated in Martin's game. I saw the shoe."

"Cheated," he says. "No, not cheated. Martin Baxter always come to gaming parlor with his math genius. I merely stabilize the game."

"What about that guy at the poker table? Were you stabilizing his game?"

"Him? No. Somebody pay to get him into debt with us. After thirty-day grace period, we sell them his note."

Sirens go off in my head. Suddenly Martin's debt takes on a whole new dimension. The syndicate was just the middleman. They didn't have any interest in him personally. So who did? "Who paid you to get Martin into debt?"

Vlad scrunches his face like he isn't going to tell me but soon relaxes it back into a smile. "What the hell, I like you better than her."

"Who?"

"Snooty French woman from Grumwell. Like all French. I never trust the French."

"Wait, what French woman from Grumwell?"

"You don't know?"

I shake my head.

"Don't worry," he says. "You meet her soon. She give instructions for us to detain you."

"Detain me? Detain me for what?"

Vlad shrugs. "If pay is good, I don't ask why. *Why* is…how you say…anathema to business." Vlad and his goons inch closer. "Now I'm afraid we must detain you until she arrives."

The bar of the door presses into my body armor as I back into it as they advance. Then, CRACK!

Wait, that isn't me.

CRRRACK!

Vlad and his men stop cold. "What is that?" he asks.

Just then the door that won't open is ripped clean out of its frame and dragged away by the revving engine of an old Buick.

"What the hell is this?" Vlad exclaims. "Go get him!"

But I am already through the exit and bolting for the car's open window. Dex waits for me with both hands on the wheel and his foot poised over the pedal. Ready to slam the gas the moment I'm in.

Ten feet from the car I have to make a snap decision how to enter the window—head or feet first. There is no time to stall. I dive in headfirst and push off the door with my hands to get as much of my torso into the car as I can. Dex guns it. My armor causes me to rock back and forth in the window frame as the tires kick dirt and the car takes off, towing behind it the back door of the syndicate that is still tied to the rear of the vehicle.

Vlad's men pull their guns. Fire.

The metallic grind of a heavy metal door being dragged along asphalt is loud enough to drown out the report, but I see the muzzle flashes through the dirt cloud near the building. They get off two rounds. One goes nowhere, the other ricochets off the car. That's it for now. We get away as Dex speeds the car up the road.

Legs still dangling out the passenger side window, I practically have to yell over the dragging door. "That was subtle."

Dex offers a not-so-subtle smile. "You know me, Jack. Subtlety is my specialty."

I pull myself into the car and turn around to check out our tow. "I'm surprised it didn't rip the bumper off."

"I anchored it to the frame."

"Should we cut it loose?"

"I kind of like it," says Dex with a sidelong glance. "It's like putting a baseball card in the spoke of your bicycle tire. It serves a purpose."

"What purpose is that?"

"It lets people know you're coming."

13.

From the moment I wake up, I know it's going to be a long day.

Dex and I have to get an early start heading into the Free City, which means I have to get up even earlier to put in an appearance at school. Dexter and Pace are in the Distributive Education program, so they're both getting school credit for running the sneakernet, but for me there is no more credit to give. From the moment I arrived at Brentwood High, the administration didn't know what to do with me. I had already earned all the core credits I needed to graduate back at the magnet academy, and there was no advanced placement curriculum for me here in Brentwood, so they did they only thing they could. They put me on Independent Study and let me spend my days in the school labs working on pet projects.

It isn't too bad. The labs aren't as well equipped as they were back at the magnet academy, but at least here I don't have people constantly looking over my shoulder. Even my faculty advisor, Mr. Chupick, leaves me alone. That ends up being productive. It was here in the school labs that I built those two rodent repellers for Dex and me. That was something I never could have gotten away with back at the academy. They regarded stuff like that as juvenile. Fickle. The wares of a less serious mind. But here in Brentwood nobody cares. Granted, I could do all that stuff in my own basement. There is nothing in the school labs that Martin doesn't already have down there—and more—but that's his space. Of course it's also mine to use anytime I need, but I prefer not to. The way I see it, Martin and I each need our own space to work. The basement is his; the labs at school are mine.

All Mr. Chupick asks in return for my freedom is that I present him with each project upon completion. Which on this early morning is a piece of code.

"It's designed to do what?" he asks.

"To tag Moreau."

"What about the tracker code you wrote last month?"

"It didn't stick."

Mr. Chupick didn't know much about the undernet before he met me. He hadn't even heard of Morlock until the day I explained it to him, let alone the infamous Morlock leader named Moreau. But now he knows all about both and my mission to find the second in order to become the first. Mr. Chupick swipes through pages of code, stopping only when he gets to the math. "I see you're using a Taylor series to approximate some function, but this 7th Gen programming language is all Greek to me." He volleys the code from his trans screen back onto my thin screen. "Let me know how it works out."

Mr. Chupick's desk is covered with a mess of topography charts, something I've been meaning to ask him about since I first walked in. "What's all this about?"

"Old geological surveys. Since I can't get any information from Blackburn about the water in my well, I was hoping there might be something in the old public records."

"Those still exist?"

Mr. Chupick gives me a knowing grin. "If you know where to look for them."

I lift the corners of a few charts and flip through them. "Did you find anything?"

It's an obvious no. "These are all surface maps. I don't think there's anything in here to find. What I really need are the geological surveys that the Blackburn Corps of Engineers took after the hydrofracking disaster." Mr. Chupick puts it aside. "Are you running today?"

"I am." I check the time. "In fact, I have to get going."

Mr. Chupick eyes me like he already knows that today's run is different because as of today I am no longer running to pay off the syndicate. Today, I'm running for the cash. Today, I'm running for me.

"You know, Jack. There was once an Ancient Greek

philosopher who demonstrated mathematically that no matter how far you run, you can never truly reach your goal."

"How's that?"

"It's called Zeno's Paradox. Let's say that you have a goal, and that you are now x distance away from that goal. Before you can cover that distance you first have to cover half that distance. And before you can cover that half-distance, you first have to cover one-quarter that distance. And before you can cover that quarter-distance, you first have to cover one-eighth of that distance. And so on. And so no matter how near or far your goal may be, you're never more than halfway there."

"Because abstract space can be parsed infinitely?"

"Not just space," says Mr. Chupick. "The goal doesn't have to be a distance, it can be a dollar amount too. And when your goal is a dollar amount, a funny thing happens. Even when the goal is never out of your sight, it will always be just beyond your reach."

I think I know what he's getting at.

"Zeno's Paradox." Mr. Chupick gives me an easy smile. "Just something to keep in mind."

14.

My plan was to do the entire run with Dex, but halfway into the Free City my wing starts to buzz, so at the last minute we decide to split up. I'll pick up my load first and then rendezvous with him on the sneakernet to give him extra support for his run. Once his cargo is secure, I'll deliver mine. If all goes well, we'll have plenty of time to grab some Free City pizza before we head back to Brentwood. And then later on tonight, I can lay it all out for Martin. Give him the note. Show him my tag. Let him know that this is how I'm going to save up my tuition for NEIT, and that's that. And once that is settled, I can tell Martin all about his blackjack game being a setup and find out about this French woman from Grumwell—who she is and why she would hire the syndicate to gain leverage over him.

Like I said: long day.

To my surprise, my pick-up point is TerraAqua, a business you wouldn't think would need Arcadian Transport's top dollar *when security is the only option* service. I can't imagine the water collective dealing in anything that high value. But they're the client, and they've agreed to pay the bill, so who am I to question their motives? Besides, if it does end up being a light run, I should be grateful to draw it. Easy money doesn't come along very often. Mind you, that's assuming I even get to it, because after nearly ten minutes of me waiting for her to sort it out, the receptionist still has no clue what's going on.

"You said you're here to pick up?" she asks again.

And for the fifth time, "yes."

I check my watch. My rendezvous with Dex is approaching quickly, and I don't want to leave him hanging.

"From Arcadian Transports?"

Once again, "yes."

"And your name?"

That's a new one. Usually I just say I'm from Arcadian Transports, and they tell me exactly where to go, sometimes even escort me there. No one has ever asked for my name before. "The Carrion," I say.

"The *what*," she stumbles, "*kay-ron*?"

"Carrion," I repeat. "The Carrion."

"I'm sorry, I need your actual name."

"That's it."

"Carrion?"

For some reason, I think of Red Tail. "That's Arcadian policy. Every runner goes by his or her handle. There's no other name to give."

"Okay," she says. "Let me…let me call upstairs."

That phone call takes another ten minutes, and I begin to wonder if maybe I shouldn't check in with Arcadian to make sure they didn't give me the wrong pick-up spot, but finally she hangs up the phone. "You can see Ms. Doyle on forty-three."

"Ms. Doyle on forty-three," I repeat and make my way past reception to the elevators.

Running data in the Free City, you get to learn the buildings pretty quick. The TerraAqua administrative offices take up floors 41-43 of the Wainwright Building. Waiting for the express elevator, I read the trans screens in the elevator lobby. One is a bulletin screen indicating time, temperature, and a bold notice that the 28th floor is under construction. The other is tuned to the Free City news stream, where they continue to discuss Blackburn's increasingly dire situation. As if the malfeasance charges last month weren't bad enough, now they're on the verge of complete bankruptcy. Apparently, if the company doesn't see a major cash infusion in the next few days, it will fold. That's what they say, anyway; but I know better. The North American Alliance cannot go even one day without an active military, and there is no other defense contractor big enough to take over all of Blackburn's operations without any interruption in service, so the Alliance Senate can't allow Blackburn to fold. They just can't. Unless of course they already have some backup plan that they're just not telling anyone about.

Up on forty-three, I am greeted at reception by Ms. Doyle's administrative assistant, who walks me through the suite to the woman's office. Mostly the people I see are undistinguishable, but there is one guy who leers at me nervously from an end cubicle. We do make eye contact, but he breaks it off quickly and disappears around his fuzzy wall before Ms. Doyle's assistant notices him. It happens quickly, but it's enough for me to register him. Forties and balding with a moderately trimmed beard, he wears a tweed coat with burgundy elbow patches and khaki pants. I don't look back because I don't want to draw attention to a man who obviously doesn't want to be seen, but as we continue to Ms. Doyle's office, I feel him watching us from behind.

"Come in," says the middle-aged woman with the beehive hairdo, knees-to-neck dress and glasses on an old lady chain. Obviously her entire look is supposed to be ironic—you don't have to look very hard to see the holes in her face where the piercings usually go, and I'm sure under all that fabric is an entire canvas of body art. "Come in. You must be Mr. Carrion."

Mr. Carrion? Wonderful. She thinks my handle is my proper name. But since correcting her would require an explanation I don't have time for, I let it slide. "Yes," I reply. And check my watch again.

"I'm sorry for the confusion," she says. "I did find a purchase order requesting data courier service, but there's no indication on the paperwork of who put it through or what it was supposed to be for."

"You mean, you don't know?"

"That's just it. No department has any outgoing cargo scheduled for today. And the purchase order was never processed, so I don't know how your people would have even been contacted. We've never used your firm before. It's just not in our budget. As far as I know we don't even have an account with you, so the money to pay for it would've had to come from discretionary spending, and there's no way a check that size would have been cut without approval from accounting."

"So why am I here?"

"That's what I'd like to know. I tried contacting Arcadian through their aggrenet portal, but no one has called me back."

That's when I realize something is off. If Arcadian hasn't contacted her back, there has to be a reason. "It's probably just a mix up I'm sure," I say. And check my watch again.

Finally Ms. Doyle gets it. "I don't want to keep you," she says, "I'm sure you have a busy schedule. I'll continue to investigate this matter on my end and follow up with you at a later time. What would be the best way to reach you?"

"Don't worry about reaching me," I say. "I'm sure it was just a simple misunderstanding. How about if I explain what happened to Arcadian, and if they have any questions they can contact you directly."

"That would be satisfactory," she says and volleys a business card from her trans screen to my thin screen. "And once again, I'm very sorry about this."

"Me too."

Ms. Doyle motions for her assistant to walk me back out, but I wave her off. "It's okay, I can find my way out. Good day."

"Good day."

●　　●　　●

I would probably be more curious about the whole thing if I wasn't already so far behind schedule. I told Ms. Doyle I was sure it was just a simple misunderstanding. Actually, I'm sure it wasn't. Is it possible? Yes. Probable? No. Not where Arcadian is concerned. These guys don't mess around. They don't leave anything to chance, and they don't misunderstand anything. There was no glitch. Somebody at TerraAqua wanted me today, right here and right now, to run a cargo. Of that much I am certain.

As if I haven't already seen it enough times—on the trans screen in the lobby, in the elevator coming up, and on the 43rd floor trans screen waiting to come back down—the status monitor on the elevator tells me that the 28th floor of the Wainwright Building is under construction. Which doesn't concern me until the elevator comes to a full stop on the 28th floor.

I check the panel. The only button lit is for the lobby. I hit it again. Nothing. I hit the button for 28 but that one doesn't even light up. It must be locked out.

The doors open.

I expect to see someone from maintenance hitching a ride down, but instead all I see is a floor gutted down to concrete and windows. Saw horses. Spools of cable. Pallets of wallboard. Folding tables set up here and there. All this material, but not a single person in sight. I wait for the doors to close on their own but they don't. I try to force them closed with the button. Nothing. So I step off the elevator onto the floor.

"Hello?"

Still nothing.

I look around. That's when I see the reason why the elevator is stuck. Someone has placed a large nut over the call button and fastened it down with a strip of duct tape. *Strange*, I think. A practical joke, maybe?

Just as I am about to remove it, the door to the stairwell flies open and a man stumbles in. I recognize him immediately. It's the guy from upstairs, the one who was looking at me from his cubicle. Only now his head and hands are smeared with blood. His own by the looks of it. He is almost out of breath, and his legs appear ready to give out like he has just run all the way down from 43. Or more accurately, like he has just been chased down. The look in his eyes is a look I know all too well. This man is being pursued.

I rush over to help him, barely making it in time to catch him by his sport coat as he collapses onto the floor. Straining for breath, he grips my arms like I am life itself.

"You're the data runner," he exclaims.

"I am."

"Good," he coughs. "I'm the reason you're here. I want to hire you."

"It doesn't work like that. You have to—"

The man grips my arm even tighter as he shoves my sleeve up my elbow. "What is your tag?" he asks.

"I'm the Carrion."

"Carrion," he says. He has already pulled out a thin screen. Now he pulls out a SQUID.

"Hey, wait a second." I try to release his grip and pull away but he is way too quick. Before I realize it, he has already placed the sensor over the chip and has started the magnet pulses. Now it's too late. Yanking off a SQUID mid-transfer could permanently damage the memory cells inside the cortex chip. I have to wait it out.

Finally I feel it. Five quick pulses indicating the completed transfer.

"Okay, now get it out!" I demand, wanting him to take back whatever it is he's just loaded into my wing, but the man grabs my lapels and stares into me with eyes that refuse to blink.

Cold. Hard. Wide. "Just let it all burn," he says.

"I don't understand."

"Just let it all burn." Each breath grows more laborious than the last. "Get this to the Outliers," he murmurs. "They'll know what to do."

Outliers. "You mean out in the squatter settlements?"

"Precisely," he whispers.

The door to the stairwell is thrown open and two security goons enter. Only these guys aren't wearing suits, they're wearing tactical vests. Full military gear. And if that isn't enough to give it away, the insignia on their vests is. These guys aren't retrievers by trade. They're soldiers.

"Halt!" screams the first as he pulls out a gun.

There is no time to weigh options. Instinct says GO!

The bloody guy in the sport coat still has me in his grip. I remove his hands from my lapels and sprint for the elevator over a second command to halt. Rip the tape off the call button. Dive through the closing doors and turn just in time to see them miss me by a split-second. The elevator moves, but the numbers can't drop fast enough.

I make my way through the lobby. Moving quickly but not so quick as to arouse suspicion. Now I get paranoid. Maybe it's just my imagination, but it seems like the reception desk gets a call from upstairs. No matter, I am already through the revolving door and out on the sidewalk. Now I have to get underground as fast as I can. There are too many relay cameras up here on the streets. Too many eyes. No one can hide up here. The stairs for the nearest station are right there, but in order to meet Dex I have to use a different station six blocks away or I'll never make it in time.

I check my watch. I have no idea what's going on. I don't have to know what's going on. What I have to do is follow my gut. Instinct says MOVE. Keep moving. Even when the cryptic words start playing in an endless loop in my head.

Just let it all burn.

Whatever it means, I know one thing for sure. Blackburn is after it. That's when I remember what Red Tail said. Blackburn is the one outfit you don't want on your tail.

This could be bad.

15.

Twenty minutes and two energy bars later I stand under a tunnel light wondering if I've already missed Dexter. The two messages I sent him went unreturned, which could just mean he has a good run going and doesn't want to stop. I open a third energy bar. Whatever this thing is that's loaded into my wing, it's either enormously big or extraordinarily encrypted to be giving me such an appetite.

Just let it all burn.

Is it a code? A passphrase? Something to say to the people at the receiving end so they know I'm legit, like in those old Cold War spy movies? And on that note, how am I even supposed to find those people at the receiving end?

He said *get this to the Outliers*. The Outliers. That rebel faction located deep inside the squatter settlements. Freedom fighters or terrorists depending upon whom you listened to. Was I really supposed to deliver it to them? Such a run would contradict what Cyril told me when I first started. So far all of my runs have been point-to-point within the Free City, just like Cyril said they would be. Now all of a sudden I'm being directed out to the squatter settlements. Something just isn't sitting right. I'm not even confident that this is the load I was meant to pick up. The logical thing to do would be to contact Arcadian for guidance, find out directly from them just what the hell is going on. The only thing is, Red Tail told me not to trust anyone at Arcadian but her and Snake. This creates the dilemma. Not knowing what is in my arm, where to go to get it out, or whom I can trust.

My ears perk.

From somewhere in the distance, it's hard to say how far with the tunnel echo but I'm guessing maybe a quarter of a mile,

I hear the whine of an engine. Dirt bike, I think. But then I hear the engine rev under the throttle and realize the pitch is too low. ATV. I'm 500 feet downwind of a switching track, so the noise could be coming from either tunnel. Or it could be coming from the adjacent track just beyond the connecting tunnel. Whenever Dex and I meet on the sneakernet, we always choose a hub with multiple ways in and out, just in case. But even if I can't pinpoint exactly where the ATV is coming from, I do know one thing for sure. It's heading straight for—

Dex.

With the echo of the ATV behind him, I don't even hear him coming until he's already out of the tunnel and leaping over the switching track with a package under his arm. Not a data package loaded into his arm, though I'm sure he's got one of those as well, I'm talking about an actual package that he's carrying under his arm. Like a shipping tube but more oddly shaped. Something wrapped in brown paper, maybe. It's too dark to see anything but shapes as he slows to a belabored step that includes a slight limp. Until he gets closer, steps into the tunnel light. And I nearly jump back in fright.

Dexter is covered in blood. Dark red smears his clothes and face. The package under his arm is no shipping tube, it's an arm. Not his own. Someone else's. Someone else's arm. Someone else's dismembered arm. Dexter is running through the tunnels with another data runner's arm.

"Dex, what the hell?"

"We got ambushed."

"You're bleeding!"

"It's not mine." Dexter swings the dismembered arm out from under his own. The raw end is wrapped with a dirty cloth but still continues to seep blood.

"What happened?"

"It's the cargo."

"What cargo?"

"*The* cargo, Jack. The one Ito and Gendo have been contracted to intercept. This is it."

"What?!?"

"I knew I should have walked away the minute I heard the details. There wasn't even a destination. The instructions were to keep the cargo readily accessible for the next twenty-four hours. Within that time, someone would make contact to arrange the handoff. Some blind alley transfer. Damn, Jack, my gut was telling me to walk away, but then the other two runners got half their pay up front. And when I saw the completion bonus they were offering…the money was just too good. I couldn't turn it down."

"Slow down, Dex. Start from the beginning."

"It was a parity run. Three runners from three different firms. Three separate loads with three separate handoffs. Mirrored."

"So any two loads can make a complete package. Okay, so what happened?"

"We weren't even supposed to see each other after the download, but we ran straight into each other at Grand Central."

"You went down through Grand Central?" You never go down through Grand Central. Too many people, too many unknowns. An interceptor could track you all the way into the tunnels without you ever knowing it. Dexter knows that. Hell, he was the one who told me.

"I had no choice. I spotted a shadow the instant I left the pickup. I had to get off the street quick. You know how many relay cameras there are around the station. I had to assume they already picked me up and were tracking me step by step. The only thing I could do was enter the station and make a break for the tunnels."

Grand Central being the midtown hub, there isn't another station for eight blocks in any direction. Dexter is right. If he picked up a shadow and the cameras were on him, it was reason enough to break protocol. Chances are I would have done the same thing. "Then what?"

"The other two must have had the same idea, because the next thing I knew, we all ran into each other on the same platform, and the only way out was on the train. That was when all hell broke loose."

"Mr. Ito?"

"Not at first. At first it was just Gendo. Man, he threw that kid against the doors and ripped off his arm like he was separating a piece of chicken. Then he threw it on the floor and stomped it until there was nothing left of the chip inside. The other runner and I ran through to the back of the train, but that was where Ito was waiting with his sword. And before that kid could even react, his arm sailed clear across the car and landed at my feet."

"So you grabbed it."

Dex nods. "I wasn't going to mess around with no samurai sword," he says in spite of his mixed martial arts training. "I kicked out the window and tossed out the arm, then jumped out after it."

That explains the limp.

The sound of the ATV grows louder, and the way Dexter throws his attention over his shoulder, I know it's for him. "This is it, Jack. This is the stolen cargo they've been contracted to disrupt."

I know it's a long shot but... "Do you have any idea what it is or who gave it to you?"

"No."

"Well we can't get caught with it, that's for sure."

Dexter takes a moment to consider the situation. "I shouldn't even have it on me. The whole point of parity is to distribute the cargo so no single runner can be intercepted. But right now I'm carrying the entire load. I need to..." Dex looks at me. "We need to secure the cargo."

He doesn't say it, but I know exactly what he's thinking. "You can't be serious."

"It's the only thing we can do. Get that cargo secure and head back to Brentwood."

"Then what?"

"Meet me in the old library tonight. We can figure it out then."

I take another look at the dismembered limb. The sad thing is, he's right. I can't think of a better alternative. "Dex, I can't exactly walk around the Free City with a severed arm over my shoulder."

"You don't have to."

"Oh, no."

The roar of the ATV is much closer now, like it could pop out of the tunnel at any moment. "I'll draw him away," says Dexter. "Once you're clear, you can remove the chip."

"You want me to cut into his arm?"

"There is no *his*, Jack. It doesn't belong to anyone anymore. Just think of it as a random arm."

Random arm? Is there even such a thing? Not that it matters, there is no time to argue. Dex hands me the cold, limp arm made tacky from drying blood. It isn't particularly heavy, less than ten pounds in total, but the weight is awkwardly distributed. No matter how you hold it, it always wants to turn in your hands. At first I put the severed end behind me, but seeing that ghostlike hand hovering in front of me by the amber glow of the tunnel light is way more creepy than blood, so I turn it around.

"You ready?" Dex asks as he steps back to the middle of the tunnel.

"Yeah," I reply, and position myself into a little niche just beyond the light. I don't think anyone passing by could see me in there, but Dexter smashes the light just to be on the safe side. Now we are in total darkness, for a moment, until the ATV emerges and the beam of a xenon headlamp cuts straight through it. It is Gendo who's riding it. From my little hiding space I watch the ATV leave the ground, sail over the switching track, land with a thud. And soon the light grows bright on Dexter.

"Hey, Jack," he says just before he takes off.

"Yeah."

"Run like hell!"

THE OTHER CARGO

16.

Twenty seconds after Dexter takes off up the track, Gendo roars past on his ATV. It's not much of a lead, but for someone like Dex it's enough. Hopefully. I have to stop myself from thinking about it, or the limp in his leg. I have to trust that Dexter will be all right so I can focus on my own run.

As soon as the ATV disappears up the track, I take off down the connecting tunnel, a tight passage that could barely fit Gendo himself, let alone his quad. But I don't take it all the way to the adjacent track. Not yet. There's something I have to do first. Halfway through the tunnel I stop at a rusted old power cabinet. Not quite a workbench but it'll have to do. I place the severed arm on top and dig my folding knife from out of my backpack. Flip it open.

"Ugh. This is going to be gross."

I push the tip of the knife into the cold, rubbery flesh. A single rivulet of blood flows down the side of the arm. It's noticeably more viscous than fresh blood, spilling in thick curtains as I cut a full circle all the way around the chip scar. These runners don't have a precisely implanted bioidentical cortex chip like I do; theirs are just a silicon module wedged under the skin for safekeeping. That's why most data runners, Dexter included, have those ridged scars on their forearms that look like cancelled postage stamps.

I peel away the patch of skin and see the module embedded in sinewy muscle fiber. It takes a bit more cutting to get at it. The muscle tissue is tough and slippery and keeps sliding under the blade of the knife. I reach in with my fingers and pull it taut, but still it requires me to saw through, and even then it stretches before it frays, and frays before it snaps.

Ugh! If I still wasn't sure what I wanted to be when I grew up, I could definitely scratch Coroner off the list.

I can't help cringing as I pull apart the strings of wet tendon to access the module, but after careful maneuvering I am able to pull it free. I hold it up to the tunnel light and examine the sticky red memory chips. Whatever is in this module is the reason why dozens of runners have lost their arms over the past few months. I grab an antistatic bag from my backpack and drop the module into it, fold it over and place it in a padded compartment.

The whole ordeal of removing this data runner's implant has been so traumatic, it almost makes me forget about the other cargo I'm carrying around, the one I never got a chance to tell Dexter about. It's only the pang in my stomach that reminds me of it.

Just let it all burn.

Whatever. That's not the priority right now. First I have to get this other cargo secure, and the only way to do that is to get it out of the tunnels and out of my hands. And before I can do that, I have a distance to run. And before I can do that, I first have to get halfway there. That's the point of Zeno's Paradox, isn't it? Whatever your goal, you're never more than halfway there. Right now I have to run through the underground to the other side of the Free City, but first I have to get halfway there.

And the remainder of the severed arm?

I leave it behind for the rats.

●   ●   ●

The north entrance of Riverfront Park, otherwise known as Riverfront Square, has as many relay cameras as any major public locale in the Free City. But between the subway entrance, the park entrance, and the never-ending traffic jam resulting from two avenues converging and two streets crossing all in the space of a single intersection, there is a bottleneck of pedestrian traffic that makes those cameras pretty much useless.

And then there's the Riverfront Café, located right on the

corner of Busy and Busier. Between all the people grabbing carryout for the park and the swarm of people hovering around waiting for a table to open up, the three cameras located inside the establishment are just for overview. Anyone tapping into the feed wouldn't have a snowball's chance in hell of spotting a face in that crowd, especially one taking measures not to be seen.

I keep my head down on my way to the restroom and lock the door behind me. The sink has a metered faucet, which means I would have to scan my TerraAqua card for an uninterrupted stream. I don't do that. After taking such pains to remain hidden, scanning my TerraAqua card would be like sending up a red flag telling everyone where I am. So instead I painstakingly wash my hands under 3-second bursts of water at 60-second intervals. At that rate it takes me three minutes just to get the soap working, but in that next minute I scrub and scrub like there's no degree of too clean. And for a moment, I know exactly how Lady Macbeth must have felt.

A pound at the door.

My hands now clean of the other data runner's blood, I pull out my thin screen and enter the following base 16 string: 52:65:64:20:54:61:69:6c. I've had Red Tail's digits on my mind for some time now, I've just been waiting for a reason to use them. This is after all the sneakernet. You don't pull someone off a run just to say *hi!*

I place the SQUID interface over the carrion crow's eye and upload the hail into my cortex chip. So far, so good. It's only when I go to scan it into the aggrenet that I run into a problem. The scanner in the restroom is wedged between the sink and the wall in such a way that I can't squeeze my arm under it. I try all different angles even though I already know it's not going to work. Scanning a card for water, no problem. Scanning a chip embedded in an arm, not going to happen. I needed another scanner.

Another pound at the door.

Ten minutes gone by, I exit the restroom to a line of extremely annoyed people. Particularly the first one, who takes a deep breath like he thinks the entire room is going to stink.

Back in the café, I get in line with a sandwich and drink that's going to cost me way more than I'd like to spend at the moment. Maybe one day soon I can budget a small portion of my earnings for minor luxuries like a $20 sandwich or a $30 movie, but today it's just an unforeseen expense.

I get to the register and the attractive young girl rings me up.

"Excuse me, what kind of bread is that?" I ask.

The instant she turns around, I pull up my sleeve and run my tag under the scanner attached to the register. The bird's eye blips as the scanner picks up the cortex chip and instantly returns an error code. I retrieve my arm just as she turns around. She eyes me with curiosity, then the register. "That's weird," she says as she hits the clear button. Then, to answer my question, "that's a honey brioche. I can have them make your sandwich on it if you prefer. It should just be about five or ten minutes."

"Sure, why not."

Then she notices the tattoo on my arm. "Nice ink," she says.

"Thanks."

She takes a closer look, observing the purple sheen in the raven crow's plumage and the way it always seems to have one eye on her. "Wow, that's really fantastic coloring."

"It's scorpion ink."

"Really? Where'd you get it?"

"It was custom job." I authorize the food purchase on my thin screen. "The guy's not around anymore."

"Oh," she replies with a hint of disappointment. "That's too bad. I'm looking for something really different. Everything around here is just so…blah. You know?"

"I guess, yeah."

She smiles. I return it awkwardly as the receipt with my order number appears on my thin screen. There's a tiny round table wedged into the corner that nobody seems to want because it's barely big enough for a couple of beverages. I take it and wait for my food.

17.

I've already finished my sandwich and drink, and a blueberry muffin, and half a cappuccino on top of that when the girl with raven hair and azure eyes enters the café and heads straight for me. I notice at once that she's not darting her eyes in every direction like I sometimes do. She does it with much more subtlety, using her peripheral vision instead. That's definitely her experience at work. There's no question she's been at this a lot longer than I have.

She comes to my table and drops her shoulder bag onto the floor beside my backpack. "What's the story, J-Bird?"

"Where to begin…"

Red Tail lifts the plate full of muffin crumbs and empty sugar packets and observes the plate of sandwich crumbs beneath it.

"Do you want anything?"

She just looks at me. Blinks. "You're loaded up."

I nod.

"You're walking around the Free City with cargo in your wing?"

Again, I nod.

"Are you insane?"

"We're data runners," I remind her as I open up my backpack and remove the antistatic bag. "Insanity kind of goes with the job." I hand it to her.

She stares at it. It's pretty clear she knows exactly what the crusty brown smears are inside the bag, even if it doesn't faze her. "This is a Mammoth Mark II bio-implantable memory module…" She turns it over and examines the etch pattern on the logic board. "Revision 6."

I am amazed that she knows the exact make and model of the memory module by sight. I didn't even know that.

"Where did you get this?" she asks.

"It's one load in a two-to-three parity cargo. My friend Dexter is currently running the only other arm. They got intercepted by Ito and Gendo, who crushed one load on the spot. Dexter got away with his load and this one still intact."

"Where is Dexter now?"

"Running his cargo."

"So why did he give this load to you?"

"Because," I say, tapping the chip in the bag. "You know that thing somebody stole that's so big it could bring down an entire megacorporation? The thing that's so damning, the people looking for it had to go outside their own internal security and hire Ito and Gendo to disrupt it?"

"If it even exists."

"It exists all right, and this is it. This is that cargo. Dexter handed me this load to secure while he lured Gendo away. I called you because I thought you might have more information about what it is, and because you told me not to trust anyone else out there."

Red Tail stretches the bag and reexamines the module through the film. It's pretty clear she doesn't know any more than I do.

"You don't know who Ito and Gendo are working for?" I ask.

"Nope.

"Do you have any idea what the cargo might be?"

She shakes her head. "But Snake might. He can probably even reassemble the cargo, but we have to get the parity load in Dexter's chip first."

"That's not a problem. I'm meeting him tonight."

"Where?"

"Back in Brentwood. The old library on Main Street."

"Okay, I'll contact Snake and we can take it from there. In the meantime, you better get back en route and deliver your cargo. You're still on the sneakernet right now." Red Tail is already halfway out of her chair like she thinks we're done here.

"Yeah, that could be a bit of a problem."

"What do you mean?"

"What do you know about the Outliers?"

She sits back down. After that, I tell her everything. TerraAqua. Ms. Doyle with the beehive hairdo. The pickup for which there was no record. The nervous man in the sport coat. The elevator stop. Getting loaded up. Getting chased into the elevator by Blackburn.

"And then?"

"Then I went down to meet Dexter, and that's when all hell broke loose with Ito and Gendo and this other cargo."

Red Tail considers my story carefully. Almost too carefully, like she's considering angles I'm not even aware of.

"I mean, it isn't unheard of to be called in for a pickup without the company knowing about it." I'm thinking of my very first run, where the security guy stopped me on the way out and told me it was against company policy to use data runners.

"It isn't unheard of, but it is highly unusual."

"What about these Outliers?"

"What about them?"

"Do you know anything about them?"

"Such as?"

"Who they are for one thing."

"They're a rebel faction that grew out of the squatter settlements."

I pick it up immediately. All of a sudden Red Tail is playing that game. Answering a question with a question. Acting like she's confused when in fact she knows exactly what I'm talking about. I know that game well. Martin did it all the time when I was a kid. Anytime I asked him anything about my mother Genie, he would play that same game.

It's pretty clear I'm heading down a road she doesn't want me on. I'll have to come back to it. If there is something at the end of this road, I'm not going to get there directly, so I change the discussion to logistics. "Okay," I say, "so how am I supposed to make this delivery? Aside from not having a contact, I don't even have a delivery point. All he said was to get it to the Outliers. He may as well have told me to get it to Old Kansas City."

That's when I get an idea. "Maybe I should just call it in to Arcadian for their instructions."

"No, don't do that!" Red Tail blurts.

I have no intention of doing that. I only say it to see her reaction. And Red Tail's reaction is very interesting to say the least. "Alright, what gives?" I ask. "I've trusted you up to now, but if you want me to keep trusting you, I need to know what's going on. Why am I not trusting anyone else at the firm?"

Red Tail sighs. She knows she's cornered. "A few weeks before you started with us, Liddy intercepted an unauthorized transmission originating from the Arcadian node."

"Data?" I ask.

Red Tail looks at me like I'm an idiot. "All transmissions are data, you dodo."

"What kind of transmission?"

"Communication signal. Whatever it was, they used military-grade scrambling, but it looks like somebody on the inside was contacting somebody on the outside."

It takes a second for the words to sink in, and even then, I have to be sure I am hearing her correctly. "You're saying that somebody inside Arcadian is a spy?"

She confirms. "We know it's not the Birdwatcher, since she found the signal. We know it's not you, me, or Snake. That leaves something like thirty-seven runners suspect."

"Cyril?"

"I'm pretty sure it's not upper management either. No, it has to be a runner." Red Tail's expression turns serious. "One of our birds is a mole."

"So how close are you to finding this mole?"

"Very. Snake's working on that right now. If all goes well, we should close in within the next twenty-four hours. But until then, you can't let anyone know about this." She waves her hand over the entire table to include both cargos. "Any of it. You have to keep it all under wraps."

"What do I do about the cargo in my arm?"

"I'll ask the Birdwatcher. Liddy doesn't make clerical mistakes. If she sent you there, it was for a reason."

"So until we get an answer I just have to lug this thing around?"

Red Tail reaches into her shoulder bag and drops a few energy bars on the table. "I'll try and have an answer for you by tonight. In the meantime, keep your blood sugar up."

Red Tail does a quick scan around the room before she gets up. "I'll go out first through the front. If there's a shadow on us, I'll draw it away. Wait five minutes and then find the back way out. Got it?"

"Yeah, I got it."

"And Carrion…"

"Yeah?"

"Keep an eye on your wing."

I hand Red Tail her shoulder bag that now contains the other part of Dexter's parity cargo. "You too."

18.

I know getting on the train is risky. But then so is hoofing it around the tunnels when I have no clue what I'm carrying or who else might be after it. All I know for certain is that Blackburn will be looking for me, and depending upon how important this thing is, that could mean as little as two soldiers or as many as the entire Military-Alliance Complex. There's no way of knowing. So yes, getting on the train is risky, but it's a calculated risk.

The crosstown train accelerates into the tunnel. Soon my train catches up with another train, paces alongside it for a few seconds, then dips further into the Free City underground.

That's when I see the expensive loafers perched atop the other train, and the perfect cuffs with the clean break that can only belong to one man. With the trains practically adjacent and barely a two-foot drop between us, he simply steps off. A split-second later I hear the muffled thud of a soft landing on the roof. No one else seems to notice it, or if they do they dismiss it as random train noise. I'm the only one who knows because I know he's there for me.

This time I haven't pinned myself against the back doors with nowhere to go. This time I've done it smart, having already checked both cars forward and rear for immediate trouble. Both were clear, but just to be sure I stand by the forward door, giving me a clear line of sight straight through to the next car. Standing there also gives me instant access to the segue if needed.

I throw open the door and enter the tight section between the two cars. The metal links on either side of me feel like pipe but hang like rope. They're slippery on purpose, to prevent exactly what I'm about to do. I climb over the accordion cage and use the uppermost link to gain footing.

My foot slips. I nearly tumble headfirst onto the steel grates bridging the two cars but manage to hang on. The second time I use my heel to lock on, which lets me push off and grab the roof of the car as my other foot propels me onto the top of the train.

The top of a train is no place to be unless you have no choice. There's wind, debris, sudden beams that can decapitate you in an instant, and a slippery rooftop with a convex bulge that can send you tumbling into oblivion with just one missed step. It'd be one thing if I were just going to lie on my stomach and ride it into the next station. But when I turn around and see Mr. Ito standing behind me—not kneeling, not crouching, not lying flat to hug the train—but standing straight up as if the dangers aren't even of concern to him, that's when I grasp the true peril of my predicament.

Mr. Ito is facing forward, so I'm the one who has to constantly whip my head around to check for anything low coming up behind me that could take my head off. So far so good. The tunnel's been wide open and clear. "You're too late," I scream over the barreling rush of wind, "I already handed it off."

He says nothing.

"The cargo is out of my hands."

Mr. Ito smiles.

"I'm serious."

"I know you are serious," he says.

"So what's this about?"

"The arm your friend gave you…is not the arm I'm after."

"You—" But I'm not sure what he's getting at. "What?"

"Yes, Gendo and I were out to disrupt that cargo. We've been looking for that cargo for some time, so finding it makes today a very good day. But that is only part of the contract. We have two cargos to disrupt. The first was your friend's parity cargo. The second is the other cargo."

I look down at my arm, at the bird staring straight out at Ito, and I suddenly realize I am hungry again. "You're after this…"

The wide eyes and crazy grin are a clear indication that Mr. Ito is done talking. He unsheathes his Katana.

"But this is Blackburn's business. They're the ones who are

after this…"

As Mr. Ito advances to the gap, I back away. That is when it all comes together.

"You've been contracted by Blackburn! That's the megacorporation this data could destroy."

"Bingo," he says with a twirl of his steel. "Now you may want to bite a bullet or something. I hear amputation by sword is very painful."

There is only one direction to run. Forward. I turn to meet the wind head-on and make my feet work to put distance between us as I leap over the gap onto the next car. Mr. Ito is now only half a train car behind and closing. After all, that is how you do it, isn't it? Half the distance at a time? Up ahead I see some beams that I could easily arm grab and dyno up to. That would put me out of Mr. Ito's reach, but not out of the reach of his sword. I'd be a sitting duck up there, and I am quite sure that slicing through sitting ducks is Mr. Ito's specialty. I let it pass and keep going. But for how long? I can't see more than one car ahead through the darkness, and for now the cars keep coming, but it won't be long before my feet run out of train. And then what?

I breathe a sigh of relief as another car emerges through the darkness.

I have to come up with a plan. I have to think of something fast. Turn around and engage my pursuer? It's worked before. I keep going. If I hit the lead car I'll have no other choice but to do that anyway, so I may as well keep going.

A low beam. I dive forward and hug the roof. The wind ruffles my hair as it sails over me. I pop back up. A few steps later I turn and see Mr. Ito do a sideways somersault over the oncoming obstacle and land on his feet like a cat with his katana. I keep running. Faster.

Another car emerges from the darkness.

There's no choice now. I have to get off this train or he'll have me trapped.

We enter a large track exchange, and suddenly I see the front of the train two cars up. More than that, I see the light of an oncoming train on the next track. It's going to be close.

The headlamp creeps closer.

The wind begins to change.

Until all at once, a second rush of wind from the side nearly knocks me off balance. Mr. Ito too, who has to swing his sword just to hold on.

Two feet away the other train passes, and I wait. More than the distance between the trains, it's the difference in speed you have to account for. That's what will cause you to botch the landing and roll off the train to grave injury. That's why I wait wait.

"Mr. Ito?"

"Hai."

"Just let it all burn."

He furrows his brow with confusion. "*Wakaranai*," he says. He doesn't understand. He doesn't know anything about this cargo. He doesn't care to know anything about this cargo. He just wants to destroy it. For the money.

Wait… until the time is just right.

Mr. Ito approaches with raised sword. "*Oyasumi*, Carrion-*kun*." *Goodnight, young Carrion.*

I leap. Off the train and into the air like I'm jumping for the other train, but instead I grab the crossbeam over my head and muscle up. Throw my torso over the beam and retract my arm just as Mr. Ito's sword strikes. It misses me by less than a centimeter, hitting the beam so close that I can feel the warm spark of steel-on-steel contact on my skin.

Mr. Ito turns and runs against the train but soon realizes the futility. He stops and stands, sword by his side, tip pointing away from his ankle, a receding silhouette on top of the train. "See you soon, Carrion-*kun*," he yells just before he disappears into darkness.

When both trains are gone, I begin to move. It's too dangerous to drop from where I am. If the ground was flat and I had room to roll out of it, maybe. But from this height, with all the rails and ties and bolts, not to mention the flood channel and the fact that I can't even see the ground well enough to do a precision landing, it'd be way too easy for me to catch my foot on something and break my ankle. Or worse. So instead I use the beam to make my way over the tracks until I find a spot where the ground is more stable. Remove my bag and drop it down.

I get to my feet, step off the beam and perform a Turn Down. My legs swing wildly to shake out the excess momentum as my strained fingers grip the rusted beam. Hanging by my arms, the drop is now only twelve feet. I release, land, roll.

I check the time. I have to get moving. With Blackburn after me, the sneakernet is no place to lay low. I figure I'll be safer once I'm out of the Free City and back in Brentwood.

19.

The front door to my house is ajar.

At first I think it's just Martin back from his trip, but he would never leave the front door unbolted, let alone ajar. Never Martin, who at any given time has who-knows-what going on down in the basement; that's how I know something is wrong.

I push the door open. Wide open. Leaving plenty of room for me to make an escape if I have to. The first thing I see is the living room. It's been ransacked. Every little thing has been turned over, every big thing toppled. Even the sofa cushions have been ripped apart. The high-end trans screen and entertainment stack that came with us from the Free City have all been trashed. Trashed instead of taken, which means this was no robbery. No corner was left untouched.

No corner left untouched. The deductive part of my brain kicks on. Okay, it's obviously not a robbery, so that means they were looking for something specific. And they wouldn't keep ransacking the place once they found what they were looking for. So if everything—and I do mean *everything*—in the room is upturned, that can only mean one of two things. Either A: they found exactly what they were looking for in the very last place they looked for it, which was incredibly unlikely; or B: they didn't find it at all. I go with B. Whatever they were looking for, they didn't find it at all.

Oh no, I think as it suddenly dawns upon me. *Basement.*

I enter the kitchen. The first thing I notice in all the mess is the biometric entry system for Martin's workshop smashed on the floor. They didn't get in that way. I suppose that's a good thing, since it's already been established that dismembering a thumb is still the easiest way through. At the very least, it means

Martin still has his. But that sense of ease disappears the moment I turn the corner and see the giant hole blown through the wall.

Blackburn. Those singe marks. That ashy detritus. This could only have been done by a helio gun. And that means it could only have been done by Blackburn. I am sure of it.

I race down the steps to find Martin's entire workshop in upheaval, much worse than the living room upstairs. Everything is a mess. Whatever order there once was, whatever lines of separation once divided his various tasks and projects, it has all been put through a blender with the lid off.

Then it hits me. *Martin.* Where is Martin?

I start up the stairs to look for him, but halfway up I see something that halts me mid-step—something I have never seen before because it was previously covered by an old filing cabinet. But now that the filing cabinet is on its side, the thing hiding behind it can't be ignored. I guess the soldiers from Blackburn who ransacked the place saw nothing strange about a heavy-duty cable running down the wall in a workshop like this. But to someone like me, or anyone with a trained eye, that isn't just any old cable. It's industrial-gauge optical fiber.

I grip the railing with both hands, run three steps up and kick my legs over, push off and turn to land. It takes me a minute to wade through the wreckage of Martin's workshop, but when I get there I follow the cable until it disappears behind the bottom of the filing cabinet. I kick aside the mess of files and slide the cabinet out of the way.

"What the hell…"

The cable disappears into the wall, which means it must go down through the floor. Down through a concrete floor? I clear aside all the papers and examine the floor. It's barely discernable but it's there. So faint you wouldn't even see it unless you knew to look for it, but it's definitely there. A seam. So now I wonder how I'm going to lift this thing. I'd need a suction cup attached to a handle to move it. But then I think about Martin, who would've had something much simpler in mind. Push instead of pull. I push down on the front corners. Nothing. I run my fingers to the back where it meets the wall and press down. Sure enough, the entire section of floor pivots back an inch. Just enough to get my fingers in there and lift away the entire section of floor. And when I do, I just stand there amazed.

"Holy crap, Martin!"

In the back corner of the basement, under the concrete floor, through the foundation of the entire house, there is a hole. I can't even imagine how he did it. He must have gotten a jackhammer down here sometime when I wasn't around. But that isn't even the surprising part. A hole I could understand, but nothing could have prepared me for what I see at the bottom of that hole.

Three feet down, Martin has unearthed a primary trunk line. It's big, maybe a foot in diameter, and it's been stripped along the top where a large oval slice of heavy rubber sheathing and three layers of inner shielding have been removed. The fiber lines dropping into the hole are Martin's own and have been meticulously spliced into the trunk line. At the other end, they feed into a jury-rigged PBX relay next to Martin's primary workstation.

"What the hell have you been doing down here?"

It's as impressive as it is incredible. Not only has Martin spliced his workstation directly into the aggregate Internet, but the way he's done it, there are no packet-switching monitors to trick. No layers of security to sneak through. In the Open Systems Interconnection model, this would be considered Layer 0. One big data stream that Martin can enter and exit at will, like his own personal backdoor to the entire aggrenet.

There's something else. I'm so taken by Martin's handiwork that I don't see it at first, but then I do. A file. A brown file hidden behind the trunk line. It's wedged in tight so I have to give it a good pull to remove it. There is a large *G* on the front of the folder, the company logo unmistakable, as is the faded red warning stamped across it. SECURITY EYES ONLY. And then in smaller letters above and below: L10 CLEARANCE REQUIRED.

"Grumwell internal security…what the hell?"

I have no idea what Level 10 security means, but I have the folder, and I open it. And when I do, the first thing I see makes me gasp. A photograph. Not of the young woman I vaguely remember from when I was an infant but an older version of the same. The dark hair and hazel eyes are unquestionably the same, but now the lines of time have begun to set in. But there's something else there too. Not maturity, something different. Something like what you see in young soldiers after they come back from their first tour. It's a kind of hardness. A coldness that can only come from having a sense of purpose that is so singular. So acute. As much as this is the same woman from my distant memories, it also isn't. Because as much as I recognize those features, her expression is that of a complete stranger.

"Genie."

But that's not what it says. As I begin flipping through the pages, the first thing that doesn't make sense is her name. Not *Genie Nill*, as I've always known it to be, but rather *Genevive Bonillia*. I run my fingers over it. "Genevive Bonillia." It even sounds foreign. Okay, so at some point she truncated her name, but why? And why would she pass that on to me?

It's strange how something as simple as a name can raise so many questions, but as I rifle through the documents I realize that's only the tip of the iceberg. One thing is clear. Whoever she was, my mother was very high up in the Grumwell concern. It's hard to decipher exactly what the pages mean; most of them sound like corporate intelligence. Not just marching orders either, but strategic design for Grumwell's internal security.

I don't know, maybe it's just the musings of an overactive imagination, but the way those papers are hidden—secretly buried in a hole in the basement—I think it's safe to assume that this folder has something to do with why she left the way that she did. Tiptoeing away in the dead of night, never to be heard from again. Maybe the information in this file is somehow even responsible for it.

When I was a kid, I would often wonder about my mother—who she was, where she was, what she was doing right now, and most importantly, why none of it could include Martin and me. But over the years my curiosity waned. I just resigned myself to the fact that I would never know. But now that curiosity has come back with a vengeance. Now I'm wondering about my mother all over again.

No fewer than a dozen questions pop into my head, but even they will have to wait for now. I stuff the file into my backpack and resume my search for Martin. I don't know what's going on, but whatever it is, I can see now that it involves more than just the parity load that Dexter is carrying and the other cargo locked in my wing. Whatever this is, it has as much to do with Martin as it does with me. And somehow I know, with Genevive as well.

The sound of heavy footsteps echo above my head. They're not hurried, more tentative, and judging by their location, they have just come through the front door. It could be anyone. I take three giant steps over the clutter, vault over the railing and race up the stairs into the kitchen. Whoever it is has moved into the living room. Before checking it out, I sneak around and put myself between him and the front door to make sure I have a clear lane out of the house in case I need it, but the moment I see who it is standing in the living room, I know I won't.

"What are you doing here?" I ask.

Of course he doesn't answer. He just points his thumb at the door to indicate he's there for me. Sent by Cyril, no doubt.

"Enough is enough, Bigsby! What the hell is going on here?"

But Bigsby just stands there with his spiked blonde hair, dressed as always in black, staring me down with those unblinking slate eyes as he twirls the car keys around his finger. It's the closest thing to a response I'll get.

"Fine. Let's go."

●   ●   ●

The moment he turns off the main road, I know something is wrong. "What's going on, Bigsby? Where are we going?"

Bigsby shoots me a glance in the rearview that is barely discernible in the slightest slant of light that breaks through the all-encompassing darkness. But in that brief glimmer, I see an altogether different look in his eyes. This time it looks like he actually wants to tell me, even if he does remains silent.

The sedan's tires pop over loose gravel as we roll into a darkened construction site and stop. Bigsby holds up a remote control and presses a button that causes two sets of floodlights to fill the car with white light that forces my eyes shut. Blinding. The more I try to open them, the more it hurts. I try the door but that's been locked from up front.

"Dammit, Bigsby!" This time it is not a question but a demand. "What the hell is going on?" And this time I can see that I'm about to get my answer. As my eyes adjust, Bigsby turns around and stares me down over the shoulder of the seat.

And finally, he speaks…

"A wise old owl lived in an oak. The more he saw the less he spoke. The less he spoke the more he heard…"

Now the barrel of a gun appears over the top of the seat. This one is not aimed at my chest. Presumably because Bigsby knows exactly what I'm wearing over my chest. This gun is aimed at my head. Right between my eyes.

"…why can't we all be like that wise old bird?"

SILENCE IS THE ONLY REAL SECURITY

20.

I yank the door latch until it nearly snaps off in my hand. Nothing.

I kick the windows, but they're made of bulletproof glass. No way out there.

Bigsby watches with amusement as I slide across the seat and try the other side to the same results. I'm boxed in.

The thing that unnerves me even more than being trapped is the way Bigsby keeps his gun trained on me at all times. Staring down the barrel of a gun is nothing like having one pointed at my chest, especially when I am wearing top of the line body armor that has already proven its merit. This is different. There is something very ominous about that long, dark pipe chambered with a slug that has my brains written all over it. It messes with my vision. Puts pressure on my focus like a finger pressed between my eyebrows. It gives me a headache.

Why couldn't he just raise it to my forehead or lower it to my mouth? Either one would give him the same result. But no, with a steady hand Bigsby holds the gun on point, right in front of me like a splinter in my field of vision. My lungs collapse. I press myself into the seatback. My head pounds. I can't breathe.

Bigsby laughs. He knows exactly what he's doing.

"You Arcadian runners really make me laugh. You run around with your little bird tattoos thinking you're tough as nails because you move cargo from one end of the Free City to the other. You act like it's so rough, but none of you have the faintest idea what it's like to really run. Between enemy lines 300 klicks inside the Islamic Republic. Past the watchtower gunmen of Pax Islamabad. Through the mine fields of old Kandahar. You little chickadees wipe the sweat off your brow after being chased by a couple of suits from Caliphate Global." Bigsby's lip curls into a sneer. "You don't know what it's like to have the Caliphate on your tail for real. To watch your best friend get beheaded less than ten feet away. You don't know what it's like to wake up each day knowing that before the day is done, you will feel the warm stickiness of another man's blood spray across your face. None of you have any idea about these things, but you all think you do, and that's the funniest thing of all."

Suddenly I realize, Bigsby's sneer is personal.

"And *you*, the Carrion."

Bigsby smacks the bridge of my nose with the slide. Not hard, just enough to get my eyes tearing. "Ow, dammit!"

"You piss me off even more than the others. If I had to listen to that fool Cyril blather on about how good you are just one more time, I would have broken cover just to shoot him myself. You really have everyone fooled with all that hokey pokey crap. Let's see you hokey pokey your way out of this one."

I take a moment to calm down. Breathe. Remind myself to keep my wits. Bigsby is just one more obstacle to work around. Just one more thing in the way to get over, under, or around.

"You were a runner for Blackburn."

"I've been running for Blackburn ever since I was fifteen."

"And now you're a spy?"

"For a smart kid, you really are dense."

I'm not dense. Red Tail warned me about a mole in Arcadian and Bigsby is it. But he doesn't know that I know that. The dumb questions are just my way of stalling until I can figure out a move. As long as I keep Bigsby talking, I have time to think. "How could Blackburn infiltrate Arcadian like that?"

"Blackburn is everywhere. There is nothing we don't have our hands in. And once this cargo is secure and our plans come to fruition, the Complex will be stronger than ever."

"That's funny. The way I hear it, you guys are on the verge of bankruptcy."

"Kid, pretty soon money will be the least of our concerns. That's why nothing can get in the way of our mission." Bigsby pulls back the hammer with a resounding click. "And right now, that means you."

"What is so important about this cargo?" That question isn't a stall, I really want to know. "You owe me that much. I deserve to know exactly what it is I'm about to get clipped for!"

Bigsby appears amused by this. "We could sit here all night and debate exactly what you deserve, but the truth is I don't know. All I know is that the cargo you're carrying could jeopardize the entire Complex and was important enough to have me break my cover. My orders are to intercept it by any means necessary…" He tightens his grip on the gun. "Including full destruction of courier and content." Bigsby takes aim. "You may be the Carrion out there; in here you're a fly in the ointment."

Fly in the ointment. Wonderful.

A blast of light hits us from the side windows. Not me directly, since I'm down in the seat, but it hits Bigsby well enough to blind him momentarily. That's it. Without even thinking I parry his arm away from my face. His hand hits the headrest. The gun goes off. And suddenly…everything…slows…down.

Flash of muzzle fire.

Deafening report.

Spider web across the rear windshield of the car.

High-pitched ringing.

Plume of silken smoke.

It all happens in seconds that feel more like minutes.

The floodlights coming through the front of the car are stationary, but the ones coming through the side grow brighter as they push toward us. It's a big yellow construction vehicle, some kind of crawler that lets out a flatulent rip each time the engine is revved. But the sound is dislocated through the ringing in my ears.

The front of the bulldozer bears down until it's all teeth coming at us.

Well, more to Bigsby than to me. The dozer takes a sharp turn and hits us at an angle so the shovel misses most of the backseat when it comes crashing through the passenger side. Good enough to save me from decapitation as the front of the car gets crushed. Metal twists all around me in a haze of dust and light. That's when I hear it, even through the noise in my ears—

Bigsby screaming for his life. The dozer pushes forward, tearing off the roof as the entire car crumples and snaps all around me, until I am sandwiched between the front and back seat.

The engine stops revving.

Trapped between the seats, I squirm.

I can't see or hear anything. Can't feel my body well enough to know if anything is injured. Can't even tell which way is up. Whatever light comes through is all cut up by metal and scattered. But one thing is for sure, I sense no movement other than my own inside the wreckage.

The bulldozer starts revving again. This time in reverse, pulling the shovel back until a mangled piece of metal that was once the rear door is removed. Almost immediately I hear movement outside the wreckage. Somebody walking around from the other side. I follow it around with my ears until her petite figure is crouched in the crushed doorway of the old sedan. And I have to admit, as messed up as I am at the moment in every possible way, all of that is wiped away the moment she leans in, and I see the smile on her face.

"Come with me if you want to live," she says in what can only be her best attempt at an Austrian accent.

I just stare at her dumbfounded.

"What, you've never T-screened *The Terminator*?"

"Of course I've T-screened *The Terminator*," I say wriggling between the seats to pull myself out, "I just didn't expect you to be quoting it at this very moment." My legs are wrapped too snugly to gain any leverage. All I can do is pull myself along the ground with my arms until I'm out.

"It seemed appropriate."

Finally I get to my feet. I nearly fall over. Red Tail reaches out to grab me, but I balance. The entire world rocks back and forth. I can't be sure if it's from the ringing in my ears or the hole in my stomach, although neither one is helping. I reach back into the car and pull my orange backpack through the collapsed seat, but fall to my knees before I can get it unzipped. Red Tail does it for me. Pulls out a flattened energy bar and rips it open with her teeth. Peels back the wrapper and shoves it into my mouth.

"Easy," I sputter. "That's my uvula."

"Your uvula?"

"The little ball that hangs at the back of your mouth."

"Yes, I know what a uvula is."

I wolf down the energy bar in four bites. The rocking begins to subside almost immediately. I know this feeling. It's definitely the chip screaming for more fuel and should settle in another minute or two.

The floodlights on the bulldozer switch off and the door opens with a long metallic creak. Then out jumps Snake, whose boots crunch the gravel hard as he circles the lifeless mangle of car to observe his handiwork. "So much for that."

"When did you figure it out?"

Red Tail answers. "When he came after you."

"What about Cyril?" I ask. "Is he part of this too?"

Snake shakes his head like it's not even a possibility. "Cyril presents himself as a recruiting agent for security reasons, but Arcadian is actually his firm."

"And he had no idea about his own personal assistant?"

"No," Snake replies, "and he's going to be pissed when he finds out. Cyril handpicked him for the job."

"Martin," I suddenly blurt. With the ringing down to a low hum and the energy bar kicking in, I start to regain my senses. "My father, Martin Baxter."

"He's fine," says Snake. "He wasn't there when they turned over your place."

"How do you know?"

"We had eyes on the people who did it."

"So it was Blackburn?"

"Oh it was definitely Blackburn. But now we've got a bigger problem."

"What's that?"

"It's Dexter," says Red Tail.

"What about Dexter?"

"They got him."

"When?"

"A few hours ago. They grabbed him right as he got back

to Brentwood."

"Then I have to help him."

Snake doesn't even have to say it. I can see it written all over his face.

"That's exactly what they want you to do," says Red Tail. "The only reason they're holding Dexter is to lure you in."

That much I have already figured out, but it doesn't change the fact that they have him. "I still have to try. I know it might not mean much to you, but Dex and I are Brentwood Dragons. We have a code. Dragons don't leave each other hanging. We don't leave each other behind. I know it's a lot to ask, but I can't do it alone."

"Do you even hear what you're suggesting?" asks Red Tail. "Didn't I tell you that Blackburn is the one corporation you don't want to mess with?"

"You did, but it's not like I had any choice in the matter. It was Arcadian who sent me to TerraAqua and got me loaded up with this." I hold out my arm and raise my sleeve. "Whatever I'm carrying in my wing, it's big enough to take down the entire Complex. That's my leverage. They won't do anything to Dexter as long as this cargo remains unsecured."

"Listen to me, Carrion. It's an impossible situation."

"It's difficult," Snake interjects, "but I don't believe any situation is impossible."

Now Red Tail is the one who's surprised. "You're saying that you want to step into their trap?"

But Snake's exterior is cool as ever. "I'm saying that sometimes the best way to outmaneuver a trap is just to spring it. There's room to work here."

"But those aren't our orders," says Red Tail, after which she and Snake exchange a private look.

"What orders?" I ask.

Red Tail waits for Snake to answer.

This is the second time Red Tail has clammed up on me. "If one of you doesn't tell me right now, I walk away from both of you."

The flexing tendons in Snake's neck animate the giant spider web tattooed across the surface. "You know us as Arcadian Aves. The truth is we're more than that."

"I know. You're Morlock too. She already told me."

"That's true. But that's not what I'm talking about. The two of us," he says pointing between himself and Red Tail, "we're Outliers as well."

"You're—That means you're the one—" I look down at my arm and think of the bloated little cortex chip floating around inside. "This is meant for you?"

He nods.

Red Tail continues. "We have orders to bring you to the handoff point to extract the cargo." She turns to Snake as if to remind him. "That's priority number one. No exceptions."

"Orders from whom?" I ask.

"Janus," she replies. "He's the captain of our unit. He's the one that cargo is meant for."

I clutch my hair in my hands in a way that immediately reminds me of Martin. "I don't get it. If you're an Outlier then why am I the one carrying this?"

"Security," she answers. "You're carrying it precisely because you're not an Outlier."

"Do you at least know what it is?"

Both shake their heads. "That's the truth," says Snake.

"Wonderful."

"We're wasting time," says Red Tail. "Whatever it is, we have to get it to the rendezvous."

I'm about to protest when Snake beats me to the punch. "No, we have to rescue Dexter first. The Carrion's right, you don't leave your people behind."

I must have gotten to him with that sentiment. If I had to guess, I'd say that Snake is ex-military.

"He's not one of our people," she says.

"Isn't he?" replies Snake. "He's a data runner who climbed out of the squatter settlements. That should sound more than a little familiar."

Red Tail grows solemn. Like she's ashamed she ever questioned it.

"We're all on the same side here," says Snake.

Snake, Red Tail, and I exchange nods. We're all in agreement. We get Dexter first.

21.

According to Snake's intel, Dexter is being held deep inside Blackburn's urban combat training zone, otherwise known as Red Hook.

Red Hook is the peninsula that sits across the Upper Tri-Insula Bay, way over on the other side of the Free City. Surrounded by docks, it now consists mostly of abandoned warehouses and torn-out tenements—what you might call the standing remains of severe urban decay. Back in the Old-50, Red Hook had already turned into a crime-ridden neighborhood. As soon as the North American Alliance was formed, the whole thing was seized and turned over to Blackburn. Just like that. Anyone still living there was handed a settlement check and ordered to vacate. Shortly thereafter, Blackburn sealed off the entire peninsula from the rest of Independent Long Island and established it as a training ground for exercises in asymmetrical urban warfare. Now the entire area has no official locality— none of the training zones do—it's all sovereign territory of the North American Alliance, leased to and operated by Blackburn, Ltd. This one is known as Blackburn Facility 117, or just BF-117. That's officially. Unofficially, even the soldiers and personnel within Blackburn still call it *Red Hook*.

In just a few short hours I begin to get a handle on Snake, who in many ways reminds me of Mr. Chupick. The only difference is, unlike Mr. Chupick whose specialty is putting things up, Snake's is taking them down. But like Mr. Chupick, Snake never needs to rattle off his credentials because his experience is evident in the stuff he knows. Not just the technical details necessarily but his entire knowledge base. Case in point: since this operation is unlike anything we've done before, Red Tail and

I both assume that everything we know about running data is automatically out the window. But Snake disabuses us of this notion at once. "It only looks that way on the surface," he says, "but the strategy is still the same. Apart from the fact that our cargo is an actual person, and our pursuers an entire army, this is just like any other run. Our fundamental aim is to avoid getting drawn into a fight. The ammo will be stronger, and the stakes will be higher, but the three Es still apply."

The three Es. Evade, Elude, Escape. Red Tail and I know them well, but somehow hearing them again helps. Thinking of the operation as just another data run on the sneakernet makes us both feel better about it, which I'm guessing was Snake's intent. Afterwards, it is Red Tail herself who is the most optimistic about rescuing Dexter. "Don't worry," she says as we get into our tactical jumpsuits, "we'll get him out."

The plan itself is daring. There is zero room for error, but we knew that would be the case with any plan we came up with. At least we have a plan. I have no idea what I would do without their help, especially when Snake reminds us of one very important thing just before we move out. "Remember, Red Hook is sovereign territory of the Alliance."

Red Tail and I both nod like we understand, but actually we don't.

"That means that none of the weapons ordinances of the Free City, Independent Long Island, or the Northeast district will apply inside Blackburn's fences."

Now we understand.

"They will have plasma cutters and helio rifles, and they will be able to fire them at us."

"Great," I say.

Red Tail hands me a black nylon kit bag and slings another over her shoulder. "We wouldn't want to make it too easy."

● ● ●

Snake meanders the SUV into the Battery Tunnel that will

deposit him just north of BF-117. Red Tail and I sit in the back. We won't be in the vehicle when it emerges on the other side of the bay. We'll be dropped off halfway through, where a service tunnel will lead us into the maze of steam pipes and sewers that we can navigate all the way to where Dexter is being held. But first we have to get dropped off, and this happens before I even know it. Snake slams the brakes without warning. "Go!"

I throw open the door and jump out. Red Tail hops out behind me. The instant she's clear I throw it closed and Snake peels out down the tunnel. Red Tail is already working the service door as the din of approaching cars grows behind us.

"Red."

"I know."

"If we get seen going in—"

"I know, I know."

The lock pops off the door and I catch it before it can roll into the road. She pulls open the door just as the next set of headlights comes around the bend. We shove through and close it behind us.

● ● ●

"So you and Snake are pretty tight."

The tunnels en route to the training zone are dark and dank, so chatting is my way of keeping things light and airy. My detail is to navigate our passage using the map on my dimly lit thin screen, but for now that's at least 3 klicks of straight tunnel. Red Tail remains focused on the passage ahead, checking every inch with her torch as we move through it, but she is more than capable of doing both at the same time.

"I don't know where I'd be without him," she says as her light swings arcs around the passage like she's done this before. She knows exactly what she is looking for. "One thing is for sure, I wouldn't have made it this far."

"Why is that?"

"Prospective Aves usually don't get approached until they're eighteen. The recruiters start watching them around sixteen or seventeen, but it takes a while to narrow it down to the one or two most fit to survive the sneakernet."

She's looking for sensors. Looking for cameras. Looking for anything that might trip an alarm at the facility and let them know we're coming.

"They signed you at seventeen because you were an exception," she adds. "I was an even bigger exception."

"How old were you?"

"Fifteen."

Fifteen? At fifteen I hadn't even discovered parkour yet. "How is that even possible?"

Red Tail pauses to study some pipes, but I know she's really debating whether or not to tell me the story. I can see them too, they're just pipes. "Back when I was living in the settlements, I used to come into the Free City to pick pockets."

"You were a thief?"

She turns the light so it blasts me in the face. "I was a liberator of disposable wealth."

"My mistake," I say behind a shielding hand. She turns the light back to the tunnel.

"One day I happened to pull a bump-and-grab on Cyril, and he caught me red handed."

"What did you do?"

"I ran."

"And he chased you?"

"He had to. I still had his wallet."

"Hold on a second. You try and pick Cyril's pocket. He catches you. Instead of dropping the wallet and making a clean getaway, you take off with it still in your hands?"

"Times were tough."

"What happened next?"

"What happened next was I found out Cyril's got a lot more under the hood than he lets on. He didn't think twice about leaping off the platform and chasing me into the tunnel. He chased me all the way to the next stop. The only advantage I had was size. If you think I'm small now, you should have seen me back then. So when the next train came, I dove into the crotch between the platform and the track and waited for it to stop, then rolled to the other side and climbed up between the cars. So when the train pulled out, I was on board."

"So you got away."

"No. Cyril knew exactly what I was up to. He boarded the train two cars up and stayed out of sight to make me think he was still back on the platform. When I got off at the next stop, he grabbed me before my foot even touched the platform. His hands and face were covered in grime, his clothes were ruined, and his hat must have gotten lost in the chase because he no longer had it. I thought he was going to drag me straight to the transit police, but you know what he said to me instead?"

I am all ears.

"He said 'you know what your mistake was, kid? You never should have gotten on that train. Next time stick to the tunnels, you'll live longer.'"

That sounded oddly familiar.

"When Cyril found out I was living in the squatter settlements, he knew he had to recruit me on the spot or risk losing me forever. Out here you can watch people for a few years before bringing them in, but you can't track anyone in the settlements. So he took me in right then and there. A few days later I got branded."

"On your calf."

"That's right."

"Because your forearm was too small to hold the cortex chip?" I guess.

This seems to impress her. "Who are you, Sherlock Holmes?"

Sure, why not. "I guess that would make you Dr. Watson."

"Irene Adler," she replies with a cleverness I can hardly refute. Irene Adler was the woman who famously outwitted the world's greatest sleuth in *A Scandal in Bohemia*.

"I couldn't believe it," Red Tail continues. "The money was great. I was able to get my entire family out of the settlements and into a low-rent suburb. Actually we were all set to come out to Brentwood, but at the last minute we found a better deal somewhere else."

The thought of Red Tail at Brentwood... she would have been a great lab partner, a great Dragon. The very idea twists my stomach into a strange knot. Not like the hunger pangs that come from chip—this one is better.

"Because I was so young, Cyril always teamed me up with other people."

"So what happened?"

"Well, as you can imagine, most of them weren't too thrilled about having a fledgling tagging along behind them. On more than one occasion they told me to wait somewhere while they went ahead to check things out and then never came back for me. The only person who made a genuine effort to look out for me was Snake. He was the one who took me under his wing and showed me the ropes. He taught me all the dos and don'ts. Things I never could have learned on my own, like how to read a crowd. But most importantly, he taught me to trust the little hairs on the back of my neck. Now we look out for each other."

Red Tail's light flashes upon the tail of a rat running away from us further down the tunnel.

"You have to give me the schematics for that thing."

"I'll build one for you. How did you two end up in the Outliers?"

"I don't know," she shrugs. "I grew up in the settlements, Snake's a dissident. How does anyone end up in the Outliers?"

Once again she gives me the passive response, answering without really answering, only this time it isn't going to fly. "Come on, Red. I'm the one carrying your cargo. The least you can do is tell me who I'm carrying it for."

She sighs. "Do you even know who the Outliers are? I mean, beyond whatever you may have heard on the news streams?"

It's not until that moment that I realize I don't. I really don't know anything about them.

"It was before our time. After the big restructuring."

The big restructuring. It happened in the wake of the Old-50 when the new North American regions were formed. The entire northwest up through British Columbia became the new

Province of Cascadia. The large stretch of territory between the Ozarks and the Gulf joined the Republic of Texas; the old South came together to form the New Confederacy; and the entire Great Lakes region became the People's District of the North Star. Long Island played the wild card when it claimed independence instead of joining the Northeast district, but then that allowed the old City of New York to become the new Free City of Tri-Insula. And soon after all of that, the North American Alliance was formed.

Of course, not every stretch of territory folded nicely into a new region, and those that didn't became settlements. Out west, those scattered settlements became the reservation towns of the New West. Out here they became the squatter settlements.

"Things were getting really bad," continues Red Tail. "Devolving into chaos. People had given up. There was no hope. And without hope, there was no reason for order. But then one day, a gypsy woman marched into the settlements. Not much is known about her except that she was raised in the tent camps of the eastern block Eurozone, but it was she who secretly formed the Outliers. She was the one who united the poor, tired, hungry masses to fight the new corporatocracy. She made us realize that human dignity is inalienable, and as long as there is still breath left in your body, there will always be something left to fight for. And over the years, as the corporations have taken over everything, it has only united us even more. The Outliers are stronger today than ever."

"And this gypsy woman?"

"No one I know has ever seen her. She's careful to remain invisible. Anyway, that's what we're all about. What about you?"

"What about me?"

"Playground rules," she quips.

I guess that's fair. It is after all my turn. "You showed me yours now I show you mine?"

"Quid pro quo."

"What do you want to know?"

"You're really dedicated to all that parkour stuff, aren't you?"

"What gave it away?"

Red Tail flashes a look at my sarcasm. Considers it. Smiles. At least she can get as good as she gives. "What I mean is, it's not just for sport, is it?"

"No, it's a way of looking at the world. You've already experienced it. We all have. It's something we're born with but lose along the way. So that's what parkour helps us get back in touch with. It isn't just a process of discovery, it's the process of rediscovery as well."

"I don't follow."

"You remember when you were a kid on the playground? You were basically already doing parkour, you just didn't have a name for it. All kids do it. We run. We jump. We tumble on the grass. We see a tree stump and we hop over it. You don't think of it as a vault, but that's exactly what you're doing. You see a wall and you try to run up the thing like it's a ladder to the sky. And when gravity does call you in, you drop back to the earth with happy resignation because at least you gave it your best shot. You gave it your all, and deep down you already knew that that was all you could ever really do. And even if you didn't touch the sky, at least you came three feet closer than you were before, and you took that for everything it was worth.

"But then we get older and something changes. Something makes us lose our connection to the world around us. We train ourselves to walk in straight lines. To go around walls. We resign ourselves to the fact that we can never really touch the sky, so even reaching for it is pointless. We get older, and instead of moving ourselves to accommodate the earth, we move the earth to suit our needs. We hit a certain age and all of a sudden a boulder is no longer a beautiful obstacle, it's just a thing in our way. Sooner or later we stop running, stop climbing, stop reaching for the sky. We stop pushing ourselves toward unattainable goals because common sense tells us that the only logical thing to do is push ourselves toward the attainable ones. If running through the world like kids on the playground is a kind of dream, then at a certain point we just stop dreaming.

"That's the real dedication to parkour. Sure, for some it is just about the money and the competition, but for me it's always been about reaching for the sky. That's what PK is all about. That's why I do it. Dexter too." When I turn back to Red Tail I notice her smile. She's smiling at me. And not because I've just said something funny either. It isn't that kind of smile. "Um…" I check my thin screen awkwardly. "In ten meters there should be an access tunnel on the left."

"Got it. So if parkour is its own reward, how does that jibe with being a data runner?"

"Well, even traceurs have to eat. But the way I see it, I'm not exploiting parkour to do what I do. I just do what I do and let parkour be a natural extension of who I am. If that gives me an edge on the sneakernet, it's only because I'm being me."

"How long do you plan to do it for?"

"I figure two years. Save up enough money to go to NEIT."

She raises her brow. "Wow. I wish I could go to a school like that. Financially, I mean."

I know what she means. Red Tail is wicked smart. There's no way she wouldn't ace the entrance exams. "You could. There's nothing stopping you."

But she shakes her head. "I'm doing this to help support my family. Getting out of the squatter settlements isn't the hard part, it's staying out. Unfortunately, college just isn't in the cards for someone like me."

"But don't you feel like you're missing something?"

"Not really. There isn't a single thing I'd be studying in school that I can't learn on my own anyway. And I do. When I'm not running, I'm always scouting the university portals for courses that sound interesting. Then I grab the syllabus and reading list and do the work on my own. The only thing I don't get is a grade."

No wonder she's so smart. Red Tail is an autodidact: a self-taught student.

"But when I am running, the stuff I learn out here in the field is invaluable. What you and I are doing right now, that's something you can't find in any course catalog. That's something you don't get with a degree."

"There is the utilitarian value of a degree," I offer.

Red Tail shrugs. "In a good month I make more money than most people with a degree. Granted, most of it is hazard pay. I still consider myself lucky." She takes a long moment to shine her torch down the access tunnel before we turn into it. "Trust me, it beats picking pockets for a living."

"I guess for me, school was just always the plan."

"Well, sometimes the plan changes," she says, "and you just have to adapt."

Speaking of adapting, the layout shows us just outside the perimeter of BF-117. I flip my thin screen to show Red Tail. She motions with her finger to her lips that we should move forward in silence. I agree. We switch to hand signals and proceed down the tunnel.

22.

Manhole covers are much heavier than you'd think, especially when you're trying to remove one with your shoulder from the top of a very long shaft ladder.

I try to lift it off gently but can't get leverage without my feet slipping. The rungs are all rusty and wet, which is a very dangerous combination. I try again. This time my feet slip off the rung entirely and it is only the well-calloused grip of my parkour hands that keeps me from dropping straight down onto Red Tail and sending us both plummeting down the shaft.

There's no point even trying it a third time. I really didn't want to have to do it like this, but at this point it's the only way the cover is coming off.

I tell Red Tail to move down a few rungs. Keep going. And even a few more. Until I have enough room to get a good running start. I launch upwards with everything I have. Climb the ladder, gaining speed with every rung. I hunch my shoulder and plow straight through the top like a vertical linebacker. The cast iron disk flies off. All I can do is cringe as I watch it flip through the air as if in slow motion, until it crashes onto the asphalt with a resonating clash. I look down. Red Tail's wide blue eyes stare up at me with horror and disbelief. I know she's right, but it couldn't be helped. I offer a shrug to let her know that.

I duck back into the hole and wait for any alarms to go off. They don't.

I pop back up for a peek.

Nothing.

I give Red Tail the signal to move on.

Snake has gone over everything in meticulous detail. Since BF-117 is a training zone and not an actual base, Blackburn keeps it under minimal guard when not in use. Usually those guards are stationed near the water, around the cluster of warehouses where actual equipment is being stored, or to guard any ships that happen to be docked at the time. Those are the red areas that we should avoid at all cost. The rest of the facility is basically just a combat stage that is swept at regular intervals, and we've got their schedule.

Red Hook looks and feels exactly like a video game. Everything has been placed. Like the nondescript white van parked in front of an old storefront that is way too suspicious not to be a trap in some training exercise—hostage taker, getaway vehicle, IED. It's there for a reason, as is every abandoned vehicle parked up and down the street, and the wastebaskets filled with just enough trash to potentially conceal something, and the Consolidated mailbox that isn't on anyone's route. The purpose of all this stuff is to keep training soldiers on their toes.

The building where Dexter is being held is only a few blocks away, but since our plan is to come in from above, the first thing we have to do is get off street level. It's fifty meters from the manhole to the alley, but we make it without incident. Red Tail unzips her bag and produces a grappling hook launcher and winch. She unfolds it and locks it open, loads a dart into the barrel and attaches a spindle of climbing rope to the side of the launcher. She raises it to her eye and aims the unit just over the top of the building, then places her finger over the trigger. A laser measures the distance and mechanically adjusts the firing range. The orange glow around the eyesight turns green, and a split-second later she squeezes the trigger.

I expect some kind of blast when it fires, but the dampers on this unit work surprisingly well. They should, considering this is military-grade equipment. The dart takes off like a rocket carrying a trail of rope behind it, sails straight up into the night, arcs over the ledge of the building, and lands on the other side. Then comes the part we don't see. The impact causes the dart's cap to blow off and triggers the release claws into the rooftop. Now the winch kicks in, taking up the slack until the rope is taut. Red Tail puts her weight on it to make sure the rope is secure before she detaches the winch from the launcher and hooks it into the harness built into her jumpsuit.

Clearly she thinks I'm going up the same way once she gets to the top and lowers it back down. What she doesn't know is that I'm already there. I grab the kit bag and sling it over her shoulder, and before she can even wonder what I'm doing, I run straight for the wall and Tic-Tac up to the fire escape. Dexter probably could have gotten enough lift to grab the top of the hand rail, which would have made for a much easier muscle up, but I only have enough reach to grab the bottom, so I have to kick off the wall and pull up with everything I have, conserving all my momentum as I cat-grab the upper railing, muscle up, and swing my feet over before gravity can take over.

My feet hit the landing just as Red Tail overtakes me, but it's still six more floors to the top.

I gain an edge racing up the fire escape for two more floors until the whole thing begins to lean precariously from having been ripped away from the building. I leap off the railing. Push off a window ledge. Catch the buckle of a drainage pipe and use that to launch myself up.

The trick is to keep going. Keep moving. You have to maintain your momentum. Momentum is balance and maneuverability. Just like riding a bike—the faster you go, the better you balance, the better you maneuver. That's why you never let yourself stop because if you stop, you lose it all. If you stop, you become dead weight, and the crippling hold of gravity will take you over. Then you have to exert far more of yourself just to get moving again. Every time you stop, you have to start all over again. So you keep moving.

I can feel Red Tail watching me as I climb past the point where the fire escape has been ripped in half. Poise my toe on the next buckle and jump from the pipe. Push off the window ledge. Grab the railing and vault over like it's the easiest thing in the world. Keep climbing. When I get to the top, I hop onto the railing and launch straight up. Cat-grab the top of the building. Muscle up. Roll across the ledge and land on my feet, on the roof. All of this happens seven floors up, but you can't think about that when you're climbing. You can't think about the fall.

If you want to fly… if you really want to fly… you have to take every leap like it's just two feet off the ground.

I get to the roof with just enough of a lead to help Red Tail over the top. With her feet flat on the ground, she just looks at me with a kind of dumbfounded bewilderment as she curls her hand and scurries it across the air. Hand signals aside, I can practically hear her voice in my head, as clearly as if she'd said it out loud. *What are you, some kind of hamster?*

Come on, I wave.

We cross the roof and arrive at the first of four gap jumps, each about four feet across. The first thing Red Tail does is look over the edge, straight down the side of the building until the vertigo makes her step back. Now it's unavoidable. I have to break our silence.

"You can do this," I whisper. "Forget about the height. It's just like running on the ground. Jumping over puddles to keep your feet from getting wet. Don't give it a second thought. And whatever happens, don't hesitate. Insist on the jump or don't do it at all."

She nods.

"Do you want to go first?" I ask.

"No," she says. I can tell she's apprehensive. Apprehensive but not afraid. "Let's do it together."

I throw our bags over to the next rooftop and move back to join Red Tail, who has given herself way more head start than is needed. Too much actually. Too much time to think. Too much room between her and the ledge to contemplate the jump. I know this because I've been where she is right now. With Dex by my side, I have been in her shoes exactly. I nudge her forward several steps to close the distance until we have enough room to gain full speed but not enough to slow down afterward. When we're in position, I take her hand and give it a gentle squeeze. "Remember," I say. "There are no limits, only plateaus."

She nods.

"Go!"

I take off, pulling her with me, running with her hand still in mine so she has to run just to keep up. I only let go when I'm satisfied she's with me.

We plant together.

Launch simultaneously.

Sail across the gap like two birds in flight.

Clear the other ledge with feet to spare.

Stick the landing and roll out.

Before Red Tail even has a chance to process it, I gather up our bags and shuffle her across the rooftop to the next gap. I throw the bags over, step back to where she's waiting for me—perfect distance this time—take her hand and pull her forward again.

Once again we sail over the gap.

The third time I don't need to take her hand. She manages it on her own.

The fourth time it's almost as if her body takes over. Not muscle memory just yet, but she'll get there.

The final distance we have to cross is not a gap between two buildings; it's a major avenue between two blocks, and there's no jumping that chasm. But at least now we have our target in sight. If our intel is correct, across the way is the redbrick building where Dexter is being held. Not as tall as the building under our feet but much larger in spread. It's nearly half a block in size with multiple entrances on each side. The oversized arched windows indicate three floors.

"What is that?" I ask as I tear open an energy bar. I offer one to Red Tail but she doesn't need it. She isn't carrying cargo.

"It looks like an old public school."

She's right. That's exactly what it looks like.

Red Tail pulls out the harpoon gun and inserts another dart and spool. Only this dart isn't a hook but a bolt, and this spool isn't climbing rope but zip line. She aims it just as she did before. The gun self-adjusts. Red Tail fires the dart in relative silence. The projectile sails across the distance with the zip line in tow and drives itself into the brick just above a third floor window. Red Tail removes the spool from the harpoon gun and secures the line to the ledge. Then she pulls out another dart.

"What's that one?"

"It's just a slug."

"What's it for?"

She loads it into the gun. "Get ready. This is going to make some noise."

I grab one of the pulleys from out of the kit bag.

"You have to—"

"Yeah, yeah, I got it." It's just a flying fox. We had one of those on the playground when I was growing up. This is kid's stuff. I fasten the strap around my wrist and give the release button a quick test before locking it onto the line.

"Wait, you're holding it back—"

The instant my feet leave the ledge I realize what she was about to say. My hand is pointing the wrong way, so when I cartwheel around the line and start my run, I'm facing the wrong way. "Crap!"

Zipping ass-backwards down the line, all I see is Red Tail standing on the ledge of the building with her arms out and palms up utterly perplexed by what I have just done. She quickly positions the harpoon gun. This time she doesn't bother with the adjustment mechanism, she just points and shoots.

The slug torpedoes past my ear with a high-pitch wind… and a moment later…blows out the window some distance behind me.

Halfway across the street means I'm halfway there, but I'm going to need Red Tail to tell me when I'm about to hit so I can release. It has to be just right. Too early I'll end up flat on the sidewalk, too late and I'll hit the building. Red Tail knows this and is giving me the signal to hold tight. Beneath me I see curb. The building must be close. But still no sign from Red Tail.

Until suddenly her fist becomes three fingers.

And I brace…

Two.

…for…

One.

…IMPACT.

I release the pulley a split-second before my crouched back

strikes the busted window. Fly through. Fall backwards for what seems like a bigger drop than it really is. Strike the hardwood floor in a shower of broken glass that tinkles like wind chimes as it rains down all around me.

Until everything settles.

By now it's just instinct—the first thing I do is check my arm to make sure the cortex chip is okay. It is. I get to my feet and look around. It appears to be an old classroom, but before I can process any details, I hear the incoming trolley carrying our gear. I go to the window and catch it just as it arrives, unhook the carabiner, and clear the pulley off the zip line for Red Tail. She is poised on the ledge waiting for me to give her the go ahead, but before I do, I look around the room once more. Nothing seems out of the ordinary. I listen for footsteps. There are none.

I turn back to the window and give her the all clear.

●   ●   ●

By the time we bust open the door to the storage room where Dexter is being kept, I know we're in trouble. There isn't a guard in sight, not even a sentry posted outside his door. There isn't a single other person in the building. And then there's the look on Dexter's bruised face when he sees us. It's not relief.

"Damn, Jack. I thought you would figure it out."

"Figure what out?"

"This," he says indicating our surroundings. I'm pretty sure he's referring not just to the school but to the entire Red Hook facility.

"If you're talking about this being a trap, we know."

"And you came anyway?"

"We have a plan."

Dexter catches sight of Red Tail. Gives her a once-over from head to toe. Grins. "So this is the girl?"

Red Tail cocks her head. "I'm the girl."

"We can powwow later," I say as I hand Dexter a jumpsuit. He quickly shakes it out and puts it on. "This better be some plan."

"I'll let you know tomorrow." I check Dexter's heat signature. It's been reduced to a faint blip by the aluminized microfiber, just like ours.

From this point on we'll need full mobility. I already have everything I need in my backpack. Red Tail takes whatever she might need in her shoulder bag. Dexter scrounges through the rest to grab a few things he thinks could be useful. The rest we leave behind in the storage closet. I give Dexter the rundown. Not the full details, just the gist of it. Red Tail is going to get him out.

"What are you going to do?" he asks.

"I'm going to draw their fire."

Dexter is visibly averse to this plan.

"Dex, they're coming after me either way, whether I come out with you or on my own. Running solo is the best chance I have of getting away clean."

Dexter still doesn't like it, but he can't argue with the logic. I may be pulling the most dangerous part of it, but it is the most practical plan. He puts up a fist. "No limits."

I bump it hard. "Only plateaus."

An explosion rocks the old school. It is way too big to be a door being blown off its hinges. Maybe a hole being blown through the side of the building. Something along those lines.

"Um, guys…I hate to interrupt this little reunion but we really have to go."

"Watch your back, Jack," says Dexter as we part company.

"Don't worry," I tell him. "I've gotten really good at this."

23.

Then again, maybe I spoke too soon.

All I see are distant lasers cutting through smoke as they come at me from every direction. I make my way to the east exit of the school. I haven't seen any soldiers yet but I assume they're tracking me with infrared, which means they're also tracking Dexter and Red Tail alongside me. That's because I'm carrying a military-issue infrared booster capable of ghosting our heat signatures and projecting three bogeys. Yet another cool toy courtesy of Snake.

I hop onto a handrail and slide down the stairs. Halfway down I feel it give, and the next thing I know the bolts rip out of the wall and nearly send me tumbling, but I manage to catch myself. Round the landing. Take the lower flight all at once. Roll out.

The wide-open space with the kitchen in back has to be the cafeteria. That's where I go. I figure the kitchen must have a back door to the alley where all the dumpsters would have been. From my right comes the bang and hiss of another smoke grenade. They're smoking up the entire school to smoke me out, but so far that's working to my advantage. I want them keeping eyes on me with infrared. With my infrared booster in play, their tactic becomes my cover. Still, it doesn't escape me that I'm being herded. The way they're coming at me from three sides, it's obvious their aim is to funnel me in one direction. That direction is east. Further into the facility. Toward the river. I can't let that happen. If I let myself get boxed in with the river at my back, I'll have nowhere to go but in.

Door to the alley. Jackpot. Now here is where it gets tricky. I'm supposed to run them away from the rendezvous point with

Snake, so I should cross into the next building and lead them through. But now that I know that that's the direction they're flushing me in, and the reason why, I have to make an adjustment on the fly. I want to give Snake a big enough window to pick them up, but I can't let myself get trapped in the process. And since they're coming at me from all three sides, there is only direction I can go. Up.

The fire escape is still intact, which makes getting to the roof as easy as climbing stairs. I get to the top of the building in no time. Below me, doors fly open at street-level and a cloud of smoke comes rolling into the alley. And through that, two piercing lasers. The first time I actually see who's on my tail is when the first two soldiers exit the building and take position. The way they are dressed, in full tactical gear, you would think I'm a terrorist carrying a dirty bomb. I'm not, but whatever I am carrying seems to be just as damning.

The way the streets are laid out below, I can only go in one of two directions. I pick one and go. Pick up speed. Ready to jump. Ten feet from the ledge, light blasts my eyes. Blind. I slam on the brakes and slide feet first on the slippery rooftop, gauging the distance by feel like a runner coming into second base through the stadium floodlights, until my heel catches the edge of the building. I shield the light with my hand.

Vortex chopper. That's why I didn't hear it. Without a rotor to chop the air, those things are nearly silent. But now that it's right on top of me, I can hear the blast of its vertical jet as it circles me thirty feet above the rooftop. Finally I am able to block the light enough to see through it. To see the rappelling line drop from the craft to the roof, and the snarling blonde kid standing at the door with dried blood all over his face and a taped gash running down the length of his cheek. In his hand is a carabiner ready to lock on. We make eye contact. He smiles with all but one of his teeth. I guess he survived the bulldozer after all.

Bigsby dives face-first out of the chopper. I have only seconds until he hits the roof. I have to act fast. The chopper hasn't changed anything. I still have to get off this building. I take four steps back and gap jump to the next building. My body armor rocks across the surface as I roll out and move on. The vortex chopper can't swoop in after me until Bigsby has cleared the line, so that gives me a few steps to get ahead of it. Not that I can outrun it, I just have to keep evading it until I can figure out how to elude it, so I can make my escape.

Evade. Elude. Escape. Because I am an Arcadian runner, and that's what we do.

I hear what sounds like a rocket being fired behind me just before a heat blast burns the back of my neck and the shaking building knocks me off my feet. I turn around. Behind me I see the chopper still hovering over Bigsby, who is caught in the line. Between us, a plume of dark smoke rises where just seconds ago was the corner of the building. Now it's a scorched hole.

I get to my feet. The chopper dips, rises, fires again.

The blast from the plasma cutter knocks me down once again as it takes another bite out of the edifice. I spring back to my feet and continue toward the edge. I have to hurry. With that plasma cutter, they could easily raze the entire building if they wanted to. Since they aren't, it can only mean that Blackburn soldiers are already inside the building and ascending to the roof.

I run. The plasma cutter fires again. I leap.

The blast propels me well over the edge of the next building and slams me into the adjacent rooftop. Bigsby finally gets loose and leaps across the first gap while I run for the next. Now I'm one and a half buildings ahead of him, but that lead won't last when the chopper comes around to intercept me. I have to get off the roof.

I leap across the next gap. The vortex chopper overtakes me. Bigsby closes in behind me. Explosion. I look ahead thinking it's the chopper firing at the next building to destabilize the rooftop, but it's not. The plasma cutter hasn't even fired. It happens again. This time I realize it's coming from the street below, and whatever it is has gotten the attention of the chopper because it swoops away just as I get to the next building.

Before leaping across the next gap I look over the edge to see what has drawn the chopper away. That's when I see the SUV come flying around so fast it pushes the anti-roll stabilizers on the rear differential to the limit. Seconds later a Humvee comes screeching around after it. Way too fast. I don't know squat about working on cars, but I do know a little about how they work. Anti-roll differentials have a very low weight capacity, which means they can only be used on light-duty vehicles. Consumer SUVs at best. Certainly not an armored Humvee.

This one flies off its wheels and scrapes across the road on its side.

Way to go, Snake!

The SUV screeches to a halt. The old bakery must have been the site for a major exercise because the entire storefront is riddled with bullet holes and grenade scars, but now it's the building from which Dexter and Red Tail emerge. The back door of the SUV opens automatically. They jump in. Snake takes off with the vortex chopper closing in.

Bigsby is half a rooftop away and closing fast, but that doesn't matter anymore. I hop onto the ledge and drop to the fire escape below. It's a big drop, so I land hard on the metal grate and slam into the railing that gives a little as the entire platform rattles. I go over the railing, catch the grate with my hands, swing my legs and drop again. This time I fall backwards onto the landing, slamming the railing so hard I think it's going to snap for sure, but it doesn't. Bigsby comes crashing down onto the top platform as I go over the top and down to the next landing, this time able to stay on my feet. Just one lache after another. Over the railing, catch the grate, drop to the next one down. Drop and land. This gives me a big lead over Bigsby, who after the initial jump onto the top landing navigates the tight stairs the rest of the way down.

The footfall of Blackburn soldiers echoes through the streets in every direction, but then suddenly they're coming straight at me. Through the smoke at the end of the street. Lasers pointed in my direction. One of them fires. With a heat trail that nearly burns off my ear, the plasma drop whizzes past my head and opens a hole the size of my torso in the building behind me. "Holy Crap!" I scream and bolt around the corner just in time to miss another that blows a hole right through the corner.

Helio guns, otherwise known as sundrop guns, follow the same principle as plasma cutters, just more compact. The bullets they fire are actually tiny drops of superheated plasma likened to a single drop of sun. Obviously not as hot or as dense as an actual drop of the sun, but that's the analogy they use. Not that the technical inaccuracies matter in the least. Judging by the size of the hole it leaves behind, just getting grazed by one would take me down for good.

Further up the street, the SUV takes evasive maneuvers through a rush of smoke. All of a sudden there is smoke everywhere. All around me. Up and down every street. Smoke like the heaviest fog bank you can imagine. Which would make sense if a hundred smoke grenades had gone off at once, but they didn't. Besides, this smoke is thicker at the feet and different in texture. Then I see why. This smoke is coming up out of the sewer grates. Of course. Naturally they would have machines like that installed under the facility to reduce visibility or even remove it altogether during exercises. Now it's being used to disorient me. And once again, all I see are lasers and shadows coming at me through a cloud of white. It also doesn't help that I'm getting lightheaded again.

Whatever eyes I had on the SUV before, it's all lost in the fog. The more important thing now is what I hear, or in this case what I don't. I don't hear the screech of its tires rushing through the streets. That means they must have made the second pickup point, my pickup point. Now I just have to get myself there before I lose my window.

All at once the vortex chopper fires into the fog as I am blindsided with a tackle, and in that one crazy burst I get thrown into the wall. Bigsby is all over me. He throws me to the ground and lands a fist on my cheek, then a knee to the gut that's taken by my armor. "I'm going to choke you till you pop, you little bastard!" he growls as he grabs me by the collar and repeatedly lifts and shoves me into the ground. "I'm going to rip that goddamn chip out of your arm and put it on my mantle!"

Just because I don't train with the Brentwood High mixed martial arts team doesn't mean I haven't learned a thing or two from Dexter. Before Bigsby can land another, I wrap my leg across his hip and turn my body to roll him off. This gets me out from under him and shifts the balance, but that won't last for long. I try to lock him down the way Dexter showed me but he's too strong. Each time I twist his arm, he somehow manages to twist it back. Maybe I'm doing something wrong, or maybe we're just that mismatched. It doesn't matter. With his field training I'm not going to last two minutes against him in a straight-up grapple. I'm trained for flight, not fight. I have to get on the move again. So I release.

Bigsby immediately goes for the headlock. This is exactly what I expect him to do, and I am ready for it. I jam my thumb into his eye.

"Aaaarg!" Bigsby's head jerks back. I wriggle free and spring to my feet. He tries to grab me before I can take off, but I am already in motion, and he can't hold on with only one hand. But I hear him get to his feet behind me. I have to turn up another smoke-filled alley, something I know is potentially a bad move, but it's my only way out.

My only way out…until the dark outline of a vehicle pulls up at the end of the alley and blocks me in. I look up. Neither building has a fire escape or drainage pipe. No ledges, no ornaments, nothing whatsoever to grab. Both walls are smooth as glass going all the way up to the third floor windows.

Damn.

I have no choice. I have to go for it. Through the rolling fog I visualize my lane. Push off the rear tire. Run up the quarter panel. Kong vault over the top.

Five steps away.

I am ready. But just before I leap, the rear door opens, and I suddenly realize it isn't their ride but mine. Snake's SUV. They must have seen me running and moved to intercept me. Instead of tracing up and over the thing, I simply hop in.

Red Tail has moved to the front seat, and Dexter's eyes are trained on the windows like a hawk. I'm not sure whether I'm going to vomit or pass out. Red Tail sees me go for an energy bar and stops me the only way she can, by handing me a sandwich wrapped in cellophane. "You keep eating those energy bars and you'll be stopped up for days."

I revel at the feast before me. Ham and Swiss on honey wheat bread. Real ham and real Swiss, not processed food, and the moment I tear it open I am greeted with a tangy whiff of Dijon mustard. It's a big sandwich. Under normal circumstances I would probably eat half and save the rest for later, but these aren't normal circumstances. I have a parasite of data in my arm.

Dexter and I get knocked around the back as Snake maneuvers the SUV through the streets of Red Hook toward the perimeter of the facility. We pick up two Humvees on our tail but Snake manages to lose one immediately with a sharp high-speed turn. And it seems like we've lost the vortex chopper, until it swoops in a minute later. Seeing it pop out of nowhere makes me wonder why it hasn't been on us the whole time, but then I see Bigsby on a line being retracted back up into the chopper and realize it went back to pick him up. Now that it has him, the thing is on top of us all over again.

The perimeter fence is fifty yards away. The plasma cutter fires a hard burst that hits between us and the fence, blowing a hole into the ground big enough to swallow the SUV whole. There is high ground to one side, but it ends halfway across the giant ditch. Snake veers for it anyway. We all see what he is doing and brace for flight. Dexter's seatbelt is already on. I zip mine across my shoulder but keep missing the buckle because I can't take my eyes off the road. Dexter grabs it out of my hand and clicks it in for me.

Snake forces the SUV into a lower gear and slams the gas. "Hold on to your butts!"

The revving engine jumps an entire octave in pitch as our tires leave the ground and we sail clear across the hole… and crash nose-first on the other side.

The impact throws us all into our belts as the front ends gets crushed, and the entire vehicle slides forward on grill and bumper until the rear end comes crashing down, nearly giving Dexter and me whiplash.

But that's not the end of it.

With my temples still buzzing, we are already crashing through the perimeter fence and busting through a line of barriers. Snake fishtails the vehicle onto an actual street and heads for the tunnel leading out of Red Hook. The vortex chopper stays on us but has to climb higher now that we are off sovereign territory and back on Independent Long Island. The best part about that, it puts the plasma cutter out of range.

"Now what?" I ask.

"What else?" says Snake. "Now we get the hell out of here."

24.

The vortex chopper does not pick us up again on the other side of the tunnel. There's no point. We're in the Free City now, and it can't fly low enough to keep tabs on us anyway. But that doesn't mean we're home free. Far from it. Where the soldiers leave off, the interceptors step in. Before we even get around Ground Zero, three non-military SUVs have already picked us up. One is on our tail, another runs parallel to us one street over, and the third has overtaken us and is somewhere up ahead moving to cut us off.

"We're never going to get through this," says Red Tail.

"Just wait," Snake replies then takes a turn so fast that it pulls us all to one side. The anti-roll differentials feel just like that moment of weightlessness when you're coming out of a skid, except in a skid that moment is fleeting. Anti-roll stabilizers make the entire turn feel like that. Unfortunately, our pursuers also have them and take the turn on the exact same line we do. "Damn!"

"What did you expect?" asks Red Tail. "This is Blackburn. We're not going to beat them with optional extras."

"Anti-roll isn't an optional extra," says Snake. "It's a post-factory modification."

Snake takes another turn just as hard. Harder. This time a light on the dashboard flashes red as the stabilizers fail and two wheels leave the road. Even still, the absolute precision of Snake's wheel handling brings it around and back down. The SUV behind us figures if Snake can do it, so can they. They bring it around at the same speed.

A piercing shriek disturbs the night just before the whole thing topples. Not slowly as if giving in to the centrifugal force bit by bit—it happens in one swift motion. The thing just flips onto its side like a toy that's been flicked by a child—the child being nature and the flick being the immutable laws of Newtonian physics.

One down, but another is still pacing us one street over, and the third is still somewhere up ahead, and I know it won't be long before others arrive.

"You have to let me off," I say.

"Are you crazy!?"

"What are you talking about?" Dexter asks.

"I don't think they have any interest in you anymore. Whatever you've got, they've written it off. It's this…" I say, indicating my wing. "This is what they're after."

"No, we have to stick together," says Red Tail.

"Why, so we can all get taken down together? You said it yourself. We're never going to get through this. But if we draw them apart, we might have a chance."

"I hate to say it," says Snake, "but I think the Carrion has a point."

"His cargo is *our* responsibility," she says. "We can't just drop him off."

"His cargo will be in their hands if we don't. We're bound on both sides by river. I don't see another option."

"Fine, then let me off too."

"No," I say. "That serves no purpose."

"Um, it will when I save your ass again. How's that for purpose?"

"Not this time."

Dexter grins. "You're taking them through the gauntlet, aren't you?"

"Yeah."

"What?"

"Look, this is going to get very dicey. There won't be time to hold your hand, and I don't want to have to worry about you."

"You worry about me! I was the one who—"

"I'm not going to argue with you, Red. I know how good a runner you are, but this is different. This time you're only going to slow me down."

"I know these tunnels just as well as you do."

"That won't make any difference."

"Why not?"

Dexter is already directing Snake where to go. I remove my backpack and shove it around the seat into Red Tail's arms. "Look after this for me."

"Drop him at the corner of—"

"I got it," says Snake, who has figured out what we're up to.

"Why not?" Red Tail asks again.

"Because I'm not taking the tunnels."

"You can't be serious," she says.

But she already knows that I am.

● ● ●

This time it's not soldiers but men in suits who are on my tail. And I do mean on my tail. Every step of the way. And that is just the way I want it.

The one thing about traceurs is that we always know the best places to trace. Go to any city in the world and find the local traceurs, show them you're one of them, and they'll happily guide you through that city's signature run. Every city has one. In Tokyo it's the Godzilla grind, an object-heavy course that begins at the famous Godzilla statue in Ginza and takes you through the streets, monuments, and malls of the most luxurious shopping district in the world. In London it's the Waterloo skip, a taxing course through the busiest railway station in all of England. Here in the Free City we too have our signature run, and I know it like the back of my hand.

The Gotham gauntlet.

Since it's a rooftop course, it's one of the most popular PK runs in the world. That's also how it got its name. *Gotham* isn't just a reference to old New York, it describes the Batman-like feel of the course itself which requires every technique in the book.

Twenty-five floors up, I take Blackburn's goons on the

training exercise of their life as I thief over a fan unit. Using one hand to vault over an object and the other to push off behind you, that's a thief. Just beyond that is a rack of scaffolding blocking my path. I underbar through it.

The next building is nine feet up, requiring either an arm jump or a pop vault depending upon how adventurous you feel. The gap is only two feet, but that's enough. There are no safety nets here. An arm jump is sufficient—leap, grab the building with your arms, muscle up. But if you want to maintain your speed— if, like me, you're being chased and want to widen your lead, you do the pop vault—leap, kick up off the side of the building, catch the ledge with your hands, and simple vault over. Perfect.

I'm all the way across the rooftop by the time they pull themselves up. Huffing already. The next gap jump is four feet across with a nine-foot drop. I plant my foot on the building and leap…breakfall across the asphalt roof next door.

I run, dyno up an overhang, slide down a vaulted rooftop and lache down to the next level.

I drop, and balance, and swing.

I pick up speed to pop vault up a fourteen-foot HVAC housing. Then stop. Reset. Gauge it carefully before I—

Precision jump a seven-inch ledge.

It isn't for amateurs. Many seasoned traceurs can't make it all the way through, but I can. There are very few things in this world I can call my own, but this course is one of them. Now the interceptors are in my territory. On my turf.

The big one can't muscle up the shiny slick aluminum of the HVAC housing. The next one pulls up just before the precision jump. It's only five feet, but when you're twenty-five floors up, all you see is down. After all, it isn't the gap that kills you but the fall. The third guy I know I can ditch easily at the Turn Down, except that two more interceptors have headed me off and are now coming at me from the other side of the gauntlet, so I have to break from the course and go a different way. Into a direction unknown.

Now I'm off the course. Running blind. I have no idea where the next rooftop will take me or if there will even be a way off it, and soon each ledge comes dangerously close to being a wall, and with no way off, my back to it.

I skid to a halt at the next ledge. Wall. The next building is too far over to make a lateral jump, but there is a terrace one floor down that I can drop to. I back up and leap. The alley scrolls by twenty-five stories below me, but I don't give it a thought as I fly across and bring my feet together for the breakfall.

I land so hard I roll straight into the stucco.

The terrace belongs to the corner office of a hip-looking company. You know the kind. They rent lofts instead of suites because they prefer exposed brick and wide-open spaces to cubicles and carpet. An aggrenet startup no doubt.

As I run through the office to the main floor, I see my pursuers make the jump behind me. The first two make it easily, the third just barely

The workstations on the main floor are scattered randomly like an archipelago of desks on a sea of hardwood. The guys behind me will have to zigzag through it but I vault over to keep a straight line, clearing all but one trans screen that I knock over after grazing it with my foot. Just before the stairwell, I pass a utility closet.

One of the goons pulls out a gun.

I rip open the utility closet and look for something, anything I can use. Grab a broom thinking maybe I can use the handle. Leave the door to the utility closet wide open and knock over a steel chair to block the path before bolting through the stairwell door. Slam it shut behind me. Slide the broomstick through the door handle and wedge it behind a pipe. I get half a flight down when I hear activity below me. I can't tell if it's Blackburn, or if they are coming in my direction, but I can't take the chance. I turn and head for the roof, passing the stairwell door just as the first goon tries it from the other side. It holds for now, but I won't hold my breath.

I get to the top of the stairs and throw myself into the door, expecting it to fly open and stay open as I emerge into the chilly night. What I do not expect is for it to bounce back into my face. Strike the bridge of my nose with a sudden flash that knocks me off my feet and sends me crashing into a pair of garbage cans. What the hell?

I groan briefly before bouncing back to my feet.

Just beyond the door I find a wedge stuck between two cinder blocks and an aluminum pale full of cigarette butts. I jam the wedge into the door and hammer it in with one of the cinder blocks before propping both of them against the door. That should give me an extra minute.

I wipe the sweat off my brow and hurry around the rooftop to check out my options. That's when I see the three soldiers dressed in full-capsule body armor, perched on a ledge three stories above me on the adjacent rooftop. Laser goggles glowing red. Sundrop guns primed. They would take me out right now if they were able. They could do that without even aiming. Hell, with the vortex chopper's plasma cutter they could crumble the entire building beneath my feet. And they want to—you can see it in the piercing shine of their glowing red eyes—they want to. But they can't because this is the Free City and firing any plasma-class weapons within its borders would be more damaging to Blackburn than anything I could possibly have in my wing. Besides, they have eyes on me. Where could I possibly go from here?

Where indeed. Two sides of the building are completely open with nowhere to go but down. The third side is where the Complex soldiers stand perched like gargoyles. The only chance I have is the fourth side.

But it's a really big drop. So big that I would probably take a minute to consider it if I had that luxury. But I don't, because right now that jump is my only option. One floor below me I hear them shoving at the door. Inching closer.

There is no turning back now.

I step onto the ledge and take one more look across the chasm as a giant thud shakes the rooftop door behind me. A garble of voices. Now a series of smaller thuds from shoulders being rammed into the door from the other side. The wedge slips. The barrel of a gun appears through the crack as if to pry it open. I can see it more clearly now, the size and shape, the markings on the side. It's definitely a Glock 21, which means it's definitely a .45 caliber.

I give myself a much bigger lead than is necessary, which I know is the very thing I warned Red Tail not to do, but I can't help it. This jump is ten feet over and twenty-five feet down, and I'm apprehensive at best. The door slips. I dig my toe into the roof.

The door behind me flies open with a slam, and all I hear after that is the mumble of their voices unfurling into a string of remarks as they raise their guns to my back. *There he is! There's the Carrion! Don't let him get away!* But I am already in motion. Committed, as the tread of my boot grips the edge of the building. I leap.

A shot is fired.

The bullet whizzes past me as I soar, suspended in thin air like I'm hanging by a thread hooked to the crescent moon, until the Earth takes over and I drop.

Feet running across air.

Arms swimming against wind.

I sail clear into the night.

25.

The muscle memory takes over.

My legs come together and up to my chest all on their own.

This landing comes faster than ever.

Spot my mark. Point my toes. Lower my legs.

My feet catch the roof like the arrester hook of a fighter jet coming into an aircraft carrier. The balls of my feet flatten into my heels, into my legs that bend all the way to 90 degrees even as I throw my bodyweight forward to catch the blacktop with the flat of my hands, a move that crushes my palms into my wrists as I continue forwards into a roll that nearly dislocates my shoulder even through my body armor. But still I have too much momentum, so instead of popping back up for the usual runaway, I push forward again into a second roll, and when I get through that, finally get back to my feet.

I feel it everywhere, but I think I'm okay. There is a limp in one knee as I stagger forward, but that's only because I hit a nerve behind the kneecap. That should pass soon enough. I immediately check the inside of my forearm, which hit the tar pretty hard on the rollout. Scrapes aside, it's going to leave a large bruise, but I don't think the impact was targeted enough to damage the chip. That being the last thing on the checklist, I think I am in the clear.

Shots are fired behind me but only two even come close, and those miss me by a couple of feet. There's cover behind the old chimneystack and I am almost there, almost safe. Until I hear it.

The CRACK steel-on-steel slide of one shot in particular.

One among several that is sharper than all the rest.

My stomach tightens with grief.

The full-arc swing of a wrecking ball strikes my back two

inches to the left of my spine and slams me forward once again, only this time it is without the slightest bit of control. This time there is no catching the roof and rolling out of it. I fly off my feet without balance or breath and land HARD.

In a single flash of memory, I think of that moment back in Brentwood. Lying on my back in the old library as Dexter runs over to see if I am all right. I remember the tears in my eyes and the sledgehammer dent in my chest. But most importantly, I remember the need to get up afterwards.

Get up, Jack.

Because even then I knew, out in the field I would not have the luxury of nursing my wounds.

Get up, Jack!

Another bullet skips off the rooftop two feet away, a second six inches closer, a third six inches away. Get up, damn it! GET UP!

But there is no way I'm getting up from that, not for another minute or two. And mostly the next minute or two is all a blur, but somehow—I can't even tell you how—despite my back that feels broken, I manage to crawl on my stomach the rest of the way to the chimneystack and pull myself around the corner as the bullets continue coming my way. So now I have cover. Even still, I have to get up. That is priority number one. With the brick at my back I push myself up the wall and back onto my feet. Barely. This isn't like it was before. Whether it's the caliber of bullet, or taking it in the back instead of the chest, this one takes all the strength out of my legs.

I peek around the corner.

On the rooftop behind me they stand, all three goons dressed in the same black suit, still contemplating the jump. Just by the looks on their faces it's clear that only two of them will even attempt it, and between the two of them, they'll be lucky if even one gets back to his feet. I'm trained for it and I barely did. But they have guns, and this rooftop is like a closed pen, which means if I don't get off now, I'll be trapped.

The rooftop door is flush against the brick with no handle on the outside. The only way it is opening is if Blackburn comes busting through from the other side, which isn't far off. With a precarious step and less than firm footing, I stumble away from the door, realizing at once the horror of my situation. It isn't that I might become trapped. I am trapped. Trapped on a rooftop with nowhere to go.

I peek around again.

Across the way, two of them have stepped aside to clear a lane for the third who I can no longer see because he has backed up for a running start. I try the door again frantically, try to squeeze my fingernails between the door and the frame to pry it open, but all I do is split them. I slam my fist against it.

All of a sudden I hear what sounds like a bottle rocket coming in my direction from somewhere below on the opposite side of the building. The Doppler effect is all vertical as it shoots up the wall. Arrives fast. A giant harpoon attached to a rappelling line that soars over the ledge and fires a booster to drive itself into the roof. It fires again, ejecting a rappelling brake from the base.

I run to the edge of the building knowing exactly who to expect. Standing on the sidewalk twenty-five stories below is Red Tail.

"Well don't just stand there," she yells.

The two goons watching me from the ledge goad the third to hurry up as I pull the brake off the anchor and lock it on. The third man finally commits to the leap. I know this because the moment I step onto the ledge with my hand on the lever and the line dangling between me and the building, I hear the foot-pounding echo of a running start. I rock back onto my heels. Balance on the corner edge with only the rope holding me in place.

The third goon comes leaping off the building with fire in his eyes.

I hop off the building and go zipping down the line as fast as the brake will allow.

I only have to push off the building three times before my feet hit the sidewalk. The instant I touch down, Red Tail grabs the brake and removes it from my harness. "Stand back," she says.

The moment I'm clear, she breaks off the safety cap and

hits the release, causing an electrical current to travel up the line and detach it from the anchor. The weight of the line pulls it over the edge and down the side of the building.

Red Tail shoves my backpack into my arms and pulls me away. "Come on."

Five blocks up the street, an SUV comes screaming around the corner. Not ours. "Where are we going?"

"The river."

The river is two blocks in the other direction. "That's no good," I say even though we're already running in that direction. "They'll box us in."

"Only if you stop when you hit water."

"You can't be serious!" Over my shoulder I catch sight of the SUV accelerating toward us.

"It's the only way."

●   ●   ●

Red Tail has already stripped down to her underwear while I'm still standing there in my pants, which is crazy because I would have thought that she'd be the one who was shy, not me. I mean, this isn't exactly the way I imagined getting semi-naked in front of her. Not that I ever imagined such a thing, but if I did. You know what I'm saying.

"Come on," she goads, and I am totally amazed by how much confidence she has for a girl who's just standing there, out in the open, wearing nothing but her underwear. Just where does that kind of confidence come from anyway?

"Come on, it's the same game," she says as if sensing my trepidation, not of the swim but of her. "I show you mine, you show me yours."

Just then a bullet zips between us. That gets my pants off pretty quick.

The critical stuff like our thin screens is already in my backpack, which is waterproof. Everything else gets left behind. Our clothes, our gear, our body armor—we leave it all on the bank of the river. Red Tail's armor is full of scuffs but no welts, which is why she grew concerned at the sight of a slug lodged into the back of mine.

Red Tail and I have already confirmed that both of us are excellent swimmers, but the way she dives in, the perfect arch in her back that inverts the moment she hits the water, it's like she's a professional. I dive in after her.

The water is pitch black and cold. Ice cold.

The trick is to keep moving. You have to keep moving. Move to fight the current. Move to fight the cold. Move to keep your whole body from shutting down. Just move. Move to cross the distance as fast as you can before you run out of steam. Because if you stop, you freeze. And if you freeze, you die.

We're not even halfway there when my back clenches and my muscles begin to burn. But not Red Tail, she is a machine. She just keeps stroking and stroking in perfect timing, breathing with the regularity of a metronome. It's only by pacing her that I manage to do the same. That's what keeps me going. As much as I want to stop for a minute to catch my breath, I keep going. As much as I want to tread for a moment in that cold abyss, I know that the moment I do, I will sink forever into that abyss and never be heard from again. I follow Red Tail like my life depends upon it because it does. If she keeps going and I stop, she will make it across and I won't.

Keep pushing. Even as my hands and feet grow numb to the very tips of my fingers and toes.

Keep swimming. Even when my spine feels ready to snap.

Red Tail pulls so far ahead of me that she's almost reached the other side.

All I can do is aim for the lights.

And keep moving.

26.

"Your lips are turning blue," Red Tail says when she returns with more wood to throw on the fire.

Most of what she finds scattered around the abandoned construction site are rotted old pieces covered with demolition dust. Good enough to keep the tiny fire going, even if they do create more smoke than heat.

As she is so fond of pointing out, Red Tail has saved my ass on several occasions. But saving someone's ass is not the same thing as saving someone's life, and this time she really did save my life. If I had been alone, I would have climbed out of the river and collapsed right there. I would have curled into a ball with my arms hugging my legs, letting the teeth-chattering shivers of hypothermia set in, all the way in, until the numbing bliss took even that away. I would have died just as I was born—scared and surrounded by dark with only my own fetal position for comfort. The only reason that didn't happen was Red Tail. She was the one who got me to my feet, threw my arm around her shoulder and pulled me up the riverbank. She was the one who found the gap in the fence and peeled away the mesh to let us through. She was the one who rummaged through the site and came back with a blanket and a piece of tarp. She got the wood. She built the fire. And when the fire got low, she went out for more wood. She was just as cold as I was, but between the two of us she was the one who was able to keep moving. She even gave me the blanket and got by with just the tarp for herself.

"C-c-can't f-f-feel m-m-my hands."

I watch her drop a few more pieces of wood onto the fire. A puff of dark smoke rises, dry and suffocating. Red Tail goes through my backpack and comes up with an energy bar. She tries to hand it to me but my hands are locked inside the dingy blanket.

"N-n-not hungry."

"After that swim you have to be."

"Too c-c-cold to eat."

Red Tail sits down next to me and wraps the tarp around the outside of the blanket, then pries the corner out of my fist and wraps it around herself so the two of us are huddled together under both layers. Her skin is surprisingly warm. Alive, from all the movement. She takes my arm and rubs it up and down to create warmth.

"You're hypothermic. We can't let your body temperature drop any further."

I'm so cold I've nearly forgotten. The cortex chip. It has temperature restrictions. 95 on the downside. I can't let my core temperature drop below 95 degrees, although right now it feels like it's already in the seventies.

Red tails finds my SQUID interface and attaches it to my arm, then uses my thin screen to get check it. "Hmm."

"W-w-what?"

"I'm not getting a reading is all."

"Is that b-b-bad?"

"No, it just means that your cortex chip has gone into hibernation to consume as little power as possible. It's a safety mechanism that triggers automatically when your core temperature falls below ninety-eight. It just means that we have to get you warmed up again before we can access the chip."

Red Tail wraps my arm around her midsection so the chip is pressed up against her, warmed by her heat.

"Don't worry," she says. "Just tell your girlfriend that your life depended on it."

"D-d-does that ever w-w-work?"

She smiles, nearly laughs. "If you have to ask that then you really don't know too much about us, do you?"

"I d-d-don't have a g-g-girlfriend."

"Can't be tied down to just one, huh?"

"N-n-no." I avoid eye contact even though I can feel her looking at me, but I can tell she understands where I'm coming from.

"Yeah, I guess running the sneakernet on top of going to school doesn't leave much time for anything else."

"I'm not in school. N-n-not r-r-really. I'm just g-g-going t-t-technically."

"Relax Carrion, I'm just t-t-teasing."

She huddles in closer, pressing us together, establishing even more points of contact to share our body heat. Although at this point it's really more Red Tail sharing her body heat with me. Unless the laws of thermodynamics don't apply, all the energy flows in my direction. The only thing I can't figure out is how this petite little girl can generate so much of it. "Hey Red?"

"Yeah."

"C-c-can I ask you s-s-something?"

"You can ask."

"W-w-what's your name? Your r-r-real n-n-name?"

She leans away and cocks her head to the side. "Why should I tell you that?"

"If y-y-you tell me y-y-yours then I'll t-t-tell you m-m-mine."

She smiles.

"What?"

"Nice try, Kemosabe. I already know your name, J-J-Jack B-B-Baxter."

Dexter called me by name, that was how she knew Jack. The rest she just assumed from when I mentioned Martin Baxter at the construction site.

"N-n-not B-B-Baxter. It's N-N-Nill. J-J-Jack Nill. From my mother's side."

Or maybe it was Bonillia. The file from the basement is still in my backpack, in the hidden compartment. But if Red Tail came across it when she was digging for other stuff, she didn't mention it. Anyway, there's no point getting into any of that since I don't even know myself.

"It's Cassandra," she says suddenly. "Cassandra Evers. Cassie or Cass, whatever suits your tongue best. I really don't care."

"Cass. I l-l-like that."

I've been looking at her sidelong the entire time. Not

avoiding eye contact, just not sure enough to make it. Out there, on the run, contact is easy. This is different. It isn't just the closest I've ever been to her, it's the closest I've ever been to anyone. The closest anyone has ever been to me. There's something about learning her name that seems to change things between us. Now we're no longer just two Aves flying for Arcadian. Now we have names.

I turn and look into her big blue eyes. Her face is so close to mine that the tips of our noses are already brushing. A bit closer and it could be our eyelashes. Something stirs in my gut. Excitement. Not the kind that comes from leaping buildings and dodging trains, this is a whole different kind of excitement than that.

Cass puts her hand on my cheek. "We really do have to keep your heart rate up."

It's already beating a mile a minute. She must feel it. She has to because I can feel hers as she pulls me closer and guides her lips to mine. And we kiss. Softly. Delicately. The tip of her tongue meets mine. She tastes like the river. I'm sure we both do.

We kiss for the first time and keep going. Keep kissing. And isn't a first kiss supposed to end at some point? I know it should but I don't want it to, so I keep going. And so does she.

27.

Dexter clears his throat.

I don't know how much time has passed, just that Cass and I have dozed off in each other's arms huddled under the blanket and tarp. The fire is down to embers now, but it worked. Everything we did worked. We're still cold but at least the shivers are gone.

Cass lifts her head off my shoulder and palms the corner of her eye. "Where's Snake?"

Dexter lowers the kit bag hanging off his shoulder. "We'll rendezvous with him shortly."

"Are they still on him?" she asks. The concern in her eyes is genuine. Snake obviously means a lot to her.

"I think we lost them," he says. "But just to be sure, he's going to circle around while we take the tunnels." Dex kind of grins a little. And is it my imagination or does it seem to be directed more at Cass than at me? "Everything you need is in the bag," he says, and leaves us to get dressed.

●　　●　　●

I'm not sure how our clothes have been picked out, but Red Tail's black leather pants and form-fitting sweater make her look smashing. Meanwhile, I'm back in cargos and flannel, and a crazy mess of hair that makes me look like I just took a dip in the river. "Was this your idea?" I ask Dexter, holding up a loose corner of my shirt.

Dexter and I walk side by side with Red Tail leading the way. "Martin's," he replies.

"Say what?"

"Your father, Martin Baxter…he was waiting for us on the other side."

"How?"

"I don't know, but it looked prearranged. Him and Snake, I think." Dexter's voice drops to a whisper even though we're in a tunnel and everyone can hear everything. "I know you work with these guys, but how well do you really know these people?"

"I trust them," I tell Dexter.

"That isn't what I asked."

"I know it isn't. I know that Red Tail and Snake are Outliers. I know that my cargo was stolen from Blackburn and that I was loaded up with it to deliver to one of their contacts. Apart from that, I know as much about my cargo as you do about yours."

"My cargo's been cracked."

"What?"

"That was the first thing Martin did when we picked him up. He paired my load with the load in the other chip and unlocked it."

"He did?" says Red Tail from ten feet up. Like I said, tunnel.

"Yeah."

"So what was it?" I ask.

"You're never going to believe it."

"I don't think anything could surprise me at this point."

"This will. This one is personal. That cargo I was carrying… it doesn't just hit close to home…it is our home."

"What are you talking about?"

Dexter pulls out his thin screen and puts it in hologram mode so we can all see. "It's surveys," he says. "Geological surveys taken by the Blackburn Corps of Engineers."

The kind of data we're looking at would look much better on a larger trans screen, but when you're down in the tunnels you have to take what you can get. Each survey is a three-dimensional image covering every subterranean stratum from the surface all the way down to the natural gas reservoir. "These are hydrofracking surveys," I say. "When were these taken?"

"*After* the disaster."

The basic idea behind hydrofracking is simple. You put

a giant spike into the ground that goes straight through your water table and into the bedrock layer. Then you inject a high-pressure stream of highly toxic and flammable chemicals called *slurry* down into the well. This high-pressure stream shatters the bedrock and releases the natural gas, which then gets pumped back up the well to the surface. If all goes well, the slurry and gas never touch your water supply, which is what happens about 91% of the time. If you live in Brentwood, you know exactly what happens the other 9% of the time. We've seen the result when a failed casing causes a massive blowout that dumps so much slurry and methane into your drinking water you can set your taps on fire.

Dexter rapidly scrolls through a dozen of these surveys, one after another, each a different town located somewhere in the Northeast district. I suddenly remember all the old charts scattered across Mr. Chupick's desk. "Wait, are these the same surveys Mr. Chupick was trying to get his hands on?"

"The same." Dexter scrolls through the remaining towns until he gets to Brentwood, rotates it around the center axis and zooms in on Mr. Chupick's farm. Raises it up so we can see the ground beneath. The first layer beneath the surface is a narrow stratum that looks like mud but flows like water in the animated graphic. That layer is labeled *Shallow Aquifer* and is conspicuously marked with a skull and crossbones—the international symbol for hazardous material. Beneath that is a stratum of stone labeled *Aquiclude (impermeable layer)*. And beneath that…a glacial-blue layer confined on all sides by impermeable rock labeled *Deep Aquifer*.

"That can't be," I say.

"It gets better," says Dexter. He taps the deep aquifer, rotates the map to an overhead view and pushes out to show me that it covers almost seventy percent of the town. Seventy percent of the town, including both our houses, is sitting on top of an untouched, untainted reserve of crystal clear water.

I'm so focused on what this means for Brentwood that I nearly forget the bigger picture. There are more than a dozen of these surveys. "Do all these towns have water under them?"

"All of them. For one reason or another, all of these towns are on the TerraAqua teat. They're all being forced to purchase their water from the water collective even though there's water right beneath their feet."

Water. Something about this strikes a chord. The way Mr. Chupick is so adamant about sharing the water from his well with the rest of the community, even though it's no longer his community, at least not the one he knew before the disaster. But it could be again. Mr. Chupick has never lost faith in that. He knows that the only thing holding Brentwood back, the only roadblock stopping the town's rejuvenation, is water. After all, every dollar that goes to TerraAqua is a dollar not going into the town. Water. "It's all about the water."

"Yeah, that's what we figured when we saw these surveys. That's the secret Blackburn has been hiding."

"But if that's the secret…" Something just doesn't make sense. "I thought the information in that cargo was supposed to be big enough to bring them down. That was the rumor, right? Somebody stole something that was big enough to bring down an entire megacorporation. We know that mega is Blackburn. But this isn't all that damning. It'd be a PR nightmare if people ever found out they were sitting on this information, but it is *their* information. They were the ones who did the surveys, so they're the ones who own it."

"That's almost exactly what Martin said."

"And?" The one thing I know better than anyone is Martin. If he raised the question, he already had the answer.

"He looked at the digital watermarks and figured out that this is only part of the information stolen from Blackburn. These surveys are a piece of the real package, but they're not the *critical* piece that everyone is after. It was just enough to create a decoy."

"A red-herring." I know the rest of the story before Dexter even tells it. It's another decoy run, only this time I'm on the other side of it. This time I've got the real load.

"Yeah. They floated this part of it around the sneakernet to distract all the interceptors while they made plans to transport the real goods, the stuff that really can bring down Blackburn.

I guess they had to wait a while until the heat died down before they could move it. In the meantime, they just kept passing the decoy load from one set of runners to another. Keeping it alive on the sneakernet."

"That's why they broke it up into a parity load…" says Red Tail.

"More runners, more decoys," I finish.

"And even if a runner gets pinched, the ruse keeps going."

Dexter grins. "You two should do this for a living."

"So if your load is the decoy…" I pull up my sleeve to reveal the carrion crow on my forearm. "The critical load must be here."

Dexter nods. "The other cargo."

All at once, my wing begins to feel heavy. Heavy with responsibility.

Until now, the longest I'd ever carried a cargo was five, six hours tops. I was just a messenger, picking up here and dropping off there. I was good at running and that gave me the ability to do the job, but it was still just a job. There was nothing invested in the people I was running for. If something went wrong and Wexler missed a patent deadline, what did I care? But this is different. This isn't just a bunch of megacorporations playing ping-pong with little bits of zeroes and ones; this is real. This affects me personally and thousands more just like me all across the Northeast district. This other cargo isn't just data, it's libation for the people who need it the most. I have peoples' lives in my hands. As sure as I am of my ability to run data, I'm not sure I'm ready for that kind of responsibility. But I guess I have to be since it's already in me.

A hollow metallic sound echoes through the tunnel. It's probably just a pipe, but we have to assume it's something more.

"We better get moving," says Red Tail.

"Yeah," Dexter agrees. "Yeah, I think that's probably a good idea."

28.

The roadside eatery where we pull over to regroup is a rundown joint. Dexter is on lookout, keeping his eyes open for any Humvees or vortex choppers that might be heading in our direction. Meanwhile, Red Tail and Snake work on figuring out how we can still make the rendezvous with the Outliers, just in case Martin can't crack the encryption. Apparently the cargo is time sensitive. If we can't crack it ourselves then we'll have no choice but to get it to the people who have the retrieval key so they can unlock it. And we have to get it to them by the designated time, or this will all be for naught. Unfortunately, the original plans didn't take into account that we would have Blackburn on our tail, so now we have to be extra careful that we don't lead Blackburn straight back to Red Tail and Snake's contact.

"Just let it all burn," repeats Martin.

"That's what he said."

While all that is happening outside, Martin and I sit at a table inside the empty eatery. The only other person in the place is the old woman running the counter, and her attention is divided between the Greek soap opera streaming on her trans screen and the meatballs she's rolling between her palms back in the kitchen. She doesn't even notice the SQUID interface attached to my arm as I shovel a second bowl of pasta into my face. Pasta with plain marinara sauce. The old woman tried to convince me that her meat was Grade A Bovine, but living in Brentwood, I knew better than to trust those certifications.

The SQUID is connected to Martin's thin screen, which lies flat on the table in hologram mode so he can work on decrypting the data matrix as we eat. Or should I say, as I eat. Martin lost his appetite at the site of raw meatballs, but I ran out of energy bars back in the tunnel and this is the first chance I've had to refuel. One thing is for sure. This is by far the most ravenous data I've ever had loaded into my cortex chip.

"Mmm. Pass the cheese please," I mutter through a saucy waterfall of spaghetti hanging between my mouth and the bowl. "And the bread too."

Martin passes both without looking. The whole of his attention is focused on the data matrix. We haven't had a chance to chat yet. I'm too hungry and he's too focused on getting the cargo out of my wing. And is it me or have the holes in these cheese shakers gotten smaller? I rip off the cap and dump a heap of grated Parmesan into my bowl, mix it together, and fill my mouth with the cheesier blend. Oh yeah, that's the stuff.

"You have to approach it like a DDx," says Martin.

"Yeah, DDx. That sounds good." I'm not even listening.

"It's a block of data, but we know they're not using modified block cipher mode."

"How do we know that?"

"It would be like making a bomb that you can deactivate by cutting a single red wire. It's too obvious. So if it's not modified block cipher, that rules out fourth-generation CCM mode and EAX3 mode." Martin turns his hand over the thin screen to rotate the data matrix that looks like a golf ball. "It's not stream cypher either, but it is a dynamic algorithm."

I feel my stomach getting too full and have to force myself to stop eating because I don't want to be sluggish on my feet, just in case I have to run again. I drop my fork into the bowl and push it away. Reconsider. Pull it back and take one more mouthful. One more after that and that's it. Now I really have to stop. I push it away again.

Martin notices. "Had enough?" he asks.

I wipe my mouth with my napkin. "It's feeding off me like a tapeworm."

"It's not big. The actual cargo is quite small. It's just very heavily encrypted."

"So I guess you found out from Snake?"

"Found out what?"

"That I've been running data for Arcadian."

Martin glances away from his thin screen but only for a second. "Jack, I've known about your involvement with Arcadian since the day they first approached you."

The surprise of this nearly makes me retract my arm off the table.

"Easy," says Martin, steadying the SQUID to keep the connection sound.

"If you knew, how come you never said anything?"

"What was there to say? You're old enough to make your own decisions. If you had asked for my approval, I would have said no. But you didn't ask, so there was nothing to say."

I go into my backpack and remove the torn-up note from the syndicate. Martin's note for the fifty grand he once owed them. I place it on the table and slide it to him, but he doesn't give it a second thought. So he knows about that as well. But there is one thing he doesn't know. "They set you up, you know."

Now Martin's expression is quizzical. "How do you know that?"

"I saw them doing it to someone else, and then Vlad confirmed it." I tell Martin all about the rigged shoe. Where I found it and how they used it against him. But again, he doesn't seem surprised. "You already knew?"

Martin turns the data matrix and zooms in on a block of gibberish before turning his attention to me. "I did a statistical mapping of the entire session," he explains. "To put it in context, imagine that the regression for any given run of cards falls somewhere within the atmosphere of Earth. There are anomalies, of course, but they trickle off precipitously once you pass the moon. Extreme anomalies occur somewhere in the orbit of Mars. Beyond that, there are only one or two aberrations that happen as far out as Jupiter, which would be the statistical equivalent of winning the lottery ten times in a row. You know when people say *stranger things have happened*? That's usually what they're talking about. The Jupiter points are the strangest things that have ever happened. In that context, based on the outcome of my game as a function of how much influence I was exerting upon that game, the data set for my session placed it somewhere in the vicinity of Pluto. The math required to describe it was way too astronomical for it to be a random occurrence. Card manipulation was a much simpler explanation. The only thing I didn't know was how they did it."

"So then who's the French woman from Grumwell?" I ask, figuring he already knows about that too.

"Pardon?"

"When Vlad tried to detain me he said he was receiving instructions from a French woman from Grumwell. The same woman who hired him to get leverage over you in the first place, apparently."

Martin shakes his head. "That had nothing to do with you. Honestly, I can't see why she would have wanted to talk to you."

"Who is she?"

"Her name is Sandrine something-or-other. She's the Chief Security Officer of Grumwell. Miles's right-hand man."

"I thought the number-two person after the CEO is usually the Chief Technology Officer."

"Usually, yes. But once you become the largest corporation in the world, with the largest GDP in the world, security takes precedence. That's always the way it is with nation-states, only in this case the nation-state happens to be a private enterprise rather than a geopolitical landmass."

"But what does this Sandrine woman have to do with you?" I ask, hoping to avoid another tirade against the evil empire known as Grumwell.

"Grumwell has been playing a long game until now trying to get me into their fold. Making such a bold move as this must mean their timetable has changed."

"Time table for what? What's going on between you and Grumwell, and what does it have to do with Genie?" Martin stops cold and fixes his eyes on me. Yeah, he's not the only one who knows stuff. And I can tell he's impressed.

"You found the hole, then?"

I reach into my bag and pull Genie's Grumwell file from the inside compartment. Slap it down on the table. Martin looks around the eatery nervously, but it's still just the old woman.

"Put that away," he says. "You shouldn't be carrying it around with you. If Blackburn finds that…"

"What was I supposed to do, leave it in the hole?"

"That would have been ideal. If they didn't find it the first time, that only makes it more secure. They're not going to go back and search the house again."

"These documents," I say tapping the file, "Genie was high up in Grumwell's security chain, wasn't she?"

"She was the original CSO. She was the reason why Miles Tolan made the CSO his second in command."

"And you were okay with this?"

Martin lifts his glasses and pinches the bridge of his nose. "I had no problem with Grumwell at the time. Back then we both thought it was a great opportunity. As a matter of fact, back then Miles and I had our own little arrangement already worked out. Once my MacArthur grant ran out, I was going to go work for Grumwell. Miles was going to set me up in my very own lab, and he was ready to give me the two things people like us crave the most—funding and freedom. The Baxter Lab would have had free reign and a blank check to develop whatever projects I wanted."

"So what happened?"

"Genie. In the course of working alongside Miles Tolan, she learned a few things. One of which was the truth about Grumwell."

"What truth?"

Martin glances up at me, but all I see is the data matrix from his thin screen reflecting in his lenses. "How about we deal with one megacorporation at a time. You've got your hands full right now with Blackburn."

But still something gnaws at me. Something about the file. About the way it was hidden away in that hole. Something about the way Genie disappeared from my memory all at once—one day there, next day gone—and yet has always been there lurking in the background. A person always chased, even if I never realized I was doing it. The hole in the basement. The trunk line.

The file. The optical fiber spliced directly into the aggrenet.

"Is she Morlock?"

"I doubt it."

"Martin?"

"Yes."

"Is she Moreau?"

Martin looks at me. "Is that what you think?"

That's not a denial. "She is, isn't she?"

Martin shakes his head. "No, Genevive Bonillia is not Moreau."

"How do you know?"

"I just do."

"How?"

"You have to trust me."

"How, Martin, how? How do you know for sure that Genevive Bonillia is not Moreau?"

"Because, Jack. It's me. *I'm Moreau.*"

My eyes stay fixed on the man long after he goes back to the hologram.

"I've been waiting for you to figure that out. I suppose you don't remember, but when you were very young I used to read you H.G. Wells to help you fall asleep."

It seems silly in retrospect. How many times had I walked passed Martin's leather-bound volume of the collected works of H.G. Wells on his bookshelf? Now there isn't a shred of doubt. I should have known it sooner. Martin Baxter is way too good to have ever been just another Morlock. He would have to be the man who created Morlock. Martin Baxter is Moreau. At the very least it explains why I was never able to find him. It never occurred to me to look for Moreau in my own basement.

The only question now is why.

Something occurs to Martin. Not just anything, I recognize that look in his eyes. It's the flash of inspiration he's been waiting for. "Hold on," he says as he implodes the golf ball and blows it up a different way. This is immediately followed by a flurry of virtual movements as he punches keystrokes and manipulates the data matrix into submission, until suddenly I feel the pulses drawing it out of my arm.

"You got it."

Martin nods. "Now let's see what all the fuss is about."

JUST LET IT ALL BURN

29.

Snake presses the accelerator to the floor to get us back to Brentwood as fast as he can even before he knows why he's doing it. He does it because Martin tells him to. That makes me wonder just how much Snake knows about who Martin really is. In his mind, is Snake taking his cues from Martin Baxter, or is he taking them from Moreau?

"We already knew it was about the water," says Red Tail.

"We knew that Blackburn had these surveys confirming a dozen or so clean water reserves," I say, "but this file tells us exactly what they intend to do with that information." The jerky road is too much for my thin screen to generate a stable image, so I switch it out of hologram mode and hand it to Red Tail. "These towns are all halfway suburbs to begin with, so each and every one of them is already suffering from blight. Blackburn's plan is to finish the job."

"Finish how?"

I reach out and scroll to a random town. "Here they're going to use the lake to flood them out." Scroll to the next. "Here they're going to let the existing power infrastructure fail. It depends upon the town. But at least half of these towns are tied to hydrofracking disasters, and those they're going to deal with in the exact same way." I scroll past the other towns to the survey of Brentwood. "They're going to use the tainted water to burn down the entire town. The entire water supply is already mixed with flammable chemicals and natural gas, so it's the perfect explosive. All you have to do is open the master valve and flood the town's pipes with this stuff and voila." I start the animated graphic to show the hazardous material making its way through the entire town. "Every tap in Brentwood is now an incendiary device. All you need is a match and BOOM."

I scroll to the end of the file, to a classified internal communication thread between Blackburn's Chief Security Officer and the Lieutenant General of the Blackburn Corps of Engineers, cc'd to Christopher Blackburn himself. The details of the first two pages are not what's important. What is important are the last few lines, which I now blow up and highlight.

In closing, the Lieutenant General expresses concern over the plan to ignite a series of blazes to burn down several North American suburbs and asks if there isn't a better way to seize control of the assets.

And the response from Blackburn's CSO…no, there isn't another way. Seizing control of the towns is the only assured way of taking control of the assets. It's the unfortunate blowback of dire circumstance, but for the good of the company, they have no choice. Just let it all burn.

"All this just for the water?" says Red Tail.

I scroll to the chart listing the projections for each water reserve, their combined total, and the estimated market value.

"Whoa."

"We're not just talking about water here, we're talking about millions of gallons in revenue. That's how Blackburn plans to pull themselves out of the financial hole they're in." I put the thin screen into hologram mode and isolate the spreadsheet cell containing the market value of all the water combined. It is very long and contains three commas. I give it a flick to spin it around. Snake takes a bump. The number fizzles out. I take the thin screen out of hologram mode. "You know how everyone's been saying that Blackburn can't survive without a capital infusion? This is it. This is their capital infusion. Once they burn out the towns, they can use eminent domain to seize both the land and the water rights. Then all they have to do is set up relays with TerraAqua and *jackpot!* Instant liquidity."

Red Tail suddenly notices the thing that got Martin up and running back in the eatery. "These dates," she says. "These dates are all…"

"I know."

"And Brentwood is the first one on the list…and

that's today."

"Can you believe they actually have a schedule for this? Somebody actually sat down and made a timetable for destroying these communities. It's…" I can't think of a better word… "Unbelievable."

"This is the Complex, Jack. They don't do anything without a timetable."

"So where are we going?" Snake asks.

I flip the thin screen over to Martin, who pulls up the survey map of Brentwood. Not the simple version we saw before showing the mere the presence of water; this one contains all the layers, including a map of all the water pipes running beneath the town. Martin steadies the thin screen on his fingertips and puts it back in hologram mode. Zooms in and rotates around the old water treatment plant that was shut down after the hydrofracking disaster. "The old water treatment plant. That's where the cutoff valve is for the town's pipes. Once they release that and flood the town with flammable water, all they have to do is trigger it."

"We can't let that happen," Dexter says with resolution.

"No, we can't." I think about Mr. Chupick. About how he turned down his settlement check when everyone else was cashing in. About how he valued his home more than any dollar amount because it was the only thing he had. About how he worked at maintaining our community when so many others couldn't be bothered. I think about Mr. Chupick's hope that Brentwood would again be the town it once was, a town where the people themselves would care enough to make it the very best it could be. We are those people: Martin and I, Dexter and his family, our friends at school and all of their families, Mr. Chupick. Brentwood is our town. Our community. "Dragons don't abandon their home."

I turn to Dexter and match his resolve with a fist. "Dragons never run from danger."

He pounds it. "Dragons never run in fear."

Snake takes his eyes off the road long enough to observe this with admiration. "That's an honorable code you guys have."

"It has to be," I say. "Sometimes honor is all we have."

30.

Snake slow rolls the SUV up the macadam road leading to the old water treatment plant. Thirty yards away, he applies the brakes. A red glow lights up the back of the vehicle as a dim squeal bring us to a stop. No one says anything. We've all been trained, independently, to observe our surroundings before making any moves, and that's what we all do.

"What do you think?" Martin whispers.

"I don't like it," replies Snake. "We're either too early or too late. Until we know which, it puts us at a disadvantage." Snake taps the steering wheel with his index finger. He's obviously trying to come up with the best possible plan. "Agh!" Snake slams his palm into the wheel. The thick of his hand shakes the entire steering column. "We have no choice," he says, "we have to go in blind."

"Okay, so who goes?" Red Tail asks.

"I'll go," I say.

"No, Jack. You got the last one back at the facility. This one's on me," says Dexter.

"There's no point in both of us going," says Martin.

"Why do you have to go?" I ask.

"In case we need to jury-rig the electrical," replies Snake. "If the need arises, he might be the only one who can bring this thing back online."

"Understood," I say, "but let's do a field recon first before we start bringing in the civilian contractors." Snake turns around and stares at me over the shoulder of the seat. So does Martin. Dexter and Red Tail both turn to me in the backseat as well. Everybody stares at me. "What?"

"There's no need for any of you to go in," Snake continues.

"The hell there isn't," says Red Tail.

"You'll need at least one of us on point," says Dexter. "Although two would be better."

"He's right," says Martin. "We'll need at least three for this."

"Okay, so that should be the person with the most field experience," says Red Tail, knowing that person is obviously her.

I object while Dexter continues to make his case. It goes on like this for another minute until there isn't time to argue anymore. And in the end, we all go.

"This is so stupid," says Snake as we all get out of the vehicle together.

Actually, it's not a bad plan. Red Tail and Dexter are going to circle around and enter through an upper window while we go in through the front. "It'll work," I whisper. "Besides, anyone who stays behind is going to be a sitting duck in there."

Snake considers this. He doesn't say it, but I can tell he agrees.

●　　●　　●

The inside of the plant is dank from abandonment. Broken lights, slick floor, rust, and moss. There's a large turbine in the ceiling that once spun under its own power but now drifts lethargically in the breeze. Every footstep, every movement, every sound seems to echo as if in a canyon. Even when Snake communicates in hand signals, there is always that pop of a joint or creak of a glove that cannot be helped. The only thing that masks our noise is the slide of the window upstairs where Dexter and Red Tail come in.

Martin points out the cutoff valve we're looking for.

All of the control equipment is covered in undisturbed grime, so if they have been here, they haven't used it. Still, we have to check things out. I take a step forward, but Snake balls a fist to stop me. He wants to check it out first. He moves in, and even though I should hang back, I follow on his heels.

Jutting up out of the floor is a giant teal pipe that connects to a network of ceiling pipes running deeper into the plant. Attached to the main pipe is a royal-blue restrictor cuff, and attached to that is a giant lever that looks completely rusted until I realize it's just painted that color.

Snake turns around and bumps right into me. Then he glares at me the same way Martin does when I don't listen. "The main restrictor," he says. "That's what's keeping the flammable water out of the town's pipes. The valve hasn't been opened yet, but…"

"What?"

"Something isn't right."

Beep.

"Shhh."

"What?"

"Did you hear that?"

"Yeah, it's coming from somewhere over—"

Beep. Still faint, but this time discernable. Snake peers into and around the restrictor. Beep.

Beep. Beep. Beep, beep, beep, beep-beep-beep-beep-beep…

"Fire in the hole!" screams Snake as he grabs my collar and pulls me back. On the second floor, Red Tail does the same to Dexter. We all run for the exits. None of us make it.

The charge blows the giant lever clean off the restrictor cuff and sends it flying through the plant like it's a six-foot wrench that's just been hurled at us by a twenty-five-foot giant. It sails clean over our heads and slams into the second floor railing a few feet away from where Red Tail and Dexter were just standing, leaving behind a giant dent as it crashes down onto the main floor like seven anvils all forged into one.

The pipe moans. Snaps. Rattles and hums. It does all the little things that pipes do, all at once. Then a low rumble fills the plant as sharp streams of smelly water spray up out of the restrictor.

"Is it going to blow?" I ask.

Martin shakes his head. "The seals are dried out. Leaks are to be expected after this much downtime, but it'll hold."

As the water pools across the floor I can smell it even more. It really does smell bad. Like a gas station, a garbage dump, and a sewage plant all rolled into one. It's hard to imagine it coming out of people's taps, but it did, and it's about to once again. The valve is open, and now this disgusting stuff that can barely be called *water* rushes from the tainted shallow aquifer into the town's main pipes. You might think that townsfolk like Martin and I who have the TerraAqua bypass line will somehow escape it. We won't. Once Blackburn lights it up, the exploding water will blow its way through. Into every pipe, into every home.

"How are they going to ignite it?" I ask.

"The main vent for the town's water system," says Snake. "Where is it?"

"About five miles down the road," answers Martin. "On the outskirts of town."

I'm relieved that Martin knew the answer to that because I didn't.

"Come on, we're moving out," says Snake as Red Tail and Dexter come back around from the outside.

Five miles down the road, I think. That's pretty close to Mr. Chupick's farm.

31.

The main vent for the town's water system is located between the water treatment plant and the town. It's basically just an auxiliary valve that can be opened in an emergency to release excess pressure before it starts busting pipes in town. That's it. Just a single valve housed in a shack surrounded by a fence. Even when the water treatment plant was in operation, it was never manned. It was never something that needed to be secured, which is why it's strange to see a vortex chopper blasting it with lights when we arrive, like it's some kind of bunker hiding a known enemy of the Alliance. The vortex chopper hovers steadily over the station.

"What's it doing?" I ask.

But before Snake can answer, the chopper guns its jet, tearing away both the fence and shack from the ground. And suddenly there he is, standing right behind it. Bigsby. I jump out of the vehicle.

"Wait!" screams Martin. Snake tries to grab me, but I'm already on my feet and running toward him, until he holds up his hand and I slide to a halt. Bigsby is holding an incendiary grenade. I have to stop. Not that I could successfully rush him, but even if I could, there's too much distance between us. He's standing right next to the open vent.

"Welcome home, Carrion."

"Bigsby, wait. Just wait." Reasoning with him is all I can do. "You know we have the paper trail proving Blackburn is behind this. You know these documents are secure and will be delivered to the Alliance Senate. Think about it, Bigsby. There is no outcome in which you will gets away with this."

Bigsby grins with teeth. "You underestimate the value of a good lobby."

"Listen to me, Bigsby. Most of these people have struggled their entire lives to climb out of the squatter settlements. They're not that different from you. You said that I don't know what it's like to really run because I haven't run through the Red Zone with the Caliphate on my tail, and you're right. You were a soldier fighting for the Alliance overseas, and you deserve that recognition. But these people are soldiers too. Maybe you can't see it because they're not in the Complex like you, but they are fighting to survive. These people…" I indicate the town of Brentwood before us, "they are the ones who did right by the Alliance. They played by the rules and worked hard. You can't do this to them. It isn't right. What you're about to do…" I pause briefly to watch Bigsby roll the incendiary grenade in his hand. "This isn't a necessary act of war, Bigsby. It's a willful act of terrorism. You're launching an attack on the very people you've been sworn to protect!"

"Hired," he says.

"What?"

"We haven't been sworn to protect anyone," says Bigsby, "we've been hired to do that job. We may be the largest standing army in the world, but we are a private army. We are a megacorporation just like all the others, and as a megacorporation our top priority will always be our own personhood. Our primary goal has to be our own personal survival. Everything else is incidental. But I'll tell you something. The truth, Carrion, if you really want to hear it…even if they gave me the abort code right now, I'd blow it anyway."

Bigsby pulls the pin.

I take a step back. "No, don't do it." But I know the minute he tosses the pin into the vent that there is no turning back. And when he releases the striker lever on the grenade, I just stand there petrified.

"I'd blow it anyway, Carrion…just to watch you burn!"

Bigsby drops the grenade into the vent and dives for cover as no less than three hands grab me from behind and pull me to the ground.

3…2…1…

The entire ground quakes beneath me. Rumbles. Shakes. All the indicators of a seismic event but without the tectonic shift. Then comes the sudden rush of heat as a geyser of fire shoots up out of the vent and mushrooms against the pre-morning dark. This is followed by another rumble—the snap of mains— and the sound of explosive energy rushing through those mains toward the town.

The air around us stinks. Martin and Snake get to their feet behind me.

"That son of a bitch," I scowl.

"No time for that now," says Snake. "Who's most at risk?"

"The hospital," says Dexter.

"The assisted living facility," says Martin. "There's hardly anyone on staff at night."

A small pop rings out in the distance, nothing like the explosion from the vent but definitely something similar. That much is certain from the orange glow that colors the darkness as smoke begins to rise. I just stand there for a moment staring at it until I suddenly realize where it's coming from. "The farm!"

Martin turns and sees at once what I mean. "Go," he says.

Without saying a word, Dex prepares to run there with me.

"No," I say. "I got this. They need your help in town."

He doesn't argue.

I put up a fist.

He barely has a chance to pound it before I'm off and running.

●　　●　　●

Living out here, Mr. Chupick doesn't have any neighbors close by. There is no one else to check on him, which is why my feet pound the road hard to cover the distance to his farm. What I do now isn't parkour, it's a flat-out sprint. Running in its purest and most basic form. There's just me, Mr. Chupick's farm, and the distance between.

Halfway there.

I am never more than halfway there.

Even as my feet cover yards that add up fast, I am never more than halfway there. Because before I can cross that distance, I first have to cross half that distance. And so it goes, half upon half ad infinitum. Zeno's paradox. It is a mathematical peculiarity to be sure, but that is precisely what makes it such a great metaphor. For me, for my life, for whatever Mr. Chupick meant for me to apply it to. Because there are no limits, only plateaus. And that is exactly what halfway is—it's just a plateau.

I turn off the road to cut through the woods, which is not the smartest thing to do I admit, but following the road will take me the long way around, and I don't have time for that.

Running. The crunch of twigs under my feet.

Running. Branches scrape across my face.

Running. Legs pumping, thighs burning, arms swinging, almost as if in slow motion.

A poem I once read back at the magnet academy pops into my head. *The woods are lovely, dark, and deep.* Just that one line. *The woods are lovely, dark, and deep.*

Over and over again as if on a loop. *The woods are lovely, dark, and deep.*

Almost to Mr. Chupick's farm, I hear the high-pitch whine of an engine coming from the other direction. And almost immediately, I see the jittering beam of a headlamp bouncing up and down with the woodsy terrain.

Even though I'm on foot, I have enough of a lead to get there first, emerging from the woods onto Mr. Chupick's land. Way over on the far side of the pasture, his house and barn are both on fire. A moment later, the dirt bike finds a ramp and comes flying out of the trees with enough air to give the shocks a full squeeze when it lands. The rider plants his boot on the ground and fishtails around. Takes off his helmet.

"Pace."

"Dexter called me about an hour ago. I was on my way to meet you guys when I saw the fire from up on the ridge."

"They went into town. We have to check on Mr. Chupick."

"Yeah. Hop on."

I jump on the dirt bike and wrap my arms tightly

around his gut.

Pace looks down. "Um…you can just grab the back of my jacket."

"Right," I say, and quickly reposition my hands to grab his jacket instead. I've ridden Pace's dirt bike before, just never on the back. "Did you take care of your house?" I ask him.

"We packed all the pipes with baking soda, but if it still blows they're ready for it. Is Blackburn really planning to burn the entire town?"

"It's not a plan anymore, Pace."

Pace guns the throttle so hard he pulls a wheelie as we take off through the pasture.

32.

I am amazed by how quickly the fire spreads. By the time Pace skids to a halt outside Mr. Chupick's house, flames are already pouring out of several windows as if they were fluid.

We run up the steps and Pace kicks in the door. Inside, there is smoke everywhere, but the fire is still contained to the rooms where it first exploded out of the pipes. We run into the kitchen only to find a wet mess of soot and ash, and a giant hose coming in through the back door. The hose is attached to a pump drawing water from the well. Pace and I follow it. Through the kitchen and up the stairs, where we find Mr. Chupick standing outside his upstairs bathroom pushing back flames like a burly firefighter.

He sees us. "The barn," he says. "Get the animals out of the barn."

Pace tries to take the hose from Mr. Chupick but again he insists that we take care of the barn.

"You stay here," I tell Pace. "I'll get the barn."

I run down the steps and out the front door, vault over the porch railing and run to the barn that is burning even faster than the house. And through the roar of that fire, I can hear the horses and sheep. When I pull open the door and enter the inferno, the first things I see are the horses neighing wildly on their hind legs and the sheep circling furiously in their pen. Whatever else there may be is hidden by smoke.

The hardware on the first stall burns my hand. I have to pull down my sleeve and use it as a glove to get at it. The instant I trip the latch, I have to dive out of the way to avoid the 800 pound animal rushing past me to get out of the barn. I move to the next one, opening the latch and getting out of the way to let that horse to freedom. Then the next. Four horses in all.

Then the sheep. I swing the pen open and move to the side expecting them to rush out like the horses, but instead they stay inside. Moving in circles but never out of the pen, even though they now have a clear path to freedom.

"GO," I scream, but they just keep bleating. I move inside the pen and try to force them out individually, but that doesn't work either. It's not until I move all the way to the back of the pen and stretch my arms wide to herd them out that they leave, all at once.

A large crack echoes through the barn as a flaming roof beam suddenly breaks off and collapses to the ground, immediately igniting the hay. Now that the horses and sheep have escaped, and their cries with them, I hear the chickens. I don't want anything to burn alive, but since it's between them and me, I'm the only bird who's going to make it out of here.

Another roof beam falls as I run. I slide to a halt. Dive back in the other direction to avoid it crashing down on top of me.

SLAM!

Instantly the flames begin to spread at my feet. I back up, pushing myself further into the barn, further away from the exit as the smoke and fire grow in between. There is only one way out and that is over. I run. Plant my foot on one of the stalls. Leap. Not over a concrete object but over fire. This time the fire is the obstacle, and I have to clear it just as cleanly as if it were a gap or a railing.

I leap over the crest of the fire, catching smoke in my eyes and heat in my lungs as the flames singe the bottom of my shoes. Land and keep going. The entire roof cracks. I leap again over a second blaze that feels much hotter than the first. Land. Run for the doors.

The roof. Comes. CRASHING DOWN!

As the horses and sheep make their way deeper into the pasture, the entire barn collapses behind me releasing hundreds of glowing embers that dance into the night like fiery particles of the devil's aura. Only there is no devil behind these infernal sprites—unless you count Blackburn.

The barn is gone, but the house seems to be under control.

At least there aren't flames pouring out of it anymore. I'm about to run back inside when the front door opens, and Pace emerges half dragging Mr. Chupick on his feet. I run up the porch and wrap Mr. Chupick's arm around my shoulders to help him.

"The barn," he coughs.

"It's gone. The horses and sheep are clear, but I couldn't get to the chickens."

"We put out the fire upstairs," says Pace.

Mr. Chupick keels over and launches into a violent coughing fit. We try to help him but he refuses our assistance. "I'm fine," he says. "You two need to go."

"We have to get you to the hospital."

"The hospital," Mr. Chupick wheezes in horror. "There may not be a hospital in twenty minutes."

Pace bumps my arm. "Come on."

I'm still reluctant to leave Mr. Chupick like that, even though I know he'll be okay. "Go!" he insists.

Pace kickstarts the dirt bike and digs half a donut into the ground as he turns it around and pulls up next to me. "We'll come back for him later. I swear."

That'll have to do. I jump on the back and grab his jacket as he guns the throttle, and we go zipping through the pasture.

● ● ●

I peer around Pace's shoulder as we race into town where an orange glow reflects off the hills in the distance. This isn't the creep of dawn coloring the sky just beyond the hills, it's the brilliant glow of Brentwood on fire. All the little flames from individual buildings have joined together with a singular purpose—to burn down our hometown.

The bike leans as Pace takes a turn I wasn't expecting. "What are you doing?" I yell.

He points out Main Street in the distance, which is lit up like a bonfire. It makes sense. That's the section of town where the most pipes run, so it would be the section of town with the most explosions. Now it's ablaze, smoke and flames pouring out of every window of every building.

"I don't see any fire trucks," Pace yells back.

Most of the buildings in that section of town are boarded up, like the old Library. "There's not enough resources," I shout. "They probably decided to just let it all burn."

"That's why we have to be sure," says Pace.

I know what he means. It isn't just the PK club that uses those buildings to train. Lots of kids from school use that space for a variety of reasons. Just because those buildings are supposed to be empty doesn't mean they are. I slap his shoulder. "Hit it."

The bike lurches forward as Pace opens up the throttle and sends us screaming toward the fiery center of town.

33.

Coming down Main Street is like driving straight through a furnace. The air is baking hot and the flames are even hotter. I'm about to tell Pace to head to the hospital since no one could survive inside one of those buildings, when I hear something. Barely. It's something like a cry. It's so faint that Pace probably can't hear it through his helmet and the roar of the fire and whine of the bike, but I do. I punch his shoulder to stop. He hits the brakes so hard that the rear tire nearly slides out on the slick road.

Pace removes his helmet. "What?"

"Listen."

Nothing.

"What?"

"*Help me…please.*"

"Did you hear that?"

Pace nods.

"*Help me, I need help, somebody please help.*"

The voice is too faint to discern, but there is a certain quality about it. Timid, almost childlike. I know I've heard it before…

And suddenly it hits me. Red Tail. The first time I met her, back on the train. The voice she used to ask for the time. That was it. That's the voice I hear now, calling for help from inside the building. I pull Pace off the bike. "Come on."

Pace and I run into the three-story redbrick building. Inside, ripples of flames pour off the walls and fill the air with hot, gray smoke that immediately catches in our lungs.

"Where was it?" Pace coughs.

"It sounded like it was coming from upstairs."

A long, hard crack echoes through the building, the sound

of something in the structure destabilizing. Pace and I make our way up the stairs to the second floor, where the fire and smoke are just beginning to appear. "Hello?"

"*Up here*," calls the voice from the floor above us. "*I'm up here…please help.*"

Pace is already on the move, but now my suspicions begin to kick in. And when we get to the top floor and see no one, I know right away that something is amiss. "Hello?"

"*Over here. I'm trapped. Please help.*"

It's coming from the far side of the floor, just beyond the load-bearing wall. Pace is about to run straight over, but I hold him back and instruct him with a hand signal to make a wide arc around the wall. That way we can see what's back there without having to stick our necks out.

"*Over here*," calls the voice as we come around. "*Over he-ere*, Carrion-kun."

"Jesus!" screams Pace, who nearly buckles backwards. Me, I was already expecting something like this.

Mr. Ito leans on his katana as if it were a cane. He smiles. "*Help, help*," he says in the voice. He breaks into a laugh. "See, I knew that little girl was important to you. If Red Tail-chan in trouble, Carrion-kun will run into the fire to save her. Too easy, *deshyo?*"

Yes, it was too easy. I should have known better. But then again, so should he. "You're too late," I tell him. "The cargo has already been removed."

"Yes, I already figure that," he says. "But we have a contract with Blackburn to disrupt you, and we don't stop until that obligation is fulfilled. In this business, reputation is everything. Mr. Ito has not failed a single job yet, and this will not be the first."

"Blackburn contracted you to disrupt the cargo, not me!"

Mr. Ito seems amused. "You are Arcadian, Carrion-kun. You *are* the cargo, and the cargo *is* you. I don't stop until your wing is clipped."

Pace backs away as Mr. Ito twirls his katana into his hand, rips off the scabbard and throws it aside like he doesn't have the slightest intention of recovering it afterwards. By the look in his eyes it's obvious only one of us is leaving this building alive.

"Run now!"

The thing to remember is this: when I tell Pace to run, it isn't an indication of panic. When a traceur says run, it's a call to action—an instruction to do exactly what we do best. When I tell Pace to run, I'm telling him to trace.

We go in separate directions and Mr. Ito follows me. I run straight at a column like I'm going to hit it and keep going, vertically, all the way up to the ceiling. That's how you have to approach it, believe that you can in fact run straight up the column until you hit the ceiling, even if you are just taking two steps and kicking off. That forces Ito to turn sharply to follow me, swinging his katana through the air behind me. I run straight for another pillar. Two steps up and kick off, this time throwing in an aerial twist as I change directions. Again Ito swings his sword at air as he is forced to turn. Up another pillar and kick off—360—another whoosh of the katana. Again and again. Midair breaks that are nothing for me force Ito to make hard turns. Tiring his knees. Tiring his legs. Tiring him out. This time he strikes the pillar well after I'm gone.

Pace has already made his way down to the second floor. I vault over the railing and Turn Down but don't have a chance to shake it out before Ito's blade comes slicing through the bannisters. I let go just in time to keep my fingers and drop wildly down to the second floor. I hit the deck heels-first and fall backwards, slamming my arms into the floor to break the fall just like Dexter showed me. Then without so much as a blink, I roll back and Kip-up just as Mr. Ito comes dropping down from above.

The second floor is ablaze. The smoke is thick and suffocating; it burns my eyes so badly I can barely see where I'm going. But from somewhere inside that smoke, I hear Pace's voice calling me. Until all hell breaks loose.

A section of ceiling falls and blocks my path with a lattice of beams. I grab a stove-hot two-by-four and underbar through it, singeing my hands but getting through just the same. However, when I land on the other side, the smoke grabs my face and makes me lose my bearings. All I see is a wall of white lit up by orange flames.

"Jack!" screams Pace. I can't even tell from what direction.

Mr. Ito comes somersaulting over the rubble behind me. It's a sideways somersault that's supposed to land him in stance, but even he is not immune to the smoke-filled air all around us. He misses his landing and falls. I pick a direction and run. But for all the effort I exert trying to see through the smoke around me, it never occurs to me to watch out for the floor beneath. Three steps later my foot hits the floor and keeps going, straight through the floorboards. I keep scrambling even as my knees drop below floor level, and all I can do is grab a fractured beam and hang on as the detritus drops into the blazing inferno below. I hang on by a single arm.

Then I see him. Directly below me. Like a monster in a pit, he waits patiently for my grip to run out. Gendo. He doesn't even care that he's standing right below me. He wants to be sure it isn't the fall that kills me. He wants that pleasure for himself.

"Jack, hang on!" Pace calls out from somewhere above. At that exact moment, patent leather toes and a blade of folded steel appear at the edge of the hole. And that's when I realize, I'm not just hanging on by an arm, I'm hanging on by my wing. If Mr. Ito wanted to clip and kill me in one fell swoop, he would get no better chance than this.

Mr. Ito smiles as he taps the tip of his katana on the splintered boards of the torn-away floor. "*Chyoto warui*, Carrion-kun. Nowhere to go, *deshyo*."

Mr. Ito doesn't raise his sword. Instead he just lets me hang, waiting for my grip to run out. He won't have to wait long. The burn in my arm has already migrated to my head.

Dizzy. The air stings my eyes shut between each blink.

Dizzy. The rest of my body floats in nothingness.

As I cough and choke and tighten my grip, the entire building goes topsy-turvy until I don't know which direction is up. And with the loss of direction, the pain in my arm loses all meaning, until I begin to wonder why it is I'm hanging on at all… if the floor is just inches below my feet.

Just a short hop to the floor.

"Jack!"

I breathe the dragon's hot breath.

Just let go and float gently down to your toes.

"Jack, hang on!"

My fingers slip, from the base knuckles to the middle knuckles.

All you have to do is let go.

From the middle knuckles to the tips of my fingers.

Let go.

The moment my fingers leave the beam, the entire world comes back into focus. Like the free fall itself shocks me back into cognition.

All I see now is Pace, who blindsides Gendo right out from under me, clearing a space that is barely big enough for me to land, but it's enough. I drop straight down onto it, catch the ground and roll across debris that stabs my shoulders and back.

Gendo already has Pace in his powerful grip, but even still he does not scream for help. He screams for me to go. "Jack, go! I mean it. Get out now!"

A searing crack rips through the building, shaking the foundation, rattling the entire edifice as the roof finally gives and crashes into the third floor.

"Jack, go! Get out!"

There's no time to do anything else if I ever want to see the light of day again. I scramble to the door and turn just in time to see a heap of flaming roof come crashing down on top of Mr. Ito and straight down onto—

"Pace!"

The heap of flames engulfing them blows me out the front door with an explosion of smoke and fire that knocks me off my feet. I see a flash of yellow at my side. My sleeve is on fire. I try to pat it out before suddenly remembering—stop, drop and roll. I roll back and forth in the dirt until the flames are smothered.

C-RRR-AC-K!

"Pace!" I scream frantically.

All at once but in slow motion, like a controlled demolition, the walls collapse and the rest of the building comes crashing down on itself until all that is left is a burning heap of wood and brick in a cloud of smoldering ash.

"Pace!" I scream again. But it's no use.

I hear nothing but the snap of burning wood because there is nothing more to hear.

34.

With the sky turning an early shade of blue, the entire town smells of smoke. Not the pleasant kind that rises out of chimneys in the dead of winter—this smoke smells dirty. It is the smell of things that were never meant to be burned. If not people's lives then surely their livelihoods.

As I ride Pace's dirt bike through the drenched remains of Brentwood, it is clear that entire wings of the hospital and high school have been lost. But they are the lucky ones because they were essential enough to get the first response. Not as lucky are the two grocery stores that have burned to the ground, not to mention all three churches. Gone.

People tried to fight the blaze. You could see them still huddled around the smoldering remains. The residents of Brentwood did whatever they could. Unfortunately, it wasn't enough. The fire spared nothing. Not everything was completely destroyed; some buildings were reduced to ash while others were left standing with little more than smoke scars, but there was no rhyme or reason to any of it. Some things burned a little, some burned a lot. But in one way or another, everything burned.

Everything burned, just like they wanted it to.

It is now, finally, as I make my way through town, that my stomach twists into a knot and my quivering hands begin to shake the dirt bike. A feeling of numbness wraps around me like a suffocating blanket. It is now, finally, that it hits me. Pace is gone. Killed in the fire helping me escape. He could have easily made it out, but he chose not to leave me hanging at the tip of Ito's sword. Pace was a Dragon to his very last breath, and this is something I will never forget. And now, through the trembling in my hands, I feel something else break through the numbness.

Something raw. Something primal. Something visceral.

Pace is gone. And all that is left in the wake of his passing is anger. Pure, unadulterated anger.

●　　　●　　　●

Finding Snake, Red Tail, and Dexter is as easy as riding straight toward the vortex chopper circling near them.

"Where's Martin?" I ask.

"Taking care of your house. Where's Pace?" Dexter asks.

It's one of those times when I don't even need a mirror, I can feel the look on my face. Dex understands immediately. I don't even have to tell him the circumstances. He seems to get that too. There's a little thing we say whenever a Dragon has to leave. Since I've been one, we've only had to say it once. But I say it now, for Pace. "Dragon once…"

Dexter joins in, "Dragon forever."

Snake's hands are full. Literally. He's got soot all over his face and an elderly woman wrapped in a blanket in his arms. They've gotten everyone out of the nursing home. Now they're moving those who need medical attention to triage, and since there aren't enough gurneys to go around, it's a job for the biggest and the strongest—Snake and Dex among others.

"This is bad," says Red Tail who has been coordinating logistics with others around town. "Everything went up at once. The water spread the flames like napalm."

"All the old buildings on Main Street are gone."

"There wasn't enough manpower," says Dexter.

"We couldn't fight the whole blaze," says Red Tail. "We had to let some of it go."

"Just let it all burn…"

Red Tail purses her lips like I don't appreciate the difficulty of her task. "Not all," she says, "but we couldn't save condemned buildings when hospitals and schools were on fire."

It's not that I don't understand that, and I do appreciate all of their efforts. I'm just extraordinarily pissed that even one building went up in smoke because none of them had to. Mr.

Chupick didn't have to lose his barn. And even more importantly, we didn't have to lose Pace.

It was all Blackburn's fault. And as the vortex chopper flies over us, I make eye contact with the person responsible. It was Bigsby who dropped the grenade into the mains to start the fire. Bigsby and no one else. Whatever the orders, it was his hand that did it. And I know he wasn't just following orders, he was happy to do it. He told me so himself. Bigsby has been gunning for me since the moment we first met. For him, setting my hometown on fire wasn't about Blackburn's plan, it was one more way for him to come after me. And now that Brentwood has burned, and I am smoked out, he knows there is nowhere left for me to go. And that is exactly what I am counting on.

"Where was the drop supposed to be?" I ask Red Tail.

"The mischief plant. Why?"

The mischief plant. How fitting. The vortex chopper circles around and doubles back. "He'll be on my tail the whole way."

"Why?" asks Red Tail. "There's no drop to make. You're not loaded up anymore."

"Yes, but Bigsby doesn't know that, and he'll want to finish this."

Red Tail pulls up a map. "It's twenty miles away on straight roads. He'll be on top of you before you even make it out of town."

I turn the handlebars and rap the gas tank with my knuckles. "Not if I cut through the woods."

"Whatever you're going to do, do it quick," says Dex as he tracks the vortex chopper. "Snake's intel says there's more on the way."

"What are you going to do?" Red Tail asks.

"I'm going to put that rat where he belongs."

Suddenly Red Tail's eyes light up.

"What are you doing?" I ask as she rips off my backpack and digs through it until she finds what she's looking for.

"Here," she says and pulls out the rodent repeller.

"What do you want me to do with that?"

Red Tail turns the box onto its side and digs her thumbnail

into the switch that inverts the signal. Flips it. "I think it's time to test this thing out."

"I don't even know if it's going to work."

"It will," she says. "It'll work because you built it."

The vortex chopper comes screaming over us. The bay door flies open, and the blonde kid who burned my town hooks onto a rope to drop down.

Red Tail backs away from the bike. "You just have to get it on him somehow."

"How am I supposed to do that?"

"You'll figure it out."

"Go, Jack!" screams Dex. "Move!"

I kickstart the bike with a huge turn of the throttle. Dig my heel into the dirt. Slam the shifter down and kick up a rooster tail of dirt as I turn the bike and head for the woods.

●　　●　　●

Clutch. Toe the shifter into third.

Clutch. Up to fourth.

I try to use a long stretch to get up to fifth, but before I know it the terrain forces me to let up on the throttle.

Clutch. Stamp it twice down to second.

In the full light of morning it isn't hard for the vortex chopper to track me through the woods. Obviously I can't see it when it's directly on top of me, but every so often when it gets ahead of me, I catch a glimpse of Bigsby leaning out of it. He must be thinking that he has me; that I've started on a road with a limited amount of fuel in my tank, and all he has to do is wait me out.

What he doesn't know is, I know exactly where I'm going.

And I'm just about halfway there.

35.

There's a reason why so many people who grow up in the squatter settlements don't eat red meat, why Dexter and Red Tail won't even go near the stuff. There is a reason, and it has nothing to do with ethics.

I grew up in the Free City, where the markets were reliable and you could trust any package that was certified 100% Grade A Bovine. Or at least I thought I could trust it. Then I came out to Brentwood. It was no secret that the North American Agriculture Collective was entirely funded by the very producers they were tasked with inspecting, and for that reason the labels on lesser grades of meat were always a little fudged. But if you listened to the people in Brentwood who actually worked at the mischief factory, they had a different story to tell. According to the folks around town, all of it had mischief. And if that was the case, if the meat that was supposed to be mischief-free had even the smallest amount of mischief mixed in, then you had to wonder about everything the NAAC endorsed. And if you couldn't trust the food you were putting into your mouth, what could you trust?

The mischief plant is located about ten miles outside of Brentwood, and I lead the vortex chopper all the way there. Since most of the plant workers are residents of Brentwood and most of them are otherwise occupied this morning, the place is barely in operation.

The dirt bike putters like it's almost out of gas when I slide to a halt in the back lot separating the processing plant from the mischief pit. I kill the engine and lower the kickstand. Pull the signal emitter out of my bag and get ready. The vortex chopper that's been on my tail the entire way swoops over me. A rappelling line hits the ground a few feet away and down comes Bigsby.

That's my cue. I don't even wait for his feet to touch down; I leap off the bike and grab him while he's still on the rope. Raise my elbow and drive it straight into the wound on the side of his face. Follow it with a punch that disorients him just long enough for me to shove the signal emitter into his vest pocket undetected, then I release. He hits the ground just after I do, but the extra seconds he takes to clear the rope is all I need to get a jump on him.

I run.

He chases.

No matter. I'm just half the distance away from the mischief pit, and there is nothing in between but playground, and I know I've got this. All Bigsby has to do now is catch me. And he will catch me, exactly when I want him to. Because this is my run, and I'm the one making the rules.

I'm not sure how or why, but something had changed. This isn't like all those other runs when I was tracing to get away. This time there are no Es. I am not running to evade, elude, escape. For the first time ever, since my very first job as a data runner, I don't feel like I'm trying to get away from the person on my tail. Just the opposite. I want him to catch me.

Up ahead is a very large dividing wall. I leap. Wall run up the concrete. Arm grab the top and muscle up.

Ask a hundred different traceurs what they love most about parkour and you'll get a hundred different answers. But if you distill those answers down to their essence, you will find the same idea at the heart of each and every one. Freedom. The freedom to be, without limits, to the very best of your ability. The freedom to move without fear or reticence and live your life one leap at a time. The freedom to unbind yourself from all those paths that have been constructed for you by society and find your own way through the obstacles. The freedom to write your own physics, accepting nobody's rules of gravity and space but your own. The freedom, finally, to unshackle your human spirit from the tyranny of grounded steps and let it fly. Freedom—in all its form and function, all its beauty and art, all its magic and allure—parkour is all about freedom.

Even the freedom to stop running if the time ever comes. Stop thinking about all those half-distances and just enjoy the view standing still. Sometime maybe, but not right now, not for a while.

Bigsby doesn't follow me up the wall because he sees the fence fifty yards away, and the giant sign indicating rats, and he just assumes I'm going to come down on his side of it. It's the wrong assumption. Running along the top of the wall, I let him close the distance between us until he can keep up on his own, and the chase becomes a footrace to the pit. And the closer we get to the pit, the more we start to see the random escapees. On the ground, along the top of the wall, they scurry everywhere.

Rats. Oversized rats. Farmed for consumption. Harvested for their meat. I nearly gag.

Bigsby goes for his gun.

"Go ahead and shoot," I yell before it's even out of his vest. "You can't beat me any other way. You never could and you never will. You will *never* be half the runner I am."

Bigsby growls like a mad dog as he releases the gun and raises his hands like claws to attack the approaching fence. I get there first. Leap off the crest of the wall. Throw a midair 360 as I soar over the top of the fence. Land and roll out. It's not that hard of a landing but it feels that way without any body armor. Getting used to wearing body armor was easy. Getting used to not wearing it again, that's harder.

The mischief pit is just that. A giant pit full of large rodents kept at bay by electronic fencing until they are ready to be processed. Thousands of them. Scrapping around in a pool of dark hair accented by long and leathery tails and the pinks of their feet. A shiver runs up my spine. I hate rats. That's why I built the repeller in the first place, so I wouldn't even have to see them. But now it's like I'm making up for all the rats I've avoided at once. I feel them at my feet. Feel their beady little eyes watching me as I run along the embankment, waiting for me to slip. Ready to pounce. It's nearly enough to make me second-guess my lane, but then I remind myself that I have to do it. I commit, because it's the only way.

Dexter could go a different way. He could do it without ever leaving the embankment. He could flip that mental switch from flight to fight and in one instant hit the brakes to take on Bigsby mano-a-mano. Dexter could get Bigsby into the pit without ever having to set foot in it himself. Unfortunately, Dexter's wheelhouse is not my own, so I have to go another way. I have to go through. There is no way I can wrestle Bigsby into the pit without him breaking my neck first, so I have to run him through it. I have to go through.

Easy, I remind myself. *It's just like any other obstacle. There is nothing stopping you. These rats are not limits. They're just a plateau...*

I leap, escaping Bigsby's fingers by a knuckle as they reach for my back. And now he has no choice. There is enough gravity and momentum between us to pull him forward with me before he even has a chance to think about it—because I'm sure if he did have a chance to think about it, he would never follow me in. But he does. I launch into the pit with all the grace of a bird in flight while he stumbles in after me like a drunken ostrich.

It is without question the strangest landing I have ever made. Everything moves. Everything squeals. The squirm of the pack makes me stumble, but I manage to stay on my feet as the rats come rushing past me like a raging river. One on top of the other, running like every one of them is clawing for the last piece of cheese in the maze. That's the work of the signal in Bigsby's vest. It isn't just attracting them, it's inciting them to attack. That wasn't my intent, but I'd be lying if I didn't say it was a happy accident.

Bigsby screams in horror. It's like nothing I have ever heard before. I'm sure a soldier like Bigsby who's been inside the Caliphate has heard it many times, but never like this, never from his own lips. I mean he really screams in horror.

As hordes of rodents continue to wash past my ankles, I turn in time to see him fire his gun wildly into the air. And when a trio of rats dig their claws and teeth into his hand and wrist, the gun goes off again. The empty shell casing arcs out of the ejection port in a drift of smoke and lands in the mischief of rats. Disappears. A rat digs its teeth into the soft web of his thumb and forces him to drop the gun. That too disappears.

Rats. Claw past Bigsby's waist and up his torso.

Rats. Up his arms and across his shoulders.

Rats upon rats. Climb across each other when there is no more surface on Bigsby to climb, when even his face is covered and all that is left of him is a mound of vermin that takes two steps in no particular direction and drops. And somewhere in that mound of vermin, through the din of squeals echoing across the concrete walls of the pit, I swear I hear him scream one last time.

36.

I have to buy some gas off the plant manager before I can get back. The tank capacity is just under two gallons, so I toss him twenty bucks to make it square and then take the main road back to the smoldering remains of Brentwood. It's twice the distance as cutting through the woods, but it's a straight shot in fifth gear so I actually get back in half the time. Just in time to join the confusion.

The vortex chopper from before, and two others just like it, are being forced out of the sky by something I have never seen before. Something that looks like it should still be a concept on paper, not a physical craft zipping around before my eyes. It isn't just a newer and better vortex chopper; it's the next step in the evolution of military aircraft.

But whose military? Certainly not Blackburn's.

The mystery craft fires electromagnetic pulses at all three of Blackburn's vortex choppers, forcing each one of them to land in a storm of sparks. Land, not crash.

"How are they still able to fly?" I ask Snake, who is the only one left at the nursing home after Dexter and Red Tail left to help out at the hospital.

"It's a brand new form of targeted EMP called the *smart pulse*," he says. "The mechanism can differentiate between various types of circuits, giving you the ability to fire a targeted pulse that can shut down the weapons and navigational systems but still leave the craft operational enough to land safely."

"I've never heard of that."

"No, it's not something you would ever read about in a white paper. That logic is still supposed to be at the drawing board. There are only a few people in the world who have the resources to build something like that in complete secrecy, not to mention the craft itself." Snake turns to face me. "Bigsby?"

"With his own kind."

Snake understands exactly what I mean. "Good. I never liked that kid."

I am so focused on the aerial show that I haven't even noticed all the soldiers who have crept in around us. Soldiers everywhere, almost as if the entire town is under martial law. Only their gear isn't Blackburn gear. This gear is lighter and slimmer, more compact, and I'd be willing to bet even tougher. Something tells me I am looking at the next step in that as well.

It isn't until a few of them run past us to secure the Blackburn soldiers climbing out of the vortex choppers that I see the unmistakable G on their uniform. "Grumwell?"

"Jesus," says Snake. "They did it. They really did it."

"When did Grumwell get into the paramilitary security business?"

"That was always the next step in the doctrine, but no one ever thought they'd do it. And even if they did, we always figured we'd be right on top of it. Damn!"

"On top of what...what doctrine? Snake?!?"

But Snake's attention is not on me, and when I look up at the Grumwell aircraft and see the one solitary soldier rappelling down, neither is my own. A woman. That much is unmistakable. She doesn't come down haphazardly like Bigsby; this one lowers herself slowly, giving herself time to observe her surroundings and take it all in. It isn't trepidation, it's discretion.

She touches ground and removes her helmet to reveal the long dark hair braided underneath. More troops in the fancy new gear seem to emerge from out of nowhere, and now many of Blackburn's troops have turned their guns against their own, like they were sleepers for Grumwell the entire time. One Blackburn soldier puts his back to the grounded vortex chopper and fires a short burst of gunfire at Grumwell until a sonic burst drops not only him to the ground, but also the two soldiers on either side of him who had already surrendered.

That is the first and last of any resistance. Grumwell's

troops now way outnumber Blackburn's. Blackburn has no choice but to surrender. But it's more than that. As I watch the others carefully, I realize it isn't just because they're outmanned and they know it. Judging by the actions of the ranking officers who have just gotten off their radios, it seems like they are under company orders to surrender.

"What the hell is going on?"

"You know, Carrion, I think we're about to find out."

"Carrion?" The woman from Grumwell is about thirty meters away from Snake's whisper, but she hears us like she's standing right next to us. She turns to me. "Monsieur Nill," she says in an accent worthy of the words *crème brûlée*. "My name is Sandrine."

Of course it is. Who else would it be?

"I was hoping to meet you at the gaming parlor, but you slipped away from our mutual friend before I could get there."

"What can I say? I'm not a fan of unauthorized detention."

Sandrine smiles. "From the son of Martin Baxter?" She pronounces his name *Mar-teen*. "I would expect nothing less."

All around us guns are dropped as Blackburn's soldiers get zip-cuffed.

"We'd like to thank you for your services," she says.

"My services?"

Sandrine removes a device from her vest, something small like the size of those old serial-bus flash drives. "With all that's happened here, you haven't had the chance to check the news stream lately."

Sandrine taps the device, and even Snake is taken aback by what we see.

An impossible burst of light shoots, nay *fires* from the tip and projects a flawless, cinema-sized hologram of the Grumwell logo into the air above the grounded vortex choppers. And I do mean flawless. The image density is as good as anything you'd see in a commercial theater, only this image isn't coming from a roomful of projecting equipment.

"Wow, I had no idea you could lens something so small!"

"Forget the optics," says Snake. "How in the hell do you

power something like that?"

At that moment, Snake and I are thinking the exact same thing. We want one. Not to use—we want one to rip apart so we can see what's going on inside.

"Free City news stream," Sandrine instructs the device. She doesn't even have to tell it where to route the audio. The device does that automatically. All of a sudden every speaker on every device within earshot delivers it. From the thin screens in people's hands to the PA systems on the vortex choppers, the sound comes from everywhere at once.

Now everyone's eyes are on the massively projected Free City news stream.

The first streamlet shows the very thing I never thought would ever happen—Christopher Blackburn wriggling his shoulders and shouting obscenities as he is hauled away in handcuffs. Likewise for the CEO of TerraAqua in the second streamlet, who is escorted from his office with his suit jacket over his head. The third streamlet covers what looks to be an emergency session of the Senate Subcommittee on Alliance Security, even though it's clear by the empty room that that meeting has ended. After that are several more streamlets covering the global takeover of Blackburn by the new Alliance security initiative known as *Grumwell Liberty*. All at once, all around the world, everything that previously belonged to Blackburn Limited is instantly acquired by Grumwell Liberty in what can only be called the ultimate hostile takeover.

"Is this us?" I ask. "Did we do this?"

"No," Snake replies. "You don't build something like that overnight. This has been in the works for some time."

"So you didn't know about it either?"

Snake shakes his head with equal parts amazement and disbelief. "We were so focused on staying one step ahead of Blackburn. Grumwell was ten steps ahead of us the entire time."

It reminds me of chess. The player who thinks two moves ahead will often believe he's pulling ahead on material even as he walks a slow road to the inevitable checkmate. That player is us. We thought we were pulling ahead by getting this cargo to the

Alliance Senate, but Grumwell had already captured the Senate from the inside.

Another streamlet pops up of Miles Tolan giving a press conference. Sandrine reaches into the light and swipes her fingers across the projection to expand the Tolan streamlet to full size.

"Integrated active motion sensor," mutters Snake. "Light Projecting Display in an ultraportable form. You're basically looking at a giant transparent screen without the physical layer."

Giant is an understatement. There is no question about it. This LPD technology will make all t-screens go the way of LCDs, and the CRTs before them. Even if it is just a prototype, just knowing it exists suddenly makes the thin screen in my backpack feel like a hunk of junk.

Miles Tolan. A graying gentleman in his late forties with eyes like black dots from a felt-tip marker. Hair slicked back. Beard trimmed close. Pinstripe suit pressed to perfection. The audio kicks in mid-sentence. "—that we are all infuriated by the egregious and unconscionable actions of Blackburn Limited and TerraAqua. I am as angered as anyone by these deplorable actions. Blackburn, acting in collusion with TerraAqua, has not simply conspired to burn down North American suburbs to steal the water rights; they have conspired to commit acts of domestic terrorism against the citizens of this great Alliance. That means all citizens—not just the citizens living in these towns, but all of us. All of you and even myself. They have launched an all-out assault on the very citizens who form the backbone of this great continent." Miles Tolan stops to shake his head *no*. "This cannot abide. Not now. Not ever. These actions must be answered for. There must be accountability."

"Watch. He's about to paint Grumwell as the hero in all of this," says Snake.

"How do you know that?"

"Just watch."

Tolan continues. "I'm sure many of you, like myself, have watched with disgust as the allegations against Blackburn have amassed. Of late and for many years now. Allegations that Christopher Blackburn has, both personally and through his company, engaged in dealings that are in direct conflict with the best interests of the Alliance. Allegations that Blackburn has dealt with the Caliphate. Allegations that the very army contracted to defend this great Alliance has been selling its services to those who would do us harm. And I'm sure that many of you, like myself, have watched these scandals with a feeling of helplessness and despair, because what other choice did we have? Well, my fellow citizens, I am a very fortunate man. Fortunate enough to have the resources at my disposal that I could do something about it. Fortunate enough that I could build the solution. Fortunate enough that I can now offer you the choice we never had before.

"That choice is Grumwell Liberty, or what we like to call the *Fortress*. No longer will the North American Alliance be forced to subcontract the management of our most prized asset—our own security. Today, by unanimous vote of the Senate Subcommittee on Alliance Security, Grumwell Liberty has agreed to an unprecedented unilateral initiative to be the sole defenders of the North American Alliance. We will be the standing army that this great coalition so greatly deserves. As of today, there are no mercenaries. No guns for hire. As of today, the North American Alliance *is* the Fortress, and the Fortress *is* the North American Alliance. Witness today the largest nation-state in the world and the largest private enterprise in the world coming together as never before—intertwined like a double helix to form the DNA of a brand new global power structure. Witness today the birth of the Grumwell-Alliance Fortress."

Cheers. In every streamlet, even all around us, people cheer.

"My god, they're taking over the whole thing," I say.

"Now you see," replies Snake.

"There is one more thing," says Sandrine, who once again hears us through all the commotion with her combat-grade earpieces.

"There is just one more thing I would like to say," continues Tolan as if on cue. "There is one person who deserves a great deal of recognition for bringing Blackburn and TerraAqua to justice. He's not one of our people here at Grumwell nor was he an inside man at Blackburn or TerraAqua. He's a young data runner by the name of Jack Nill. And through his efforts, even putting his own life in jeopardy to do it, young Mr. Nill was able to deliver the evidence that brought these actions to light. Jack, wherever you are, the Alliance owes you a debt of gratitude."

It is a very strange thing to see yourself in cinema-sized dimensions, but that is exactly what happens when my Brentwood High yearbook picture fills the air above the vortex choppers, looming overhead like the mug shot of some fugitive on the lam. The only thing I can't figure out is what the hell he's talking about. I was carrying the evidence, yes, but it wasn't me who delivered it. "I don't get it," I say. "I appreciate the credit, but he must know I had nothing to do with it."

I see at once that Snake doesn't share my sentiment. Just the opposite. He closes his eyes and shakes his head.

"What?"

"It's not a favor," says Snake. "You've just been burned. The one thing you absolutely need in order to be a data runner is anonymity. That was the most valuable asset you had, and he's just taken it away from you. Fame is like kryptonite to a data runner. You can't run cargo when everybody knows your face."

I look up at the screen, at my face, at the grim smile on Tolan's, and for the first time I know what it is to walk in Martin Baxter's shoes. I know what it is to have the CEO of Grumwell sitting across from you playing the other side of the board. Miles Tolan. My opponent. The man who moves the pieces against me.

Sandrine kills the projection as the rest of Blackburn's soldiers are marched away. Most of them will probably be folded into Grumwell Liberty; but I'm sure a few of them, the loyalists, will be dealt with differently.

"Monsieur Nill," she says. "Please inform Monsieur Baxter that Miles's offer to him still stands. There is nothing that has transpired here today that will be held against him if he chooses to come to us now." She goes to leave, but before she does, turns back to me. "This goes for both of you," she adds.

"What's that supposed to mean?" I whisper.

"It means that Martin Baxter isn't the only one Tolan is after," Snake answers.

Sandrine restrains a smile. "À tout à bheure, *mon chéri.*"

NEVER MORE THAN HALFWAY THERE

37.

One week later, Cass and I sit on the rusted merry-go-round in the run-down old playground of Brentwood. Or I should say, *Burntwood*. Barely a week gone by and the nickname given to Brentwood by the media has already stuck, even among the people living here.

We had a service for Pace early that morning, which is why I'm still wearing my black suit. Dexter was there too, but he had to leave in a hurry. Our town may have been burned but the rest of the world kept on. Still plenty of data needing transport, still plenty of loads to be run. Not that my wing had buzzed once since Tolan's press conference, but if there was an official dismissal from Arcadian, I was still waiting to get it.

Cass looks around the playground. "So I guess this is one of the few places that didn't get touched by the fire."

"Only because there was never any water here to begin with. The kids always had to bring their own."

"I heard there'll be some money coming in from the settlement. Maybe even enough to rebuild the town."

"Maybe."

"You don't think so?"

I shrug. "Money doesn't make a community, it breaks it. The first time Blackburn destroyed this town by poisoning the water supply, everyone took their settlement checks and left. Then we moved in. Now they've done it again, and once again there's a settlement deal on the table. Maybe some folks like Mr. Chupick will reinvest it into Brentwood, but if I know most of the people around here—for sure the ones who are walking around calling their home *Burntwood*—they're going to take the buyout and leave. And all of this," I wave my hand at the last remains of a town that has seen more than its fair share of disaster, "will be left to weather into the ground."

"But you and Martin will still be here."

I shrug, remembering Mr. Chupick's words when I asked him why he never left Brentwood. "Where would we go?"

"Hey, don't look so glum. In spite of the fire, you did help bring down Blackburn. That's no small feat."

Another shrug. "Does it make any difference?"

"What's that supposed to mean?"

"Does it make any difference whether our national security is under the thumb of Christopher Blackburn or Miles Tolan? The megas are like a Hydra. You cut off one head and two more pop up to take its place. It's the definition of futility."

"No," says Cass. "No, that's not right. It's a difficult struggle but it isn't futile. Hercules did it."

"Hercules wasn't real."

"Neither was the Hydra."

The merry-go-round squeaks as I toe it around one arc minute at a time. Cass falls silent. I know she has something on her mind, something that's been on her mind the entire afternoon, I've just been waiting for her to get to it.

"There's something I have to tell you," she says finally. "Cyril is moving me off the Free City beat. I'm going to be running internationally."

"As of when?"

"As of right now. I leave for London tonight. It's a big step up from point-to-point. Huge. The loads are even more high-value and the stretches much longer..."

"But the pay is much better," I finish.

Cass smiles, and in that smile I can see how much she enjoys what she does. Sure she does it for the money, we all do, but for her the promotion is also a validation. She's incredibly good at what she does. Getting the chance to run the global sneakernet is proof of that.

"Hey, you're a great runner," she says. "I'm sure it's only a matter of time until you get the same bump. We'll be running side-by-side again in no time. Then you can teach me some more of those moves."

I return the smile halfheartedly. Cass thought it was funny that I got my picture broadcast all over the news stream. Just like me, she didn't realize the broader implications of what that meant. I don't say anything. She's on top of the world right now, and I don't want to ruin that. "Yeah, I'm sure you're right."

"Yeah, I'm sure I am." She ruffles my hair with both her hands. "You're the Carrion. You'll be flying the Eurozone in no time."

Ever since the construction site, I have imagined kissing her again. I imagined every little detail. The where and the when and even the how. Whether it was day or night, even the awkward moment just before. But now that the moment is finally here, there is this giant chasm between us that I never could have imagined in a million years. I never thought that the next time I kissed Cassandra Evers, it would be a kiss goodbye. Over the past six weeks I was hit by a lot of things I never saw coming, but none of them punched me in the gut like this one. She's the first girl I ever really liked.

In the distance, I see the spec of a vehicle coming our way.

A long wet kiss that tastes like raspberries. Three short pecks from her lips to mine. Another long one from me to her. Two more short ones that are both me and her. She puts her hand on my cheek and touches her forehead to mine. The electricity gives me goose bumps.

One more time, for the last time, Cass kisses me goodbye. "See you soon, Jack."

● ● ●

Before I even have a chance to process what's happening, the black SUV with darkened windows pulls up. Bulletproof glass from what I can tell. I know who it is even before the back door opens and he gets out. Cyril.

"How's it going, Jack?" he asks as he holds the door open for Red Tail.

She gets in without looking back.

"You tell me."

I fully expect his trademark smirk, and he doesn't disappoint. "You're quite the trend these days," he says.

"That wasn't my fault."

"Who said anything about fault? There's no one to blame, it's just the way things played out."

I have to hand it to him, the man is nothing if not pragmatic.

"It's quite unfortunate, though. I had very high hopes for you. You could have been one of the great ones, Jack."

"It's not over yet, Cyril. I still can be if you'll just give me the chance." But the look on his face says it all. "This is so unfair."

"Who said anything about fair?" he replies. "Do you remember what I said to you when you asked me why we were so hard to locate?"

"You said they can't compromise what they can't find."

"That's right. So what does that say about a data runner whose face has become the bitstream of the month?"

It says he's about as useful as a one-legged man in an ass-kicking contest. "So that's it?"

"That's it. I really hate to do this, Jack, but consider yourself clipped."

And just like that, Cyril lets me go.

"Wait." I pull up my sleeve to reveal the Carrion Crow on my arm with a cortex chip for an eye. "What about your gear?"

But Cyril just smirks. "Keep it."

I stand there confused.

"You're a smart kid," he says. "I'm sure you'll find some use for it." Cyril opens the door of the SUV just enough for himself but not enough for me to see Red Tail sitting inside. "By the way," he says, "I had to find a new assistant to replace that little prick Bigsby."

I acknowledge the information with a perfunctory nod. What do I care? It has nothing to do with me.

Cyril taps the driver side window. The door opens and out pops—

"Dex! What the hell?"

This time it's not a smirk but a full-on smile that Cyril offers as Dexter takes the door from his hand. "I'll give you two a minute," he says and disappears into the vehicle. Dexter checks to make sure Cyril's leg is clear and shuts the door behind him.

"Dex!" The excitement is genuine, bittersweet but genuine. "When did this happen?"

"This morning." Dexter pulls up his sleeve to reveal the fresh scorpion ink across his thick forearm. It is a very large bird in flight. Wings arched high. Beak large and designed for tearing. Something fierce and aggressive that you wouldn't want swooping down on you in anger. Clearly it is a bird that has been on this planet for a very long time, with no plans on going anywhere anytime soon. "Griffon Vulture," he says. "What do you think?"

Griffon Vulture. From what I see on his arm, it looks like a bird that is equally adept at fight as flight. "I think it suits you."

Dexter lowers his sleeve. "Hey, Jack. It's too bad it had to turn out like this. I was hoping we could run together like before."

"That would've been nice."

It's funny. Sometimes people drift apart slowly, over time. Like when the close friends you start high school with become the distant strangers you don't even recognize on graduation day. But sometimes it's just the onslaught of circumstance that pulls people apart—not over the passage of time, but all at once.

"I was really looking forward to showing you this next time I saw you," says Dex with a sentiment I recognize at once. It was the exact same sentiment I had while saying goodbye to Cass. Dexter never imagined that the next time he saw me would be like this.

"Don't sweat it," I say. "Just remember, you're the one representing the Dragons on the sneakernet now. Do us proud."

"Always."

A moment passes that is only broken by the sound of knuckles tapping the other side of the tinted window. Dexter motions that he has to go. He gets into the driver's seat of the SUV with Cyril and Cass in the back as I turn in the other direction. But just before he leaves, Dexter rolls down the window. "Hey, Jack!"

I turn back.

"You know that getting clipped isn't any kind of limit…it's just another plateau."

I suppose I already knew that, but hearing it brings a smile to my face.

"Be sure to look after the Dragons. You're the club captain now."

"I will." But there's something else I want to say to Dex. Something to encourage him the way he's always encouraged me. A few words of wisdom to encapsulate everything I've learned about the sneakernet. Unfortunately, I have no such words, and I can't find them quickly enough, so I settle for the next best thing. "Hey, Griffon!"

He looks over his shoulder as the vehicle pulls away.

"You watch your back out there!"

38.

It takes more than a week to get the house back in order—first from being ransacked, then from being burned. Structurally, we're in pretty good shape. All the bathrooms and most of the kitchen will have to be redone, but the rooms without wet walls have only cosmetic damage. The bannisters on the main staircase have all turned powdery black, and all the walls are stained brown from water and smoke, and no matter how much air freshener we use the whole thing smells like a wet chimney, but in the end the house is still standing. Just like Martin and me.

Now, down in the basement, through a giant hole that was once a heavy door guarded by a biometric security pad, Martin manages to get his systems back up and running. Back online. Hardwired directly into the aggrenet. And for the first time, standing there looking at it from the top of the stairs, I see Martin's basement for what it really is. Not a workshop at all.

"So this is the Morlock lair," I say. "Where the mythical Moreau controls the undernet."

Martin looks up to see me looking down from above. "The best way to hide the truth is to shroud it in myth," he says as he continues ratcheting together a switch. "And for the record, Moreau does not control the undernet. He has his thumb on the pulse, just like a good sysop should, but the undernet is out there. You, Dexter, Red Tail, Snake, you're not just surfers on someone else's infrastructure, you guys are the nodes and relays that make up the undernet. That's what separates it from the aggregate Internet. That's what makes it better. It isn't owned. It's the sum of its parts." Martin stops to consider this as he moves to another screw and continues ratcheting. "It's more than the sum of its parts."

I take an eyes-wide-open look at what Martin has done with the place. It's just a musty little basement enclosed by dirty walls, but it's enough, and it's private. If nothing else, it's a place where a man like him can work. Whether it's Martin Baxter or the shadow they call Moreau, it's a place where he can really get something done. And isn't that all a mind like his ever really needs out of real estate?

"So we're definitely staying then? We're not going to take the money and run?"

Martin confirms. "It's where we belong. Moreau can be much more effective out here and protected. You were right about this being our home, Jack. Leaving is the easy way out."

I descend the stairs to Martin's worktable. "You know, you still owe me a reason."

"Reason for what?"

I shake my head. No more question games. "You know what I'm talking about."

"You want to know about Genie."

I have all the pieces; I'm just missing the big picture. "You said something about her finding out the truth about Grumwell. And then Snake said that taking over Blackburn was all part of some plan. The doctrine? That's what you were talking about, wasn't it? That was the thing that Genie found out."

Martin nods. "It's called the *Grumwell Doctrine*, and it is the unwavering belief that the only successful global empire can be the empire of the corporation. Put simply, it is Arthur Grumwell's plan to take over the world, to acquire whatever he can and destroy whatever he can't until the world's largest private enterprise is also its biggest global superpower. The Grumwell Doctrine is his personal mission to create the next world empire under the banner of a single corporation. His corporation."

"How come I've never heard any of that?"

"Because Grumwell is exceptionally good at selling everything they do. You saw how everybody reacted to Miles's speech the other day. He painted Grumwell as the great savior that the Alliance so desperately needed, and everybody just cheered. The public loves Grumwell, and Miles uses that affinity to his advantage. Grumwell's greatest asset is the awe they inspire; with that they can get away with almost anything."

"Even taking over the world."

"Even taking over the world."

"And when Genie was the CSO of Grumwell, she found out about the doctrine."

"She did."

"And she wanted no part of it?"

Martin shakes his head. "If it was that simple, she could have just quit, walked away, and been done with it. But the thing about Genie, and certainly the reason I fell for her the first time I ever met her, is that she has a fire inside her. When she has a passion for something, there is nothing in the world that can stop her from pursuing it. Genie couldn't just walk away. She couldn't just stand by and let it all happen. But she couldn't put you in danger either, so after I scrubbed her identity, Genie did the hardest thing she ever had to do in her life. She kissed you goodbye and went off to form the Outliers."

At once I recall Red Tail's story. "Genevive Bonillia is the gypsy woman who marched into the squatter settlements to form the resistance."

Martin nods. "It's a Castilian name, but the roots are Romani. Her family truncated it when they immigrated to North America from the Eastern Eurozone, so when came time to give her a new identity, we just reverted back to the old one."

"So, I'm part gypsy?"

"The correct term is *Romani*," says Martin. "And yes, that's the other half of the blood pumping through your veins."

I'm stunned. Genie. Genevive. The Outliers. They're all the same. Just like Martin, Moreau, and Morlock.

"I want you to know something," Martin continues. "She did it for you. For all of us. She left so that we could all have a better future. On the surface, the Outliers may seem like just another protest group fighting for rights to things now owned by private enterprise, things like the water we drink and the air that we breathe, but deep down they are so much more. The Outliers are an uprising. A revolution. They are the all-out resistance to the Grumwell Doctrine, and their goal is to bring back the constitution of the Old-50. A true government that is of the people, by the people, and for the people. Only this time we won't make the mistake of allowing the corporations to disguise themselves as people and usurp the whole thing."

"And how does Morlock fit into all of this?"

"That was my idea. I couldn't let Genevive fight this battle all on her own, but I couldn't put you in danger either. Then one night I was reading you to sleep with *The Time Machine* and I came up with the idea of creating a singular beast made up of millions of individuals. People just like you and me. A beast that will continue to grow no matter how many nodes they stamp out. A beast that will spread itself around the entire globe. That is the digital resistance."

I think I understand. "Genevive Bonillia does it with boots on the ground, Moreau does it with little bits of zeroes and ones."

"Precisely."

"And she's still out there doing it?"

"For security reasons she stays hidden, but just like Moreau and Morlock, Genevive Bonillia leads the Outliers from within." Martin moves the switch aside and gets started on another piece of equipment. "So how did it go with Hermes Agency?"

"As expected." Back when Dexter was running for them, they would have given anything to get me on board. Now they won't even touch me. No one will. "You really have no idea why Tolan did that?"

"I told you before, that's the way Miles operates. He will never drag you kicking and screaming, he'll simply remove all other options until you have no choice but to go to him. I don't know what his game is at the moment, but for now he's ensuring that all roads lead to Grumwell…for both of us."

Martin is right about one thing. Whatever his game is, Miles Tolan has certainly backed me into a corner. I had already decided to keep running with Arcadian for a year or two to save up the money for NEIT. Now even that's not on the table anymore. I suppose I could still eke out a living proofing code, but after everything I had seen and done, after running the sneakernet, could I really resign myself to being Bartleby the Scrivener? The answer is as simple as looking at my parents. Martin could never do that, and apparently neither could Genie, so I guess that sort of mind-numbing task work just isn't in my DNA. I need something bigger.

"I've been thinking a lot about Zeno's Paradox lately," I tell Martin.

"Which one?" he says. "There are nine of them."

"Nine?"

"Yes, although most are restatements of the same principle, so reductively there are really only three."

"I'm talking about the one where you're running for some goal, and before you can reach it, you first have to get halfway there. And before you can do that, you first have to get a quarter of the way there. Etcetera, etcetera."

"The dichotomy paradox," says Martin.

"Right. Anyway, I was thinking. The paradox is designed to show that a finite distance can never be crossed because it can be bisected infinitely. So no matter how far you travel, you're never more than halfway there, thus ensuring that you're never more than halfway to your goal. But the whole idea is really contingent upon the subject standing still the whole time, isn't it?"

"What do you mean?"

"I mean if you stand there looking at all those half-distances you have to cross and keep adding them up in your mind, then of course any effort to achieve your goal would seem futile. I don't know, Martin, I think in a way the paradox is supposed to represent life. Every goal in life is unachievable if you just stand there focusing on the distance between you and it. But once you start moving, once you start crossing all those half-distances, picking up speed as they get smaller and smaller, you just do it. You set your mind to chasing down your goal and put yourself in motion. Let the math take care of itself."

"It does."

"What does?"

"The math. It does take care of itself. If you just apply a little bit of calculus, you see that the series *one over two to the nth* converges to zero."

"Right," I say realizing that Martin has just proven my point. "Because calculus is the mathematics of movement. The paradox only exists when you're standing still in Euclidean space. But once you start running and apply the mathematics of change, suddenly this insurmountable distance gets crushed under the curve of motion. It's like, the solution to the paradox isn't some complex mathematical proof—it's just to put one foot in front of the other and get moving, and that movement will carry you to the goal before you even realize the math says no."

"That's a very interesting perspective," says Martin, "but how does it apply to your current predicament?"

"It applies because that's what I have to do. No matter how far the goal may seem, no matter how much space there is in front of me, I just have to put one foot forward and start moving. And once I do that, I have to keep moving. Keep moving, keep going, using the momentum to my advantage. And I guess the distance will take care of itself."

Martin stops what he's doing. He knows I'm about to lay something on him. "And what's the goal here, Jack?"

"Mr. Chupick already said that he would fix my attendance record so I wouldn't have to go through the motions of showing up anymore. But the truth is, school isn't just about showing up anymore. I have a commitment to the Dragons. With Dexter away and Pace gone, I'm afraid the club will fall apart without me. And the school could use my help fixing up the place. The whole town could. So maybe I'll work with Mr. Chupick for a while getting things back to normal. And while I'm doing that, maybe do some coursework through the university aggrenet portals. I may not get the grade or the credit, but it's like you said, *knowledge is the shared intellectual property of all who seek it.*"

"And after that?" Martin asks suspiciously.

After everything I've learned, there is no stopping me now. I can't just stand here staring at the distance between us knowing what I know. I can only move forward. And for me moving forward means only one thing. "I want to find her."

He raises his eyebrows. "You can't be serious." But he can

see that I am. Martin taps the table twice like he wants another card. "Jack, I think you need to stop and think about this for a second."

But stopping is exactly what I don't want to do, even for a second. Stopping will only make it seem too far away, too difficult, too insurmountable. Stopping will only make it seem futile because it's only when we stop that we realize we're never more than halfway there. So now I need to move.

When I first started on the undernet there was one thing that drove me more than anything—looking for Moreau—and I didn't stop until I found him. Even if he did turn out to be Martin, and the distance between us was zero the entire time, I found him. Now I need to find the other person I have always wondered about, the one who is little more than a distant memory.

"I'm serious," I tell him, and the way I say it makes it perfectly clear that I am not seeking his permission.

Martin may think I am the same person I was before, but I'm not. Even if I'm not running data for Arcadian anymore, I am still a bird. I will always be a bird. That ink is permanent. And as a bird, the time has come for me to leave the nest.

"I'm going to find her, Martin. I'm going to find my mother."